THE
RADIO
OPERATOR

THE
RADIO
OPERATOR

A NOVEL

ULLA LENZE

Translated from the German by Marshall Yarbrough

HARPERVIA
An Imprint of HarperCollinsPublishers

THE RADIO OPERATOR. Copyright © 2020 by Klett-Cotta–J. G. Cotta'sche Buchhandlung Nachfolger GmbH, Stuttgart, Germany. All rights reserved. Printed in the United States of America. No part of this book may be used or reproduced in any manner whatsoever without written permission except in the case of brief quotations embodied in critical articles and reviews. For information, address HarperCollins Publishers, 195 Broadway, New York, NY 10007.

Translation copyright © 2021 by Marshall Yarbrough.

HarperCollins books may be purchased for educational, business, or sales promotional use. For information, please email the Special Markets Department at SPsales@harpercollins.com.

Originally published as *Der Empfänger* in Germany in 2020 by Klett-Cotta.

FIRST HARPERVIA EDITION PUBLISHED IN 2021

Library of Congress Cataloging-in-Publication Data

Names: Lenze, Ulla, 1973- author. | Yarbrough, Marshall, translator.
Title: The radio operator : a novel / Ulla Lenze ; translated from the German by Marshall Yarbrough.
Other titles: Empfänger. English
Description: First edition. | New York, NY : HarperVia, 2021 | "Originally published as Der Empfänger in Germany in 2020 by Klett-Cotta"
Identifiers: LCCN 2020049993 | ISBN 9780063018389 (hardcover) | ISBN 9780063018396 (trade paperback) | ISBN 9780063018402 (ebook)
Subjects: LCSH: World War, 1939–1945—Fiction. | GSAFD: Historical fiction. | Suspense fiction.
Classification: LCC PT2712.E59 E4713 2021 | DDC 833/.92--dc23
LC record available at https://lccn.loc.gov/2020049993

ISBN 978-0-06-301838-9
ISBN 978-0-06-311249-0 (Int'l)
ISBN 978-0-06-311779-2 (ANZ)

21 22 23 24 25 LSC 10 9 8 7 6 5 4 3 2 1

THE
RADIO
OPERATOR

I

SAN JOSÉ, COSTA RICA, MAY 1953

EARLY EVENING. TWILIGHT. SWARMS OF INSECTS. THE WIND sweeps them into his face on the ride back; he has to squint. But still he can see her as he turns off the road, away from the green river and into the driveway: Maria. She's standing on the steps leading up to the house, looking a bit nervous, fidgety. At one point she slaps her arm.

Something else he can see: she seems to have been waiting for him.

"Mail for you, Don José," Maria calls out as he parks his moped. "On the stairs," she says. And as he's walking past her: "From Germany." He slows down.

He hasn't written his brother in three months. For the most part his silence has been met with reproaches: *We've always made an effort. It's always been important to us to stay in touch with each other.*

"Do you want to come inside for a moment? I have cold lemonade."

Carl's letter will have to wait.

He steps into the room with its dark furniture. She turns on the ceiling fan. The air stirs; it smells of dust. The small birdcage that hangs from one of the rafters starts swinging violently back and forth. The squirrel trapped inside has been trying to get out for days. Maria caught it in the garden, *con mis manos*—with her bare hands. Its bushy tail flails around like a mad painter's brush.

"When are you going to set it free?"

She looks at him, taken aback. "I like animals. Horses, dogs, squirrels."

"But all it can do is go around and around in circles. It's about to go round the bend."

She laughs at his play on words—*volverse; volverse loco*—and leans back in her chair. Her body is shaped like a barrel. No waist. Five children, all of them married. She wears a shirt that belonged to her late husband, large and boxy. He knows Maria is lonely. The nights here lie shrouded in gauzy darkness. No light anywhere. The house enveloped in a warm caress, heat trapped in the walls.

He tells her about his flight over Santa Barbara. About how they have to go ahead and map out the roads that are to be built next year—that's why they're meeting with the engineers.

"Roads," she says, "are important. There's too much dust here."

Darkness falls completely while they talk. He doesn't talk about Germany anymore. "The country is divided now?" she once asked, uncertain.

Yes, there was a war in Europe. Surely you must have heard about it! "A world war," he explained.

"There are so many wars," she said, defending herself. *We have had many wars here too.*

When his glass is empty he gets up, walks outside, and finds his way up the stairs in the moonlight. As he climbs, he reaches for the large brown envelope.

Upstairs the heat hangs torpid. He occupies a single room with a veranda that looks out over the jungle. He can't complain. Dörsam took care of everything, including finding him a job at the Geographic Institute.

He turns on the fan, throws open the windows. The sharp screeching of the cicadas assails him. There aren't many distinct sounds here. A region blanketed by the green of the plantations and of the jungle. Sometimes the rumbling of a freight truck on the government road to San José, or the boy who sells bread pedaling to the last house in town and bleating a few lonely notes into the air on his bicycle horn.

When he slits open the envelope, a magazine tumbles out. As if of its own accord, it falls open to the page where Carl put his letter. And he sees his own face.

The photo turned up all over the place back then, even in the *New York Times*. Him in front of his radio equipment, Princess on the chair next to him, both looking into the camera. Anyone seeing it would think something is wrong either with the dog or with him, because they're both the same height.

> Dear Josef (or Don José? We all had a good laugh about your new name!),
>
> A report on your case has come out in *Stern* magazine. A real-life account of the German intelligence service's activities in America. It's a whole series! There are five more issues to come, I'll send them to you as soon as I have them. That's all for now. More soon.
>
> Greetings from your brother, Edith, and the kids
>
> p.s. Täubchen now has her own room on the ground floor. She's a young lady now!

He lays the magazine out on the table and pulls the lamp closer. His eyes go line by line; he's not reading, he's looking for his name. But he doesn't find it anywhere.

Now he starts over again from the beginning, actually reading this time. It's the story he already knows, now told from the Germans' perspective: *Vaterlandsliebe*—love of the fatherland. Written like a detective novel, as if it were all just entertainment. *FBI! You're under arrest! Why not confess and get it over with? If you talk, you might spare yourself the worst!*

No wonder Carl sounded so cheery, almost excited, even. But it's not entertainment. It's his life.

Later, in bed, he just looks at the advertisements.

CAKES AND PASTRIES, CONDENSED MILK FOR EVERY OCCASION.

HEUMANN'S SLIMMING GRANULES WILL HELP YOU TOO.

SCHAUMA SHAMPOO—LOTS OF FOAM WITH EVERY USE.

GET MORE ENJOYMENT OUT OF TRAVEL AND FREE TIME—WITH

HALLOO WAKEFULNESS TABLETS.

Germany seems to be back on its feet.

He awakens in sweat-soaked pajamas. Faint gray light—the sun hasn't risen yet. He searches his room for cool air. All the doors and windows are left wide open at night, and still the temperature never disperses.

He steps out onto the veranda, reaches for the iron railing, grips the metal with his hand. Not cold, but cool.

He stares out at the palm trees, blissfully limp. Instead of New York skyscrapers, instead of German ruins, and instead of Argentinian pampas, he now has these green giants all around him. Hemming him in, keeping watch on all sides. A faint smacking sound when their leaves brush together.

Off in the distance the green river, made of glass this morning. No movement at all on the water. The river reflecting palm groves and banana bushes. There's nothing else here. Later he'll dress and ride out to the Geographic Institute. Fly over Alajuela. They're mapping Costa Rica, piece by piece: roads, rivers, lakes. They've acquired new machines, but they lack qualified workers; they roll out the red carpet for people like him. Dörsam wants to come up from Buenos Aires next month. Does it have to do with the report in *Stern*?

In Buenos Aires the Germans puffed thick cigars that made him feel ill. They talked and talked. About the conspiracy against Germany, about the government in exile that would soon oust the American puppet Adenauer. Sure. It was like a drinking song, they struck it up again and again; no one cared anymore what the words were. He was invited to the chess club and to tea and dancing at Club Union. Most of the time he kept his distance. When the opportunity came to work in San José, he took it.

Dörsam will be here soon enough.

At the washtub under the tree, Maria is scrubbing his pants and shirts. She gets everything done in the morning. In the morning, before the brutal heat of day has set in. Her body pitches forward and back. She scrubs with all her might, scrubs patiently. All the scrubbing makes little tears in his clothing. Granted, the clothes are old, most of them still Carl's. From Germany. Carl's underwear. Josef has worn them in Europe, North Africa, and South America. Carl's underwear has traveled the world, while Carl has never left Germany. He'll have to speak to Maria about the tears. But how? He doesn't want to offend her. Maria irons his shirts, cleans his room, addresses him as "Don," even though, at just fifty years old, he's too young for that. Never a complaint, even when he leaves the maps and photos from the Institute lying around on the floor. She respectfully cleans around them. She's even managed to match his old gray socks to their original pairs. Maria is easy to get along with. He can come and go as he pleases. A little chitchat in the evenings sometimes—he doesn't want to have to move yet again. How many times has he arrived somewhere and had to act as though it were his home?

2

NEUSS, JUNE 1949

THE LEFT EYE DOESN'T MOVE. IT'S A GLASS EYE. JOSEF HASN'T seen it in a quarter of a century. He'd forgotten about it.

They embrace, briefly, not too tenderly—a solemn moment. Carl wears a suit despite the heat, and over it a white shopkeeper's smock.

"Look at how thin you've gotten, my dear man!" Carl cries. "And we thought America was the land of milk and honey!"

Josef smiles and follows his brother into the redbrick house, photos of which he'd seen before the war, narrow and tall, but the bricks beginning to shift. It was cheap, Carl had said in his letter, but it hadn't been Aryanized—seized from Jewish owners and resold. That Carl had refused to do. "Something like that just can't end well."

He trudges up the stairs behind his brother. Carl has combed his graying hair back over the beginnings of a bald spot; the ends form little curls over the nape of his neck. He stops on the second-floor landing.

"We have so much to talk about! So much catching up to do! I told Edith, 'I do hope he stays a bit longer.'"

"Does that mean I wasn't supposed to stay long?" Josef asks with a wink. When he sees the look on Carl's face he wishes he hadn't.

"No, I mean it just like I said," Carl replies and holds the door open for him. Inside, it smells of detergent and pastry.

"Edith's been baking. She's just out picking up groceries, she'll be back any moment."

Josef sets his bag down on a chair and notices Carl's gaze following his hand.

"That's all you have?"

"Just this here." When Carl doesn't say anything else Josef picks the bag back up, and now he doesn't dare set it down again. Carl takes the bag from him and carries it into the next room, a kind of parlor: brown velvet curtains, dark-colored period furniture, oil paintings of land-scapes, dramatic teardrop-patterned wallpaper.

"All this made it through the war with us." Carl tries to help the conversation along. Josef is silent; he can't force himself to utter any praise. He feels a twinge of pain and steels himself against it. "Come," Carl says quietly. "You'll be sleeping in this little room back here."

The room is furnished with a sofa, armchair, and writing desk. No telephone here either. He needs to call Dörsam.

"Edith will make the sofa up for you to sleep on. What do you think, will you be able to bear it in here?"

"Of course, absolutely. How neat everything here is."

"That's Edith's handiwork! A capable housewife—that's something you won't find so easily."

In Carl's letters the word "capable" appeared again and again in refer-ence to Edith. Carl seemed unable to find any other words to describe his wife. In the photos he saw a pretty, dark-haired woman with a star-tled look in her eyes. He suspects that Edith might be a bit taller than Carl, assuming Carl still stood on his tiptoes when getting his picture taken, like he'd started doing years ago.

"Here, have a glass of water." Josef drinks and looks at Carl, who paces back and forth before him, telling him now about his business as a soap wholesaler. Business is picking up more and more, he says.

Josef limits himself to helpful prompts: "So the new powdered laundry detergent is better, the customers are saying so too?"

"Yes, and I relay that back to the manufacturer. Paul is thirteen now. Helps out with the business in the afternoons. Next year we'll take him out of school. Then he can work full-time."

Carl pauses for a moment, straightens a picture frame on the wall.

"You'll meet the kids any minute now. They really wanted to skip school when they found out yesterday that their uncle from America is in the country! The chocolate you sent them—they'll never forget you for that!"

There was more than chocolate in the thirty packages he'd sent.

Package 1: coffee, lard, powdered milk, powdered butter, powdered eggs, soap, shaving cream, tobacco, cigarettes, needles, thread, aspirin, saccharin, bouillon cubes, chocolate, pepper, nutmeg, cloves, darning wool.

Package 2: oats, flour, sugar, starch, rice, gelatin, bandages, aspirin, baking powder, chocolate, thread, adhesive tape, needles, wool, tobacco, comb, socks, razor blades.

Package 3: lentils, tobacco, chocolate, lard, sugar, jerky, honey, coffee, pepper, gelatin.

Package 4: wheat flour, coffee, condensed milk, honey, pancake mix, soap, tobacco, chocolate, cigarettes, vegetable oil.

Package 5: coffee, sugar, condensed milk, lard, cocoa, chocolate, razor blades, shoelaces, vanilla extract, yarn, needles.

Et cetera.

The money that was meant for his lawyer, six hundred dollars, went into these packages. His case was hopeless anyway. Thirty packages from 1946 to 1949; he'd heard about an agency that would put them together and ship them.

Carl sits down in a wing chair and starts rubbing a spot on the arm where the fabric is already worn. He's grown pensive.

"We're through the worst of it. But '47 was a hard winter. Soup kitchens, warming centers, the neighbors chopped their piano up to feed their stove. Then the summer after that it was flooding and hailstorms, the harvest completely ruined. Times like this, you have to grit your teeth, do without, make sacrifices, stretch every penny. Don't you agree?"

He looks at Josef, and in the look is a question. The silence swings back and forth between them. Now Josef is meant to fill it with his explanation for why he's come back from wealthy America with nothing to show for it. A poor lout. He didn't break even; he's in the red. Again he feels a slight pain in his chest.

They're released by the creak of floorboards. Both look toward the door. A woman is standing there. "Well," says Carl, "we've got time. We can talk about everything soon. No need to rush! Here, first things first. Come meet Edith."

She is thin. Thin is the first impression, then beautiful. A slightly Madonna-like, ascetic beauty. If she were a bit better nourished she could work as a fashion model. But he cannot tell her this. She holds her hand out to shake, very proper, stiff. He squeezes her hand and doesn't let go, cradles it a bit in his; let her think this is how they do it in America. He gives it another squeeze and then he does something that surprises even him: he takes her hand and lifts it to his lips to kiss it.

"Oh-ho, the boy's brought manners back with him," Carl cries.

Edith blushes, and Josef too feels his face turn red.

"Are you two hungry?" she asks. "I've baked cherry pie. Or would you care for something else, Josef?" He can sense that she's having to force herself to speak. Already she's heading toward the door to hide her face.

"Pie sounds wonderful," he says to her slender back.

"He's got an accent. Do you hear it, Edith? You sound like an American," laughs Carl.

"Coffee will be ready in ten minutes!" Edith calls from the kitchen.

When Carl gets up he gives Josef's shoulder a quick squeeze. A firm squeeze, as if to say, *Everything's all right now. You're here. You're here.* That's how it was before: they were simply there, and all of a sudden it's like it used to be, for a brief, fleeting second. Then he stands up and follows his brother into the kitchen.

He keeps catching himself staring at Edith. She wears a thin, floral-print summer dress that catches between her legs when she stands up. Her hair is set in waves, an old-fashioned hairstyle; it's been a long time since he's seen a woman wear it. She is both shy and self-possessed, the latter whenever she can set the table and serve. She does it almost forcefully.

They eat a very sour pie with lots of cherries—"We don't have any butter or sugar," Edith explains. The children, a boy and a girl, are so quiet and obviously frightened that later, when he lies down on the sofa, he can't say what they look like. He remembers, however, that the boy kept nervously blinking, clearly a tic. Carl at one point raised his hand and whispered, "Stop that!" But the son didn't stop.

He dozes off for a moment and is woken by Carl's voice: "Leave it. You'll let the heat in! Leave the door closed!" Then he hears Edith's mild voice, and again Carl shouting: "Let her live out on the street, then, if she likes the sun so much!"

Carl's shouting. He hasn't heard his brother's voice in twenty-five years. And now he sounds like their father.

When they parted twenty-five years ago, the wound was still fresh. They had removed the eye quickly after the accident at the factory. At the time, they couldn't get anything more out of Carl about what happened to him; first a yell, then he started screaming and couldn't stop. That was what his fellow welders later reported, and Carl, in the hospital bed, said nothing. A mute reproach in this silence, and this reproach was directed at life itself, or maybe America's immigration laws. The first thing the loss of his eye meant was losing his entry visa. They had learned English together, but at Ellis Island Carl would have gotten an *X* written on his shoulder in white chalk and been sent back.

In his first letters Josef restricted himself to saying how hard life as an immigrant was, how disliked Germans were, how difficult it was to find work, how high the rents were. And it was all true too.

That evening they all sit at the large dining table in the parlor. Edith serves vegetable soup and explains defensively that it all comes from the garden. Carl stares at the beer glass filled with water in his hand.

"By the way, Josef, in the next few days we have to go to city hall and get you registered."

"I think they know I'm here," he answers with a crooked grin, his teeth showing a bit on the left side of his mouth. It's his special Joe grin, and he closes his eyes for a second. It's gone. It doesn't belong here, this grin, he can tell.

"It's about the ration stamps," Carl explains. "They have to verify who you are." He grabs his beer glass and drinks, keeping his eye trained on Josef as he does.

"Josef?" Edith is standing next to him. He nods, and she gives him another ladleful of soup. He is now distinctly aware of Edith's scent. It's the same plain soap smell that envelops the whole family, but there's something else there too, something that is uniquely hers, and if he could touch the smell, it would be as soft as velvet.

"Did you never think about getting married?" Carl asks suddenly.

"Thought about it, sure."

"But never found the right one?"

"Might well have found the right one, but something got in the way."

Carl nods and doesn't probe any further. Now it's Josef's turn to speak. But Josef sees no point in speaking of a love that by Carl's standards would be a useless love, completely useless and even harmful.

"Do you like it?" asks Edith.

"Very much, thank you," he says without hesitation and smiles.

Does he like it? Food had always been important to him. Yes, very important. Eating could be revelatory for him, as if there were dead recesses of his being that could be resurrected by the aromas of a given meal, as if an unusual herb could tickle something in his brain awake.

"Do you know what Mama called you when you were away?"

"No, what?"

"Jö!"

Josef doesn't understand but smiles. Edith laughs, though; she seems to understand.

"You wrote to her back then and said that in America they called you Joe now. Mama came over to us with your letter and said, 'Our Josef has a new name, Jö!' I told her, 'No, Mama, you say it like this: *Dscho.*' That's right, isn't it?"

He nods. He finds the story funny, but something about it hurts. As he keeps eating he gets more and more tired and doesn't mind when Carl starts conferring about various things with Edith—a table that has to be moved, a dresser down in the cellar that has to be repaired and painted.

The girl keeps looking at him the whole time, and he asks quietly, in English, *"How are you, my little dove?"* She smiles and murmurs, *"Good, thank you,"* and keeps looking at him.

They go to bed early. It's just afternoon, American time, but he's happy at the chance to be alone. On his pillow he finds a neatly folded set of pajamas, a towel, and a toothbrush. His life is over, but they make it easy for him to act as though he still has one; he just has to play along. Carl sets the rules. Even in the letters, a web of painstakingly detailed questions—though when no answers were forthcoming Carl was quick to beat a retreat, the next letter admitting that well, certainly, he of course had little sense of the political circumstances there.

In his first letters in 1946 he had had to inform his brother that since the start of the war Ellis Island had been a detention station for enemy aliens.

Enemy aliens?

I'll explain everything later.

The room faces south, hence the heat. Even here it smells of the cigar that Carl lit up after dinner. Sharp, a bit like piss.

He opens the window and hears the train. He can only marvel. Two nights ago he was still lying in a bed always cold and damp from the sea air, all around him the rumble of the tugboats that sailed past the island and the deadening tediousness of imprisonment, a life devoid of choices. Time pervaded everything. There was only time. It was the element in which they all lived. Time as punishment. Much worse, however, were the four years in Sandstone, Minnesota—a real prison with real criminals.

Up there in the north it always felt like winter. He moved at a run. He had to, they all had to—never stand still. *Don't stop. Move!* For if ever the men did stop, that's when the fights would start.

Carl doesn't know about Sandstone. In Germany they were busy with the war, and Carl didn't seem surprised that Josef too was silent for five years.

3

NEUSS, JUNE 1949

NOISE WAKES HIM. SHOUTING FROM THE OTHER SIDE OF the wall. "How can he do that? Doesn't the boy have any sense?"

So it's about the son this time.

The clock shows 6:30. For the self he left behind in America it's just past midnight, and so he decides to turn over onto his other side.

The next time it's operetta music that wakes him. Carl sings along, if only to the most memorable bits. Edith says, "Try to be quiet," and Carl says, "This is my house. I can do as I please." But the radio is switched off. And then the door falls shut.

The next time he wakes up the clock says ten o'clock, and needles of sunlight shine in through the window. Carl's voice again. In the short pauses in between whatever Carl is saying he hears Edith say something. He swings himself up off the sofa, hurries into the kitchen. Carl turns to him and stops speaking mid-sentence.

"Ah, the gentleman awakes. Slept well?"

"I'm six hours behind you."

The look on Carl's face shows incomprehension.

"The time difference. For me it's still the middle of the night."

"Here. I haven't drunk out of it yet." Carl hands him a cup. Josef drinks, if only so as not to offend him. "If we hadn't had that coffee of yours, Josef, seriously, I wouldn't have been able to run this business. I need coffee. I need coffee more than anything in the world!"

He stops, looks Josef up and down. "Don't you want to put some clothes on?"

"I have clothes on."

"A set of sweaty pajamas. We're in the kitchen, my dear man!"

Edith turns around and stirs a pot.

"Beg your pardon," says Josef.

"Edith left some clothes in your room for you. Come, I'll show you," and with that he pushes Josef out of the kitchen.

In the room, in fact, are a pair of suit pants, a white shirt, a jacket, and a pair of underwear. It's clear that they're Carl's clothes. They're the same height, five foot three. It should all fit.

Carl looks out the window as Josef peels off the pajamas. The pants are a bit big at the waist; he has to fasten the belt as tight as it will go. As he's buttoning up the shirt, he hears Carl say, as if from far away, "So all right, let's hear it."

"What?"

"What are you doing here all of a sudden? How is it possible to just hop on a plane that takes you from New York to Frankfurt? How do you have the money for something like that?"

"For the FBI it's no trouble at all, Carl."

He thought the mere mention of it would shut him up. But Carl asks, "FBI? What's that?"

"It's the American federal police."

He starts to roll his sleeves up. Then stops in the middle of doing so and rolls them back—it could be that Carl finds rolled-up sleeves as improper as pajamas in the kitchen.

"Did you commit a crime?" asks Carl.

"After 1941, after Germany declared war against the United States, it was a crime just to be German."

He buttons the cuff of his left sleeve. Then the right. Carl stares at him. Clearly waiting for further explanation.

"There were just five of us Germans left on Ellis Island. Five enemy aliens. Plus a few Italians and one Japanese guy. They didn't want to have to keep the island in operation just for our sake."

Carl nods and looks over to the door; Edith is calling.

"The customers are waiting." As he leaves he claps Josef on the shoulder. It feels like he's been marked.

Now he tries to read Carl's steps. In the kitchen the radio starts playing. A man sings of a red sun on Capri, a fisherman and the ocean. At one point he hears Carl say, "All very mysterious." Then the front door falls shut.

He goes to join Edith in the kitchen. When she notices him she puts on an apron and bends over a pot: "You must be hungry. I can make you some eggs. Our hens have been busy."

She wears the same dress she wore yesterday. It clings to her stomach; she seems to be sweating around her navel.

He can't look away.

Edith is taller than Carl; he noticed it the night before. She must be five five. That means she's taller than him too. She seems absorbed in watching the eggs, which make a very quiet *thok* sound when they knock together in the boiling water.

Now she finally turns toward him. She hesitates for a moment. Then she starts setting the table with great vigor. Plate, salt shaker, a basket of bread—and with a final elegant flourish she places an egg spoon next to the plate.

But there is something bashful in her movements nonetheless. A strange man in her kitchen. That's what he is, and suddenly it's clear to both of them.

"Carl was very happy to hear from you all of a sudden after the war. We were always happy to get your letters."

"His letters meant a lot to me as well," he said. "To have a family." And he thinks of Carl's constant words of encouragement. Which sometimes he could only smile at. But still: they were from his brother. He didn't have another. He clung to those words, to the ragged cursive on smudged postwar paper with holes where Carl's pen had punched through it.

"I'll be in the laundry room if you need anything."

He has a mouthful of egg and can only nod. He's not very hungry; for his American self it's only six o'clock in the morning. But he wants to do what's expected of him.

After breakfast he looks up Dörsam's address in his notebook. He sits down at the writing desk, grabs some letter paper, and writes:

Dear Herr Dörsam,

I'm in Neuss, staying with my brother. Where can we meet?

Respectfully yours,

Josef Klein (Joe)

He finds an envelope, then stamps, and puts Carl's address as the return address. But then he folds the letter again and again and puts it in his pants pocket.

By laundry room Edith must have meant the bathroom downstairs. Because he can't think of anything better to do, he goes to join her. She kneels by the tub, and when he clears his throat, she turns her head to look at him over her shoulder. Her face is sweaty. Dark strands of hair cling to her temples.

"Can I help you, Edith?"

"Washing clothes isn't a man's job."

"It isn't a woman's either."

She keeps scrubbing as if he hadn't said anything.

He doesn't give up: "I would have my clothes picked up once a week. A boy would come by and then drop everything off again the next day, clean and pressed."

She keeps scrubbing.

"Nothing fancy about it. Wasn't expensive."

Again he regrets what he said. He slips out of the laundry room without another word. Soon afterward he's outside on the street.

There are no sidewalks. In the rubble and in the footstep-flattened dirt, children are crouched down playing marbles. The air smells of potato peels and dust.

The folded-up letter is crammed in his pants pocket. A few blocks away he stares at a pile of rubble, what's left of a building that collapsed. When he's sure he's not being watched, he risks a few steps into the rubble heap, crouches down, and digs a little hole with his hands. He lights the letter on fire and waits until it has crumpled into black scraps of ash. Back on the street he knocks the dirt from his pants.

At the train station, where he means to call Dörsam, government officials are standing around checking bags. He turns around immediately, heads back to the brick house on Sternstraße.

The house casts a blue shadow over everything. At the northern edge of the property is a shed. Next to it, a chicken coop. He can hear clucking and fluttering sounds coming from inside, a strange yet comforting ruckus. He sits down on the bench in the garden and waits.

He's good at waiting; for eight years he did nothing else. He closes his eyes and is overcome with sadness, sadness that has something to do with Carl, with the look Carl gives him, his two eyes drifting apart. He'd like to give Carl a reassuring pat on the back and say, as he might have in New York, *Relax. Let's have a good time.*

Someone is shaking him by the arm. He must have fallen asleep.

"If you're planning on staying with us for a while, you have to go get registered. It's the law. I'll have hell to pay if I let somebody live here who isn't registered."

Josef, still half asleep, looks up at Carl. Upstairs in the kitchen window he sees the curtains fall back into place.

"I don't have papers."

"You don't have papers?"

Josef shakes his head.

Carl starts to say something, and then, without a word, he lets out a sigh. Takes a few steps across the yard, as far as the shed, thinking. A quick glance at Josef. "If you wouldn't mind helping me move a table, that would be nice."

It's dim inside the shed, but Carl doesn't turn the light on. Once his eyes have adjusted to the darkness, Josef can see shelves lining the walls filled with boxes of detergent, tubes, bottles, and little packages of soap. It's all neatly organized, but there's still a sense of chaos, maybe owing to the strong smell of medicine, of lavender, lemon, and toothpaste.

There's a telephone on the desk. He'll call Dörsam from here.

He hears his brother's voice. "Josef? Will you come over here, please?" He finds him in a back room, an office.

"It's not heavy, just bulky," says Carl as they get ready to carry the table on its side through the shed.

"Do you want me to carry the front end?" he offers. He can feel his brother's body through the table. His hesitation.

"I can do it," Carl answers gruffly and starts easing his way backward through the door until his hands get caught in the doorframe and prevent him from going any farther. Josef doesn't say anything.

"The table is too wide," sighs Carl.

"Grab the tabletop from the inside. Then your hands won't be in the way."

Carl laughs. "My goodness, of course."

Outside in the yard Carl insists on being able to continue walking backward all the way to the house. When they're finally there, Carl wipes his forehead with a handkerchief.

"Thanks for your help."

"Don't mention it."

Carl hesitates, then he takes a deep breath and says, "We listened to Radio London."

"Radio London," Josef repeats.

"The so-called *Feindsender*—enemy radio. If it'd gotten out, I'd have been facing prison or worse."

Josef nods.

"We always kept ourselves informed about what was really going on in this country. The American press must have been critical as well?"

"Yes, always. Always critical."

Carl nods, apparently satisfied with the result of the conversation.

4

NEUSS, JUNE 1949

H E WOULD LIKE TO TELL CARL AND EDITH ABOUT IT. HIS life in New York as a free man. But they don't ask. Are they worried he might tell them something alarming or indecent? He has to laugh. Maybe they figure he's got nothing interesting to tell. Also possible. He does what's expected of him, doesn't draw attention to himself. Maybe they confuse that with insignificance? He was never able to get across what was important to him, not well.

Lauren was surprised that he had hardly any books. "But I do, on amateur radio." He pointed shyly at the stack. Finally she found an explanation: "Do you know why you're not a reader? You don't need the double consciousness."

What did she mean by that?

"You're always completely present wherever you are, and that's enough for you."

"And for you too, apparently."

She laughed, loudly. She laughed like a kid.

"And what about Thoreau?" he asked.

"You and your Thoreau."

She had still been polite then.

Later she told him he hadn't understood Thoreau. But *Walden* was his book. It was enough for a whole life. Thoreau's life in a cabin in the woods sparked a yearning within him. He read of the joy of being in nature. He sometimes saw the city as if it were made of trees and mountains, a landscape of stone and geometry. He could disappear within it. It was big enough.

Lauren asked if he'd read the other American writers and transcendentalists, Emerson and Whitman. He didn't even know the names. And the word "transcendentalist" confused him.

Thoreau's words flowed straight into him, without hindrance, and thanks to Thoreau he knew his own mind. That was enough. Most of the time talking about something was just a sign that you didn't understand it. His favorite line was:

> A man is rich in proportion to the number of things which he can afford to let alone.

But of course there is a lot he could tell them about. That he saw Duke Ellington live at the Cotton Club, that his doctor was named Dr. Weinrebe, that he stopped going to church and not a soul was interested. That he was free, because there were too many people who were all too different for anyone to be able to take anything all that seriously.

He had lived in East Harlem, in one of the less pretty buildings—a plain, squat brick box. Still, he lived on the very top floor; he had no trouble fixing his antenna to the roof. He liked the neighborhood. There was nothing glamorous about it. There, any pressure he might have felt to try to prove something was gone. He walked the streets up and down, again and again. The tall buildings looming overhead no longer seemed to mock him, as they had in the beginning; instead they seemed to watch over him in a paternal way.

His one luxury was his radio equipment, and maybe also Princess. A German shepherd. She waited patiently all day for him to come back from the print shop in the evening.

Every day he took her to a weed-choked vacant lot by the Harlem River, where she did her business between old tires and the overgrown remnants of broken foundations. It always smelled a bit rotten and brackish there, which made Princess all the more excited. She had to sniff everything. Then they went shopping. On the way to Lexington Avenue, they fought their way through the children playing on the sidewalks—hopscotch and jump rope, baseball, marbles. The kids would pet Princess, would call her by her name, and Princess with her mouth open seemed to smile.

He took her to the fish market with him, bought mullet wrapped in a giant page of newsprint. At the grocery store he bought Kellogg's Corn Flakes, and at Idrie's he bought bean pies, a specialty that had its origins in New York's Black Muslim community. At the intersection, a black cop with white gloves and sunglasses directed traffic; the butcher stood in his shop window between dangling sides of meat; the Italian hatmaker smoked under his awning. If he was lucky he'd see a showgirl from one of the clubs, catch sight of the sequin shorts she wore under her coat. Back home, he'd put on Ethel Waters, "Stormy Weather" or "Georgia on My Mind." He had seen Ethel Waters once on Lexington. Tall and regal—and even though she was already a star, she returned his smile.

One day his friend Arthur had suggested that they build a radio. For days and weeks they sat together, taking turns reading from the books they'd bought. They painted a cardboard tube with paraffin, wound wire around a spool, sketched out circuit diagrams, cut wires. The smell of oil and burnt metal, a pile of screws, wires, and electrical tape on the table in front of them, and Arthur twisting his strawberry-blond Charlie Chaplin mustache, when suddenly—he'll never forget it—a sound came out. A faint, squealing sound, a bit like chirping. They turned the tuning knob, and out came a sound like wind and the beating of rain, and as they continued turning there were sounds he had never heard before, electronic sounds, whistling, sliding, leaping, bending. It sparked a tingling feeling inside him, a feeling of happiness. Then they started picking up voices. The voices crackled like leaves in winter. "CQ, CQ"—*come quick*. A shaky, warbling man's voice singing, "Sweet Sally, Sally of my dreams."

They looked at each other as if they had summoned God.

"Voices everywhere."

"People can tell each other everything now. What's really going on in the world. Soon there won't be any secrets at all anymore."

Arthur's face lit up. He had just joined a group that was engaged in the fight against social injustice and for the Christian faith. Arthur was the son of Irish immigrants, but not at all devout. He only believed in friendship. And in German work ethic. As far as the latter went, he'd picked the wrong German, and soon realized it, but he still let Josef work at his print shop and live with him those first few years. When Arthur got married, Josef moved to East Harlem. The bars there served alcohol, despite Prohibition, for which reason Arthur often came to visit him and was soon bemoaning married life. "She comments on everything I do. Says I slice an avocado the wrong way, crossways down the middle instead of longways. I'd have been better off marrying you."

"Did you know that in California they tried to rename them alligator pears?"

"Really?"

"On account of the skin. Didn't catch on, though."

"Yeah, dumb name."

As soon as things quieted down on the street outside, he would turn on the voices in his apartment. Early morning in South Africa, a storm in Mexico, in Helsinki dead fish on the shore. He heard of a moderate northwesterly wind in Perth and catastrophic flooding along the Yellow River in China.

He was good at Morse code. The jaunty beep-beeping could be heard over anything, whether it was street noise or the neighbors' shouting. In the beginning, he would sit there with pencil and paper to work out the sequences, but soon it would happen automatically in his head. He recognized some operators immediately from certain hesitations, drawn-out tones, or a particularly galloping rhythm. Everyone sounded a bit different; everyone had their own handwriting.

It took a whole year before he could bring himself to speak. To talk without seeing anyone. To build confidence. To just sit there and talk. To send something of himself out into the world and hope for the best. And then he discovered how freeing it was. No one could see him. No one knew anything about him. Not how tall or short he was, or whether he lived in a house with a yard in Brooklyn or a tenement in Harlem.

To be only a voice, everywhere, at any time. In the beginning, he tried to trick himself into believing that this precious state, like magic, was enough to shield him from misery. With the Depression, the universal rules grew clearer; there were forces stronger than his inner life.

Arthur had to shutter the print shop indefinitely. They sometimes met at the soup kitchen by Bryant Park. Josef found a poorly paying job delivering flyers for a large furniture store. A pretty big step down, considering he used to produce the flyers himself. But he liked the work. When he got into a rhythm, when he felt more like he was dreaming than working, he could lose all sense of time. Use his index finger to flip open the lid of the mailbox and slip in the piece of paper pinned between his thumb and middle finger, his other hand free to hold his cigarette. The city became an animal with countless hungry mouths, and it was his job to feed them. By the time the economic situation had eased a bit, he had hit almost every building at least once. But he still couldn't send his mother any money; he could only send news of just scraping by. His mother asked if he didn't want to come back: in Germany a new era had begun; Germany was reborn. No. Never. New York was his city, especially now that he'd fed it.

5

NEUSS, JUNE 1949

THEIR DAYS AREN'T YET IN ALIGNMENT. THE FAMILY IS SIX hours ahead of him. He drags after them, dead tired, and at night turns restlessly in bed while they're already peacefully asleep.

Mornings at six he hears Carl whistling merry melodies. He briefly wakes up, rolls over again, and goes back to sleep until ten. Carl returns shortly before noon, at which point Josef has been up for just two hours. Once Carl says, "My dear man, we're always tiptoeing around to keep from waking you."

"It doesn't seem like tiptoeing to me. But that aside, noise doesn't bother me."

The heat has made its way inside, filling each room like a thick liquid. His scalp is burning. Sweat runs down his face.

Carl gamely continues wearing suit and smock and seems to be the only one not sweating. He looks like a character from a book.

There's a white line of salt on the nape of Edith's neck. Josef can't stop looking at it.

He spends the morning hours with her. It's going better and better between them, a good reason to get up a bit earlier every morning. Little by little they find things to talk about, from the German goods and food-stuffs for sale on "Sauerkraut Boulevard" in German Yorkville (she finds this funny) to the preparations for the daughter's birthday (sugar, butter, and cocoa need to be stored up weeks in advance!). All the while, Edith darns socks, irons shirts, peels potatoes, mops the floor. Josef offers his help, but she declines every time, amused. She sticks to her opinion that it's all women's work. He could tell her that having lived as a bachelor for many years, he has had to perform women's work himself, but she doesn't want to hear it. She shakes her head in disapproval. It's not clear if it's pity or reproach.

And so he watches. And allows himself to be a little bit intoxicated by her energy, the casual air with which she, like the conductor of an orchestra, exercises control over a hundred different things. Sometimes he thinks the Edith he's watching doesn't exist at all. She vanishes into her activity. There's something girlish about her—not a hint of sensuality, not even innocence; rather, in all her industriousness, an air of something like sleep or a trance.

At midday, the kids come home from school. When they're close he can hear them on the street outside. Laughing. This makes him happy. Walking home in the sunlight, they bring the sun in with them. But inside they go quiet. Paul is the son's name. Irene, the girl's. Josef calls her *Täubchen*, "little dove." Täubchen is quiet but alert. Her gaze is always on him, and when he returns it she is slow to lower her eyes. He tries to coax her out of her reserve with jokes. Is she too dainty for housework? he asks, as she pores over her schoolbooks at the kitchen table, where Edith is peeling potatoes. He has to fight back the urge to laugh when he sees the offended look she gives him. "How 'bout it, Täubchen, still working on that arithmetic?" he asks a half hour later. "Don't you have to go to Maikelowski's and pick up some bread?"

"Michalowski," she corrects him. *Mi-scha-lov-ski*, not *Mike-a-lov-ski*.

He laughs and looks at Edith. "She always knows best. She's going to drive her husband nuts one day!"

Täubchen doesn't show any response. But he can tell she's pleased by what he said.

"You could go get the bread yourself," says Edith.

"Gladly. Well, off I go to Maikelowski's, then."

Later he hears the kids saying, "*I haff ta go ta Mikealowski's.*"

He can't speak decent German anymore. He hadn't realized.

On the fourth day he's allowed to hand Edith her tools, though it might only be because, him being a man, she doesn't dare deny him his natural connection to tools. She kneels by the old wing chair, a gray work apron tied around her waist. The tools lie in a circle around her.

"May I help?"

She looks up, surprised. "I don't need any help."

"I know that, Edith. But maybe you'd like some company?"

"I don't know," she says, but he's already kneeling down next to her.

"I can hand you the tools."

This, even though they're all lying there within reach. She frowns. But he hands her the scissors, then a pair of pliers, then the scissors again, and looks on attentively as she removes the worn upholstery with a single cut. Then he helps her pull the fabric off the chair, their arms brushing together for a brief moment. "You're the surgeon and I'm the nurse," he says, trying to come up with some way for her to think about this whole thing, even if it's only to break the awkward silence. A sheepish smile flits across her face.

On the fifth day he gets to help Edith hang up the laundry in the yard. They move back and forth between the clotheslines and from tree to tree. The underwear, her own, she has already separated out back in the house and banished to a back corner of the balcony. He has taken a close look at them: worn out, graying white panties and small brassieres that look hand sewn.

He gets to hand her the children's underwear, then, not without awkwardness, his own (which ultimately are Carl's; it falls to Edith to decide who gets which). Edith, who has just been talking about fertilizer for the tomato plants, goes silent. Her embarrassment is so strong that it carries over to him. They can't find their way out of this silence.

When they're finished, Edith bends to pick up the empty tub and starts heading back to the house.

"Wait, Edith, let's sit down on the bench and rest for a second."

Reluctantly—she can't think up an objection just then—she sits down next to him. Her legs pressed close together like two objects that have been neatly put away. Everything about her is measured, plain; even to cross her legs would probably seem to her to be too coquettish. He, on the other hand, lets his legs splay out to either side like an exhausted construction worker.

"You're very different, the two of you. Was it always like that?"

The question takes him by surprise. He looks at Edith and wonders what she's really trying to get at.

"Yes. But it's gotten worse. Back then I was the stronger one, and then I left him behind when I went to America. I always looked after him, he was my little brother."

Her face darkens, seems to seal itself off. She doesn't say anything for a long time, and then, as if coming to a decision, she says, "He puts it very differently. He says you were always making trouble, and he was the one who had to answer for it."

"No, that's not how it was." He says it too quickly and a bit testily. Now he tries to collect himself and to speak calmly. "He took most of the beatings from our father. Two left hands—you know how it is. Something was always going wrong. A torn pair of pants, lost change, spilt milk. Then our father would have to punish him."

He seems to be calling up what to her mind is a strange image, her husband as a clumsy and abused child. He could go on, say something like: *And he still is today, plus he's missing an eye on top of that. It must take a huge toll on him trying to make up for all these weaknesses.* Instead he says, "But there is one thing we have in common. We're both short men."

Edith stares at her hands, the veins that run over her slender wrist. She has pale skin; it neither burns nor turns freckled in the sun. As if she were kept under glass.

She interrupts his thoughts: "He wishes you would confide in him."

"Ah, I see," says Josef, trying to buy some time.

"Can you do that?" she asks.

What can he say to her? *Sure, I'll do it?* Again he is silent for far too long. Edith's body tenses up; her fingers intertwine. He almost feels bad for her. Now it's clear to him that she's under instructions from Carl to ask him. And she doesn't want to go back to him empty-handed.

"I can't confide in him because I myself don't know what happened."

She looks at him in disbelief, yes, almost angrily. "Did you not have enough time to think it all over when you were in prison?"

He leans back, smiling, sneering a bit at her question. "You can't think freely in prison."

"What's that supposed to mean?"

All he says is "Hmm" and rests his arm on the bench behind her, which makes Edith slide forward a bit.

"Look, Edith, I'm not one of those people who go to prison and write great books or find God. Some people become religious in prison. Not me. I never had any kind of profound insight."

"That wasn't my question at all, Josef."

No, that wasn't her question.

He sees the dress fluttering in the sun, then he hears the door, which closes with a creak behind her.

He'd clipped articles from the newspaper. He'd started at Sandstone. Then Lauren crumpled them up right in front of him. She didn't dare go so far as to rip them up. She'd wanted him to stop. Had he? No. Of course not.

One of the first articles he'd clipped was about Canaris. The man they'd been working for. Canaris had neglected to inform Hitler that US troops were already in North Africa.

That evening he keeps peering over at Edith, trying to tell if she's still angry with him. No, everything seems the same. The children concentrate on pushing their peas onto their forks and taking care that none should fall off or, worse yet, fall from the plate to the floor. This draws a stern look from Carl. Or a question. "What did you two learn in school today?"

The son speaks fearfully into his plate.

"Look at me, please!" says Carl.

"We gathered herbs for medicine," says the son and lists off the varieties: stinging nettle, birch leaves, coltsfoot, dandelion greens. When he's finished, he blinks. Clink, clink.

"The teacher is sending the kids off into the woods with the homeless and the unemployed. If that's how it is, we can in good conscience take them out of school and put them to work in the business."

He butters a slice of rye bread, adds a slice of sausage, and takes a bite.

Notices the look the girl gives him—Carl couldn't find any better way of going about it. Täubchen has also buttered a slice of bread, but has only another filling slice of bread to lay on top.

"Now you're free and you still can't get anything good to eat," Edith says suddenly.

This isn't quite true.

"The food at Ellis Island was excellent," Josef hears himself saying. "We got everything we asked for. Hans Dörsam was our spokesman. He insisted that they honor the Geneva Convention. Starting in 1946 we got our own kitchen and our own cook, we ate *sauerbraten*, schnitzel, *Königsberger Klopse*. The food was so good that the guards wanted to eat with us. We sat in the former registry room, a giant room with chandeliers and a view of the ocean."

It's all true, but why is he telling them this?

"Why did you want your own cook?" Carl asks.

"It was to make sure that no Jew would be cooking for us." Dörsam's words.

It gets quiet, and they look at him as if they are seeing him for the first time.

"You can't talk like that here, Josef."

"No, no, you've got the wrong idea. The Germans were afraid that someone would poison them."

Carl clears his throat, exchanges glances with Edith. "Even then, one doesn't say that."

He looks at Edith as well, but she stares at her plate.

"No?" he asks and grabs the last slice of bread. "What does one say, then?" This too just slips out of him. He knows he's only making things worse.

"If you want to joke around, you're in the wrong place."

For a while the only sound is the clatter of the silverware on the plates.

He feels ashamed. He doesn't know what's wrong with him. He thinks of the water that surrounded them. It sloshed and crashed, and the wind sang in their ears. Birthday cakes with swastikas made of chocolate icing. Ingesting swastikas. "Pull yourselves together, gentlemen." Swastikas carved into doorframes. Not being able to speak. And then, when you can speak, like now, you say the wrong thing.

"They gave the kids sweets," says Edith suddenly. "They seemed very friendly, the Americans. Didn't they?"

Täubchen nods. If he'd been arrested just four months later he would have landed in the electric chair. Just like the people after him. Wartime law would have applied. A pure formality, the only difference between him and the dead. "Yes, the Americans are very nice," he agrees.

That night he wakes up. Something is different. There's a sound, and the sound slowly attaches itself to a word, and the word is rain.

The first rain in weeks.

The patter of raindrops is loud; it drowns out the creaking of the floorboards. He creeps through the kitchen to the balcony. He wants to be closer to the rain. The trees sway in the yard. Suddenly the air is cool. He realizes there's something his body is looking for, right here.

He leans against the wall, the cold brick at his back, and tries to draw the coolness into himself and hold on to it.

When he opens his eyes, he sees a light on in the bedroom. Has he woken Edith and Carl? He hears their voices. He can hear Edith.

"He's a bachelor, Carl, he doesn't know any better. He never had a woman to look after him."

"Sure, you can prattle on carelessly like him when you haven't built anything and you're not responsible for anything or anyone."

"Carl, don't get so angry."

He holds his breath. Before he can learn anything more about himself, he creeps on tiptoe back to his room.

In the morning, cool air blows through the open window. Reaches him as he lies half dreaming, half awake. Hands holding his. Musicians playing in a pavilion in the park. The taste of caramel candies. Carl in a bulky coat—it's Josef's coat; Carl, the younger brother, has to wear it. Facets of light reflecting in the tall glass of beer their father holds in his hand.

Operetta music drifts in from the kitchen. Carl's whistling accompaniment sets in. Josef picks himself up, gets dressed, and walks into the kitchen at a quarter to seven. The glass eye is lying on the table.

"Good morning, brother of mine!" blares Carl.

Edith smiles shyly in her bathrobe. "Coffee?" Her voice is still thick with sleep. Both seem like they got a late start today. Probably the storm, the heavy rain and their conversation last night. Is that what kept them awake? He feels a twinge of jealousy.

"Can I come with?" he asks.

"Come with? Where?"

"Making deliveries."

"You're not registered yet. People could ask questions."

Carl turns his back to him and puts his glass eye back in.

"That's true. Maybe. I don't know."

Edith presses a coffee cup into his hand, instead of just placing it on the table like she usually does.

She can tell I don't have anyone, he thinks.

"Tomorrow," says Carl. "But you don't talk to the customers. Not a word."

6

NEUSS, JUNE 1949
NEW YORK, FEBRUARY 1939

THE DELIVERY TRUCK IS PARKED OUTSIDE. CARL WEARS THE white shopkeeper's smock, which makes him look like a doctor. Josef has on Carl's nut-brown suit; Edith took it in so it would fit him. Now it's his. A lit cigarette in the corner of his mouth, he props his elbow in the open window. Carl gives him a look but then just puts the truck into gear. The wind smokes the cigarette for him.

He likes playing Carl's sidekick. Boxes get pushed this way and that, papers get signed, and he holds on tight to whatever Carl puts in his hand. Shaving cream and detergent jostle together in the back of the truck. The bottles clink; a comfortable rhythm sets in. At every stop Carl says, "This is my brother. He's helping out today," and before any of the customers can ask a question, Carl quickly asks what they think about the new hair tonic.

When they're in the truck, Carl has a wealth of jokes to pull from, but only of the sort that can't be told at the kitchen table: "Two friends get to talking. One of them asks: 'When you see a pretty woman, what's the first thing you look at?' The other one says: 'My wife.' 'Your wife?' 'Yeah, to make sure she's not looking!'"

The sky is totally clear. A radiant blue. It makes the town look even more ruined. Carl seems in high spirits, downright relaxed.

Did Edith talk to Carl? Put in a good word for her brother-in-law? *It just takes time. It's all new for him. And it must be a shock to suddenly come back to Germany. To a completely devastated country. His homeland!*

They stop in front of a small grocery store. A boy takes the delivery and signs his father's name.

Josef thinks of Peter, also a child.

"By the way, I used to make deliveries too. Not soap, the things we printed."

"Yeah?"

"I went all over New York."

"And now you're going all over Neuss."

He sees himself, shoulders hunched, walking through Harlem with that shy boy on that unbelievably cold day, so cold it felt like the city would shatter under their feet. February 1939. The handcart clattered over icy, hard-packed snow, but it wasn't carrying soap. It was carrying filth.

The fact that they printed everything except for Communist literature comforted him, let him think it was just a job. The flyers got tossed from tall buildings by the bucketful. They hung up in the trees and got stuck under people's shoes. The rest were handed out to passersby by speakers on soapboxes who shouted their contents into the streets.

Above them a fiery blue sky. He kept looking up at it, while next to him the boy struggled with the handcart. Josef was training him. The boy was supposed to handle the deliveries on his own soon, then Josef could go back to the heated print shop.

As often as they'd delivered to the American Nazi Party's headquarters, every time they went the address seemed to have moved a few buildings down. His eyes searched the storefronts. Sam's Famous Pizzeria. Barber shop. Smoke shop. Then finally Nancy's Beauty Parlor, a salon that specialized in hair straightening. In the doorway it smelled of food. Without a word, the hairstylist, a Negro woman, pointed to the back. He touched a finger to the brim of his hat. They had to go one floor up. A nest of cigarette butts on the floor helped him find the door. No sign anywhere. The Party operated in secret.

He knocked four times—that's what they'd worked out with Stahrenberg. The door opened. Stahrenberg extended his hand in the Hitler salute. Josef stared at his tiepin, a metal swastika. The boy hastily placed the bundle of flyers on the table. Josef had Stahrenberg sign.

In the hair salon a toddler had appeared and was pressing his nose against the windowpane. He turned to them and pointed an outstretched finger at Josef, laughing. "We used to print greeting cards," Josef said sheepishly to the hairstylist. She didn't respond.

Smoke hung in the air. The metallic winter sun was like a molten lump of coal in the sky. At the 116th Street subway station they carried the cart down the rusty stairs.

The train was packed. He told the boy to lean against the doors and keep a firm grip on the handcart. He himself stood in the middle. With effort he reached a grab handle and hung on tight as the movement of the train pulled his ribs apart.

It was just six stations, but when they reemerged into daylight, suddenly the old world had been swapped out for a new one, poor for rich, shabby for ornate. They stood in a ravine of twelve-story buildings that radiated might. Turrets and gables, castles soaring into the sky. Park Avenue.

He was nervous. A flyer meant for the Negro leader Samuel Jordan, DON'T BUY WHERE YOU CAN'T WORK, had been sent by mistake to the elegant Mrs. Dollings, director of the Park Avenue Patriots, while their flyer, AMERICA FOR WHITE PEOPLE, had been sent to Jordan. The boy had mislabeled the parcels. Arthur had screamed at the boy so viciously that he hadn't said a word since.

They stepped into a heated, brightly lit lobby adorned with gold and marble. The doorman leapt up and pointed toward the service entrance. "Mrs. Dollings is personally expecting us"—words that he had gone over in his head beforehand. They waited for the doorman to call up, the boy staring at the upholstered armchairs and mahogany table. No one invited them to sit.

The grate closed soundlessly. The elevator boy took them to the twelfth floor, the penthouse, now considered the last word in fashionable living. Once it was barely good enough for laundry facilities, storage rooms, and servants' quarters. In the perfumed hallway they were encased in that silence only the rich were entitled to. They went past apartment doors spaced a generous distance apart from one another to an open door at the very end of the hall. There they were received by a housemaid. He gave the hesitating boy a push, and when he noticed the look on the maid's face he added kindly, "Oh, go ahead, kid."

The girl led them into a parlor, the kind of room he had only ever seen in Cary Grant and Ginger Rogers movies. Oriental carpets, antiques, an enormous chandelier, and behind the glass doors a snowy balcony. Everything here was dignified and harmonious. The girl took his hat and coat. He wasn't even wearing a tie, and he'd been wearing the same shirt for a week. The skin on his face began to get hot, as if he had a bad sunburn.

He heard Mrs. Dollings's voice and quickly wiped his moist hand on his pants. But there was no handshake. She wore a long, dark dress, was tall and gaunt, and smiled in the warm-hearted, almost selfless manner of very high-placed people—statesmen, movie stars, priests—who from the lofty perch of their position are able to display great kindness toward anyone they choose.

"Good day, ma'am. How are you?" he asked, feeling that he was being hopelessly ingratiating. He was relieved when she returned the question. "Our delivery boy wants to apologize to you."

But Mrs. Dollings grasped the boy's hand and led him into the daylight shining through the glass doors. The boy wore a coat that was too big for him and shoes with busted seams.

"How old are you?"

"He's fourteen, ma'am."

Mrs. Dollings shook her head—"Nonsense, he's no more than twelve"—and then sighed and said something about illegal child labor, how it didn't reflect well on America.

Next she started waving the flyer around, AMERICA FOR WHITE PEOPLE, and started telling Josef about major changes that needed to be made. She ignored the table, as if she feared the unavoidable closeness it would bring. She remained standing, and he made an effort, as he stood next to her, not to inadvertently touch her.

"Do you see this word here? This we must avoid." Her index finger, its nail painted red, rested on the word that was to be avoided; she didn't say it aloud, and when he did, she snorted. "Everyone knows by now who we mean when we write 'alien' or 'minority.' We mustn't let ourselves be associated with the rabble, like those in the Christian Front."

He nodded sympathetically.

"The same goes for Hitler."

"What do we put instead?" he asked carefully.

"'Führer,'" she said with a clear voice.

"'Führer,'" he repeated.

"Alternately, we can also write 'the George Washington of Germany and Europe.' Or 'the humanitarian and bringer of peace.'"

He nodded, as if he were making mental notes. Mrs. Dollings was now writing on the flyer, crossing things out and making corrections.

"We now say 'new leadership' instead of 'revolution' and 'save America first' instead of 'Heil Hitler.'"

He actually had nothing to do with the content, and that was important to him. He just fed everything into the mimeograph machine. Normally he didn't make deliveries either, only when a new delivery boy had to be trained. Maybe she was confusing him with Arthur? Arthur who was full of understanding and always showed interest. Sometimes when Josef went into his office while he was on the phone, his boss would roll his eyes. "Why do we print the stuff, then?" Josef had asked once.

"Why? I have to make sure the money adds up so I can pay all of you," replied Arthur.

"You must be very proud of your country, Joe. Have you thought of going back?"

"Back? I'm an American."

Mrs. Dollings raised an eyebrow and smiled inquisitively. "You mustn't misunderstand me. We are so full of admiration for the Führer!"

"Not everyone is. The *New York Times* for example, they aren't."

She looked at him without a word, then she nodded to the housemaid. "Let me help you find the door, Mr. Klein." Josef felt her watching him as he stiffly left the room.

The truth was, in the beginning he actually was proud. He had written his brother a letter and congratulated him on the strongman who was helping Germany to assume a new significant role in Europe. The papers were saying the same thing then. But Carl wasn't having it. He never wrote a word in response.

A thin layer of fresh snow covered the street. The boy kept trying to find spots where there were no footsteps. The cart lurched from side to side. He really was just a child still.

A dull ache flared up behind his forehead. They passed by a pharmacy and he considered buying some aspirin, but he didn't want to show any weakness in front of the boy. If he had his choice he would have gone home. But they had to go to the headquarters of the German American Bund, where Hans Schmuederrich wanted to discuss the mock-ups for February 20th.

A cold wind blew from the East River. Darkness fell. The cold smelled of snow. Of fire. Of damp basements. They turned from Third Avenue onto 86th Street. The Germania bookstore already had its shutters down. He was supposed to pick up something for Arthur there, speeches from the Reichstag that Arthur had translated and then sold. Josef had started a translation once, but he had had to look up too many words, and some he couldn't even find. "*Volkszorn*" for example—*the people's anger*—seemed to exist only in German.

He and the boy kept walking down 86th, past the Schwarzer Adler, Café Geiger, the Jägerhaus, and the United Bavarians of Greater New York. From the beer halls came the sound of people enjoying themselves. Little red swastika flags adorned shop windows and the windows of the apartments above.

Two young women in fur coats walked past them, arm in arm, talking loudly in German. Reflexively he placed his hand on the boy's shoulder and steered him to the other side of the street.

They walked toward signs bearing words like "*Möbelladen*," "*Konditorei*," and "*Bremenhaus*." German words in New York's rigid street grid. Whimsical confections, like *Bienenstich* and *Frankfurter Kranz*, framed by cold geometry. In the beginning he had come to this neighborhood as one might to a grave. Did the Germans not notice? It may have started with the honest desire to cobble together an imitation of the old country, but as the memory grew less distinct with each generation, foreign elements had crept in. By now he probably didn't notice himself anymore. He felt something like comfort when he went to Schaller & Weber and ate mettwurst. But he knew it didn't taste like it did in Düsseldorf. Maybe it started with the pastureland, the sun, the wind. Because even the pigs and cows tasted different than they did back home.

They stepped inside a bright, three-story building and went up to the second floor. In German he read PRESSEBÜRO, SCHATZMEISTER, SEKRETARIAT—press office, treasurer, administration. "Herr Schmueder-rich is expecting you. Go on in, Herr Klein," the secretary called through the open door.

Schmuederrich, seated at a polished oval desk, stood up and held out his hand. He was a tall, big man. When he laughed he displayed a large gap between his front teeth that had something childlike about it, as if he still carried his baby teeth around in a little jar in his pocket. He had a reputation as a ladies' man.

There was a big rally planned for February 20th at Madison Square Garden. They were printing the flyers, posters, and speeches. Josef glanced through all of it and nodded. *Mein Bundesführer*, Josef read. *Fellow white Americans and other nonparasitic guests!* He didn't feel good. There was a buzzing inside his head. He looked at Schmuederrich, who sat across from him and proudly held forth on the security measures.

"We're expecting twenty thousand patriots! And La Guardia is providing seventeen hundred policemen for our protection! I'm liking this country more and more!"

They spoke German, which felt hard and sharp-edged in his mouth, not like English, which flowed like liquid over the tongue. They had first met last year at the Rotesandbar in Yorkville, but right away Schmueder-rich had started talking as if they'd known each other for years. "I might look like I have a small dick. But I've got a big one." And he'd gone on: "We can't do enough cheating and spreading our German seed around."

The women had squealed, *Eeek*, but with a certain excitement. A light and carefree feeling had set in around the heavyset Schmuederrich. A kind of fun.

"How's that radio hobby of yours? You're a bit of a tinkerer—am I remembering that right?"

Josef nodded. He had heard somewhere recently that Schmuederrich's American wife wanted a divorce.

"Let me see that photo again, would you?"

Josef took out the photo. He always had it with him. He and Princess in front of his radio equipment; the dog looked as tall as him.

Schmuederrich seemed to be thinking about something. "Sometime soon I'm going to put you in touch with some German businessmen. They're looking for new means of communicating with Europe. Could be interesting for you. Some nice cash on the side. Would you be interested?"

He heard women's voices speaking on the telephone in the next room and then himself saying, "Definitely. Making money with a hobby, sounds good to me," and he could feel his pulse start racing for reasons he couldn't explain.

Schmuederrich stood up, shook his hand, and said, "Then we'll see each other on February 20th at Madison Square Garden. Your boss says you're coming. I'll take care of the tickets."

No one had told him about that, but he kept the friendly look on his face. Arthur considered it important for them to make appearances at their clients' events.

"I'm sure you'll feel safe with us."

He sent the boy home, headed back to the print shop, and found Arthur smoking in his office. When he stormed inside, the jolt caused the door of the cabinet against the wall to open—suddenly Josef was looking at rosy, ample thighs and bare breasts. He was about to ask Arthur where he got off signing him up for the rally at Madison Square Garden without asking him first when Arthur beat him to the punch: "Mrs. Dollings canceled her order. What happened?"

"What did she say?"

"That she's lost her trust."

Trust. The word cut strangely deep. As if he were a crook. Only then did he hear the radio, Father Coughlin's singing cadence, as if the priest was savoring every syllable. "We have nothing against Jews," and then: "But . . ." Several million listeners.

"Turn the radio off, please. I can't listen to that guy anymore."

"Oh-ho, since when are you so sensitive?" mocked Arthur and turned it off. "We're going to another Christian Front meeting tomorrow. Think of it like church. We don't have to believe any of it. The important thing is that we're there."

"I'm already looking forward to it."

"Try making a little more of an effort, Joe."

Josef opened his mouth to say something but then just swallowed. He didn't like the way Arthur had been talking recently. He knew that Arthur was under a lot of strain, but everyone was under a lot of strain. The city seemed like it was about to combust. And it was at times like this that friendship was most important.

They smoked a cigarette together. Josef told him about Schmuederrich, though he didn't mention that Schmuederrich had floated the prospect of a job as a radio operator. He toyed with the thought of telling Arthur he was quitting if this new job was a good one. Then they could just be friends.

———

It's getting close to noon, and the truck still isn't empty. He's sweating. He'd like to take his jacket off, but he doesn't know if he can handle the look Carl would give him.

Carl stops in the shade of an empty facade that rises up like a ghost. They both get out. "It's quiet here," Carl says and hands him a buttered roll.

Josef feels the bread stick in his throat. As he chews he looks at the cracked pavement. Grass and dandelions grow in the gaps.

Carl tells him about neighbors who had twins—"Thank God that's all behind us now!"—and about the extra ration of butter that has been approved for their daughter; Täubchen is certifiably under-weight. Carl jumps from one subject to the next. Josef mumbles agreement to all of it.

They've finished their rolls. His mouth is very dry. Carl is sitting in the truck again. He runs a comb through his hair, checks the result in the rearview mirror. "This new hair tonic really is good. Are you coming?"

Josef gets in. In that same instant Carl starts the motor.

"By the way, some of my customers I'm not especially happy to do business with," says Carl suddenly, and waits until he gets a nod from Josef. "Some of them have a certain past. You understand?"

He understands. He understands and tosses his cigarette butt out the window.

"Now to Michalowski," says Carl.

"Ah, Maikelowski," says Josef, joking around, and Carl laughs, "Yes, to your pal Maikelowski."

"Your brother picked quite the time to come back—everything's ruined. Can you believe it?" Old Michalowski laughs.

"Life has a way of playing tricks on you," says Carl.

"I'm just here visiting," says Josef.

Carl looks at him, taken aback, and then hands the delivery note across the table. "If I could get your signature here, please, Herr Michalowski."

"Just visiting? I wish I were myself. But where's a person supposed to go? All of Europe is in ruins now."

"You can say that again," Carl agrees. "Another signature here, please."

"So where are you headed, then?" Old Michalowski won't let it go.

"Buenos Aires."

Carl lets out a sound that turns into a cough.

"Can you live there? As a German?" asks Michalowski.

"The Argentine government is very well-disposed toward Germans."

"But you have to learn the language, of course. Portuguese?"

"Spanish."

"Then you'll be able to speak three languages—German, English, and Spanish. My lord! You've had quite the exciting life! Makes a man start to get jealous, doesn't it?"

Carl won't look at either of them. Now he starts fumbling with the papers. "We have to go, I'm afraid."

His voice is shaky. Josef should have told him earlier. And not like this.

When they get back in the truck Carl knocks his knee against the steering wheel and curses softly. When he's calmed down, Josef says, "There's no future for me here."

"Why not?"

"Just look around. What am I supposed to do here?"

Carl cranks the ignition. He's silent the rest of the way home.

"Get out."

Carl parks the truck behind the house. Josef waits at the front door. He doesn't want to walk into the house alone. Carl comes up to join him and says as he walks, "Just how are you going to pay for it? And without papers on top of that?"

"I don't know yet." He's lying. He knows exactly how. He just has to stop stalling and call Dörsam.

"You could also work for me. Take your time. Give it some thought."

He can tell how hard it is for Carl to bring himself to make the offer. He doesn't do it because he likes the idea of having his brother around in the coming years. No, he considers it his duty.

"That's very kind of you, Carl," he says. "I'll think about it."

7

NEW YORK, FEBRUARY 1939

THE NEXT DAY THEY WENT TO SEE SAMUEL JORDAN ON SEVenth Avenue in Negro Harlem. Everywhere a roar and clatter. Smoke from open fires stung the eyes. Rats scurried past the buildings. Ahead of Josef, Arthur and the boy climbed a narrow stairway up to the third floor.

Jordan opened the door wearing a bathrobe, eyed them warily, and took a drag on his cigarette as they stepped inside. The floor was covered in newspapers. Jordan seemed to spend the day reading before climbing up on his soapbox in the evenings to warn the world about the white man.

They shoved the boy toward him. "All right, let's go, apologize!"

"He's just a kid," said Jordan. "You let kids work for you? First colored folk and now children?"

"We've brought the right flyers this time," said Arthur. The boy grabbed the bundles from the handcart, flyers with the legend DON'T BUY WHERE YOU CAN'T WORK, and set them down in two stacks.

On the shelf was a photograph of Hitler, a careworn and yet resolute expression on his face. A poster for the PACIFIC MOVEMENT OF THE EASTERN WORLD advertised a lecture, something about Japan being the ally of all black people in America. He had heard the idea going around that the Japanese came from Africa and were therefore also black, hence their supposed solidarity with their oppressed brethren in America. FIGHT THE BLACK REDS, read another poster—Japan was fighting Communism in China.

Jordan said quietly, "What about the other delivery?" Arthur pulled his chair close to Jordan and started to whisper. Josef heard him say something about a delay, and Jordan said, "It's about time we started coordinating our efforts."

"But we're in this together," Arthur continued in the confiding and earnest tone of voice he reserved for his customers.

"The day, the revolution," said Jordan.

And then Arthur started speaking so quietly that Josef couldn't hear anything more.

A blinding light flooded the street. They walked through Mount Morris Park, past the tall boulder-strewn hill that he sometimes climbed with Princess. The Harlem mountains. From the top you could see as far as the river. Black-green boulders all around, bleak, rough-edged, with patches of snow between them, spotted like cows.

They were silent, but in his head he kept batting questions back and forth. Finally he said, "What's Hitler doing on the shelf of the leader of an organization for Negroes?"

"Mutual enemies: England and the Jews."

"You're planning a coup?"

No answer.

"You're selling weapons?"

"There are lots of people who want a revolution. The Christian Front, the Christian Mobilizers, the Silver Shirts, the American Patriots, the Crusaders for Americanism, even the Communists."

Arthur stopped. A squirrel shot out from a bush. Josef watched it go. He saw the heart pumping under its fur.

"And you, Arthur, what do you want?"

"Joe, not everybody gets to live the American dream. Just look at the people in the factories. Sometimes you have to work outside the law. After all, it's the law that keeps people like us on the outside. If I only took on normal print jobs, you think I could employ you? They all pay me extra because I'm the only one who will work with them. The majority of Americans are democratic. They hate anyone who steps out of line. You just haven't noticed yet because you've made such a cozy little nest for yourself up in Harlem, like Thoreau in his cabin, as if you were the only person far and wide. You're not a part of American society, Joe. Don't kid yourself."

Josef looked at the townhouses that surrounded the park. They didn't say a word until they'd reached Columbus Circle. The weekly meeting of the Christian Front was taking place in the rectory of a church.

On the chairs inside sat about a hundred men. The air was already stale, the windowpanes covered in condensation. They were all immigrants— mainly Italians, Germans, Irish. He recognized them by their ill-fitting suits and the combative way they carried themselves. They stared toward the front expectantly, mouths open. He sat next to a man who chewed vigorously on a piece of gum. Swastikas on collar pins and on flags framing the portrait of Father Coughlin.

The loudspeakers crackled. The man up front spoke of revolution, of the people, of race, of patriotism and the nation. He asked questions, and the men shouted answers. Mostly it was the word that Mrs. Dollings didn't like hearing. Sometimes they pumped their fists in the air; Arthur joined in.

Josef turned around and looked into red faces. He thought about whether he should just stand up and leave. If he did, would they run him down and vent their rage on him?

Now the priest was calling the president "Rosenfeld" and the New Deal a "Jew Deal."

Josef turned and spoke into Arthur's ear, "But Roosevelt isn't Jewish."

"No, but he's fighting Nazi Germany. So he clearly sympathizes with the Jews."

"But America isn't taking in hardly any refugees from Europe. There's been a huge amount of criticism. It's barely twenty thousand a year!"

"Take it easy," said Arthur.

After the meeting somebody waved a flyer under his nose: "Get *Social Justice* delivered to your home once a month, just two dollars a year."

Arthur stepped in: "Joe here prints the damn things for you, you pea brain."

"So he's already a member, then?"

"No," said Arthur and smiled, "but maybe you should become one, huh, Joe?"

Reluctantly Josef filled out the form and was then swept up in a crowd of men. They called themselves the citizens' guard and were heading up to Washington Heights. For a few years the neighborhood had been known as Frankfurt on the Hudson, also the Fourth Reich. Arthur caught him by the sleeve.

"I'm only going as far as Harlem," Josef said.

They marched at a fast clip through the dark streets, heading in the direction of Central Park, and there, where they stood less chance of being heard—it was now illegal—they started shouting, "*Sieg Heil!*"

One poked at a dead rat with his foot. "We could use it, right, boys?" Laughter. One of them came up with a newspaper to wrap the carcass in. "Keep your eyes open. Maybe we'll find a few more."

One of them was an elevator attendant, another worked in a butcher shop, still another sold shoes. "Have you read the *Protocols?*" Josef shook his head. "Until you read the *Protocols* you've got no chance of understanding what's really going on in the world."

The cold was fierce. His teeth chattered. They handed him a bottle of vodka and clapped him on the shoulder.

When they drew even with the Harlem Meer at the northern edge of the park, he stopped. A wild goose fluttered up from the reeds. "I've got an appointment to keep on the radio."

Arthur gave him a nod. "See you tomorrow."

Only a few people were still out on the streets. On Park Avenue a man with a horse blanket thrown over his shoulders was trying to pee behind a parked car without anyone noticing. A woman rooted around in a trash can. In the beauty parlors there were still a few young women getting their hair straightened.

The lights were still on at Idrie's too. He bought two slices of bean pie, ate them as he walked, and enjoyed the filling sweetness. The warming smell of cinnamon covered over the impressions of that evening, the mob of men spoiling for a fight, their rage.

At home he poured some food into the dog bowl for Princess. Sat down on the one chair in his kitchen and watched the dog split and crush the little pellets, saw the remaining food get dark with her saliva.

He didn't know how old Princess was. He had found her down by the Harlem River, tied to a tree. At first he'd waited with her; she too seemed confident that her owner would come back, and eyed him with caution. She had pretty eyes; they looked like they were lined with kohl. When it got dark, when the fog began rising from the field and the dog began to whimper, he untied her and led her to the water, where she eagerly drank. He took her home, intending to come back to this same place the next day in case the owner came looking for her there, and for the next six months he passed by the spot almost every time he took her out for a walk; he was ready to give her back any day. Until one day, all of a sudden, he wasn't anymore.

She was a gentle, affectionate, friendly dog, and because there was something aristocratic about her, he had named her Princess.

He stepped on a floorboard that only creaked in winter and that he normally avoided. The wall above his radio terminal was covered with QSL cards, all the way to the ceiling. Hunting trophies. He too sent out QSL cards to confirm contacts made. As far as Paris, Stockholm, even once to the South Seas. Networks that stretched across the globe. English in every accent imaginable.

He switched on the transceiver and took a seat. Quiet signals trickled in through a flood of static and squeals. He sent out his call sign, then a CQ—*come quick*. He repeated the sequence a few times and enjoyed listening to the static and crackle of the atmosphere, the feeling that the whole world was flowing toward him.

"W2DKJ here."

It was a woman's voice.

"Good evening, W2DKJ. W4NER here, reading you loud and clear. What time is it out where you are?"

"Hello, W4NER. I'm reading you loud and clear too. It's twenty-three hundred here."

"Same here!" That meant the woman was somewhere nearby. He usually had contact with other time zones; the dead zone over New York could extend well beyond the city.

"What's your location, W2DKJ?"

"The Catskills, Woodstock."

"So that's where the New York City dead zone ends!"

"And life begins!"

She laughed and seemed very young all of a sudden. The voice was hard to read, but he liked it. It had a glamour to it, and as a way of getting her to speak more, he asked about her equipment. For a receiver she used a Hallicrafters, a Super Skyrider. She asked about his setup, and for a while they talked about antennas, something he'd never done with a woman before. Her voice was warm and inviting. His body, rigid from the strain of being around the men, seemed to relax. He'd have liked to talk about something personal with her, but that wouldn't do; others could hear them.

"Are you still there?" she asked.

It was his turn to speak. "I'm still here." A pause set in, then he wished her a good night—"Till next time, W2DKJ."

"Lauren," she said. "My name's Lauren."

8

NEW YORK, FEBRUARY 1939

BLUE TWILIGHT DESCENDED OVER THE CITY. THE LIGHTS came on around Madison Square Garden, a yellow glow from inside the office towers flowed out into the sky, and there he stood, minuscule, on the pavement down below, and looked for Schmuederrich.

He had a hard time getting his bearings. The demonstrators shouted, "Boycott Nazi Germany!" The policemen kept forcing them back, nightsticks dangling from their belts. The police horses reared up. The demonstrators briefly retreated, their banners hanging crooked in the air, FASCISTS OUT fluttering above their faces as the horses were illuminated in the flashes of the photographers' cameras.

The sirens grew louder, the chants swelled: "Boycott Nazi Germany!" He now saw men with bloody lips, men stuffing their shirttails back in their pants.

He felt a blow on his shoulder and spun around in a panic. Schmuederrich stood behind him. He wore the military uniform of the German American Bund and pointed, breathing heavily, to the entrance to the stadium. They fought their way through the people, ads for Pepsi-Cola, Planters peanuts, and Chevrolet blinking overhead. "Bloody bastard," someone shouted. "Go to hell!" Schmuederrich shouted back. A new chant started up—"Go home, kraut!"—and this one was addressed at them.

Schmuederrich shook his head. "There, up ahead, they'll let us in. They know me. Don't dawdle now, little man."

The flyers they'd printed were all over the sidewalk, caked with horseshit. He had FREE AMERICA! stuck to the tip of his shoe. BE UNITED! . . . BE A NATION, BE AMERICANS, AND BE TRUE TO YOUR- SELVES! Supposedly the words of George Washington. Today the German American Bund was celebrating Washington's birthday. He told himself this and knew it wasn't true. He touched a single patch of stubble on his chin that he had missed while shaving. His fingers kept compulsively going back to it as they neared the turnstiles, back to the rough, itchy stub of a hair. His fingertips twisted it this way and that. Once he tried to rip it out on the sly, his head lowered. He was short; his hat formed a screen.

Beyond the turnstiles the shouting abruptly stopped. It was the quiet that comes after a fight—nothing settled, just a brief ceasefire. They walked down long, dimly lit hallways, Schmuederrich counting exits, explaining that they had to get to the front, he, as a Bund official, had very good seats, almost up on the stage, and after they had walked what seemed like an entire block, they finally stepped into the stadium. He knew the sight from the newspaper. Usually the floor on which thousands of people now sat was an ice rink for the New York Rangers or a boxing ring where Armstrong defeated his challenger Montanez. But now he, who was no fan of crowds, was right in the middle of it, and he could hardly breathe. A mass of people, bright in the floodlights. A hot, burning atmosphere, almost euphoric, it swept up everything and threatened to sweep him up too. *We've done it*, their voices said, all mixing together. *We've managed to gather despite the hatred out there, the lack of understanding, the fury.*

Meanwhile the press was reporting that the devil was on the loose in New York tonight. And George Washington stood ten feet tall at the back of the stage. Couldn't say a thing in his white curly wig, his bucket top boots, his coat buttoned only halfway down his chest, as if a burst of wind had opened it. BE UNITED. The swastika was banned, but it had been smuggled in here in a new design, rising into the air like a skyscraper, three-dimensional, surrounded by American flags. BE AMERICANS.

Schmuederrich pulled him into the fourth row. People drew their knees in as they pushed past. The flat, cocked hats the ladies wore blocked his view. He sank into his seat almost with relief, a hideout of flowers, feathers, and tulle. Schmuederrich, ever gracious, greeted people left and right. He complained about the "riffraff outside" and was met with agreement.

Schmuederrich was beloved. He created this flattering atmosphere of exclusivity and importance. But what was Josef's role? What did Schmuederrich want from him? He turned to look around, and a pair of kids in the row behind them, a girl in a dirndl, a little boy in a man's suit, stuck their tongues out at him.

He withdrew deeper into himself. Suddenly regiments of flagbearers flooded the aisles. Onstage a group of storm troopers appeared, their gaze directed at nothing. The drums played a march. Enforced solemnity all around, he scarcely dared breathe. "This is incredible," said Schmuederrich. "This is like Nuremberg!"

Josef nodded. The wiry beard hair, when his fingertip passed over it, was capable of filling his entire consciousness. He could concentrate on a tiny point, allow himself to be absorbed by it. He could, like he'd done in the church pew with his parents, when a bit of lint from his sleeve danced in the light flooding in through the windows, exchange the big for something small.

Applause roared from the bleachers. A speaker assured the people that they weren't doing anything evil here. More applause. That the American press slandered them because they told the truth. Because they, like the best minds in Germany, warned against the dangerous mixing of the races—that was their duty. For everyone knew that a "standard human race," such as Communism advocated for, was an illusion, a blasphemous error that only served the goal of making the world the same everywhere, in order to more easily control it. No one here had anything against other races. But each race should protect and honor its particular God-given qualities.

He knew it all by heart. He'd had to proofread it again and again before printing it. Every time he read it he had the same thought, that the qualities they were talking about weren't something that held true for all eternity. After all, he himself had gone from being a Rhinelander to being a New Yorker.

Where was Fritz Kuhn, anyway? Kuhnazi. Chief of the Ratzis. That's how he was mocked in the press. Schmuederrich had said that they were mainly here for Kuhn.

An hour had already passed. He thought about whether he should go to Sam's Pizza on the corner of 125th afterward or get out a stop early, then he could buy Chinese dumplings and heat them up at home. Work at the print shop didn't start until eleven tomorrow morning. They had been working nonstop the past couple of days, printing flyers, brochures too. You could buy them at the tables all around, plus, despite the ban, swastika pins paired with little American flags.

He was wasting his time. He'd rather be at home, sitting on the couch or in front of his radio. Especially now that there was W2DKJ. He followed her across the frequencies; he recognized her handwriting by now, slightly halting and jumpy. Mostly updates on the weather in the Catskills. Still snow, lots of snow. "Grab your skis and head on up,

New Yorkers!" Yesterday he actually responded: "I'd love to come!"
You could say anything you wanted, after all. She laughed, then they
switched over to a different frequency, where they were alone, and she
said, "No, I'll come down there first."

Finally the applause was for Fritz Kuhn himself. His sizable belly was
held in by a belt and a tight-fitting brown uniform. He stood there at the
lectern and let his gaze sweep imperiously around the hundred-meter
expanse of the stadium.

"You all have heard of me, through the Jewish-controlled press, as a
creature with horns, a cloven hoof, and a long tail."

The crowd laughed. It was a loud, lurching sound that came from all
directions and went out in all directions, stopping nowhere, continually
renewing itself as Kuhn kept up his derision. Kuhn meanwhile didn't
make the slightest effort to rein in his German accent; he rather seemed
to flaunt it. Yorkville was teeming with such people.

"Vee doo not say zet oll Tschus are Communists . . ."

Kuhn paused. Looked to one side. A young man had jumped
onstage—he didn't get far; the brownshirts fell on him instantly, like
he was a fire that needed to be put out. The man now hung pitifully over
the edge of the stage, blows raining down on him, a tangle of legs, arms,
hands; in the middle a face twisted in pain. The police stormed onto the
stage, pulled the brownshirts off, hauled the man out. Boos, shouting,
whistles, suddenly a glimpse of a pair of white underwear, hairy legs—
they had pulled his pants down. Waves of laughter from the stadium. The
police led the man off the stage.

Kuhn didn't move. His hands resting on the lectern, bent slightly forward, he patiently watched what was happening. Then he began speaking again.

"A Jew," said Schmuederrich.

"How do you know that?"

"Look, there's a small delegation of Jews sitting up front. It was arranged with the German American Bund."

While Kuhn went on to demand a just America, a white America, an America not ruled by Jews, Josef tried to remember what kind of underwear he was wearing. Plaid?

"It was brave of him, though," he said to Schmuederrich.

"Brave? When the SA really wants to rough a guy up, it looks different. These people here know nothing's going to happen to them. Let them say what they want. He's got his little crowd of supporters. Tomorrow he'll be celebrated in all the newspapers as an anti-fascist."

A soprano performed "The Star-Spangled Banner." Immediately afterward, shouts of "Free America!" mixed with cries of the banned "*Sieg Heil!*" Schmuederrich was busy shaking hands. He waved Josef over to him. Josef pointed apologetically at his wristwatch, could see Schmuederrich's lips forming words, but he quickly fled outside.

At a take-out place on 126th he devoured a giant portion of rice and beef in a spicy sauce with a Senegalese name.

His building didn't have an elevator. Six flights of stairs. He always tried to find that day's rhythm, one that he could keep up all the way to the top.

He was half a flight to the top when he heard the ringing of the telephone. He now took the stairs two at a time, unlocked the door, and reached for the phone on the wall out of breath. The ringing had stopped. He put the receiver back on the hook. For a while he stood motionless in his dark apartment. The dog licked his hand.

He had sent his brother a photo of Princess.

> Impressive animal. But not all women like dogs. Did you think of that before you got her?

This was Carl's way of trying to find something out about his distant brother.

After standing still for some time, feeling like he'd forgotten his way around, he turned on the overhead light. Again he could see the face twisted in pain, the bright white underwear amid the uniformed men, the hairy legs, the arms pinned back.

He put on Bunny Berigan, "I Can't Get Started," poured himself some whiskey, and fell back onto the couch. He put his feet up on the coffee table and felt the stack of papers shift. Goebbels. For Arthur. He still had to translate it. No, he still had to refuse.

He grabbed a newspaper and learned that the television was the next big thing; it would change society, just as the radio had in the twenties.

The phone rang again. This time he got to it in time.

"You took off so soon, little man. What's wrong?"

"Nothing."

"Come to the Old Heidelberg next Tuesday at seven. There are a few German businessmen who want to meet you. The textile business. Could be interesting for you financially with those radio skills of yours. Dörsam will be there too. Don't let your nerves get the better of you, you sissy."

Josef knew Dörsam fleetingly from the Rotesandbar, where Dörsam usually stood at the bar drinking beer. Gray hair, bald spot, wiry, an engineer at Ford, old—the kind of person who had always been old.

He went into the bathroom and shaved for the second time that day, staring at the sad hard water spots on the fixtures. He took a rag and started cleaning. Whenever he cleaned, he felt like he was being watched. It wasn't possible for him to simply clean; he felt eyes on him every time. It was the only thing that kept him from cleaning—nothing else did—but today he made himself do it.

After he finished, he sat down at the desk with his radio. A call sign, ON4JC, came through: Jerome in Belgium. Jerome's English was quite decent. But when he realized that Josef was German, because his accent was thicker than ever before, he hissed something that sounded like "Asshole," and after that there was only empty static.

9

NEW YORK, FEBRUARY 1939

So there stood W2DKJ. A short, pale figure under the boathouse awning. He was a bit taken aback—she was very young.

"Hello, W2DKJ." He walked up to her with hand outstretched.

"Nice we can talk without everybody listening in for once," she said with a laugh. He guessed twenty, twenty-one. She was a bit taller than him. Her blond hair fell onto her shoulders from under a sturdy hat.

"May I, Lauren?" He stepped forward to join her under the awning and closed the umbrella. The park was empty and rainy—a disaster for a date. If that's what this was. He wasn't exactly sure. Plus, she wasn't pretty, not really. Her lips were too thin, her face square and boyish. He offered her a cigarette. She reached for one, and he tried some comradely conversation, asked about frequencies and times.

Then a silence ensued. She pulled on her cigarette and nodded, though he hadn't said anything. Rain beat down on the sandy path. Together they looked at a wall of water, the park in a blur behind it.

"So what brings you to New York anyway?" he asked. Then she started talking, and he quickly found out that she had made a break for it. That the aunt she was staying with on the Upper East Side still thought it was just a visit, but Lauren was checking the classifieds for apartments

and had her eye on a furnished room in Brooklyn. Lauren spoke with
the conspiratorial intimacy that sometimes sets in between complete
strangers when they know they won't ever see each other again—in a
remote harbor bar, on a train ride, on the beach. Yes, she was looking
for a job—didn't matter what kind, could be in a kitchen, as a salesgirl,
just so long as she could stand on her own two feet. Later she wanted to
go to college. He didn't know anyone who had gone to college and said
uncertainly, "That's a good idea."

Lauren looked him in the eye as they talked. She had none of the self-
consciousness of other women, the kind who played with their hair a lot,
laughed too loud, and locked both themselves and him into a perpetual
smile.

"The Catskills. That's where New Yorkers go for vacation, right?"

"My parents run a hotel in Woodstock. No vacation for us. Our vacation was coming to New York City."

"Got it," he said.

"Was it the same for you, back then? That you felt you just had to get
away? You're not from here, right?"

"No, I'm not from here."

A pause set in. She waited for him to keep talking.

"It was different. I didn't have a choice." She looked confused, ready
to object—as if he didn't understand how serious her situation was. But
he didn't want to talk about war and hunger. He wanted instead to hear
her voice, a voice that was more familiar to him than her face. "Tell me
more about the hotel."

"A small family hotel. With a ballroom, a dance orchestra, and a
swimming pool outside with a view of the mountains."

"Sounds horrible. I'd take off too."

"Cut it out, Joe," she said with a laugh. "You're not in my shoes."

He felt the sleeve of her coat brush against his when she took a step back, away from the rain, and he used the moment to glance down. She wore shoes with tall heels. If she took them off she'd be the same height as him.

He lit up another cigarette, held the pack out to her again, but this time she shook her head.

"And where are you from, Joe?"

"Germany."

"Germany," she repeated and paused in case he wanted to elaborate.

He didn't say anything. He didn't want to give in to the indignity of having to state where he stood on things, as had been expected of Germans for some time now. Finally he said, "You know, Lauren, in America you're actually supposed to act as if you were always here. I always liked that. It's only recently that things are different."

She nodded and took a step out from under the awning. "It's stopped."

They went south, the majestic Plaza Hotel in sight ahead of them. He told her that he particularly liked Central Park at this time of year, when the trees were bare, the view of the surrounding buildings clear. Lauren liked the park's hills and dales, the winding paths, and she explained that the architects who designed it in the nineteenth century had tried to reproduce the natural American landscape rather than the manicured parks of Europe. He gave her a look to show he was impressed. She pulled a New York travel guide from her pocket: "It's all in here."

She told him about the world's fair that would take place in New York two months from now, with new innovations, like television and a machine for washing dishes, and a big meetup for amateur radio operators. According to Lauren this was something you just had to go to—after all, over fifty thousand hams were registered in the US, so there were sure to be at least several hundred coming. That was amazing, almost like a family reunion. She lifted her eyes and looked at the skyscrapers, a gray set of teeth surrounding the park.

She reminded him of himself when he first arrived in the city fifteen years ago. The excitement of the beginning, the many beginnings—at that age, everything is a beginning. What had he actually been doing in all the time since then? Not much. Hadn't built anything, hadn't started anything. It was more like he'd mastered the art of disappearing. As if that was the one thing he'd succeeded at. The cabin in the woods in Harlem. Arthur was right. But things were going well for him, at least most of the time! The whole city was his.

She interrupted his thoughts: "What was your farthest contact?"

"Sydney. You?"

"Haiti. Not very far."

Where had she even learned to operate a radio? he asked. It wasn't exactly typical for women.

"Sure it is," she objected. "At my school they offered classes for girls. I even built my first radio myself."

"How long ago were these classes?" he asked.

"Oh, a long time ago. At least four years."

"Yes, that is a long time," he sighed.

She laughed. It was the first time he'd hinted at the age difference between them. A test without clear result. He told her about his apartment, that it seemed to him more and more like a radio station, like a window to the world. It was quickly apparent that they both shared the joy of turning a dial a few millimeters and drawing a whole continent closer, then turning the dial again to send it away and make yourself disappear. Feeling your pulse quicken when voices came through, never knowing whom they belonged to, observing your own reactions as if through a magnifying glass.

Was this her first time meeting with a man she didn't know? He'd have liked to ask her. Whatever the case, Lauren didn't seem the least bit self-conscious. Maybe because she was constantly interacting with strangers at the hotel? Did the thought please him? Her lack of insecurity made him insecure. Suddenly he didn't know if he was supposed to let her, the lady, walk ahead of him whenever they came across a big puddle that left only a narrow bit of dry sidewalk, or if he as the man should go first and make sure the way was clear. Once, because he hesitated and Lauren finally went ahead, he lost his balance and stepped in a puddle. His foot got soaked immediately, sock and shoe both. He tried not to show it.

He thought of the women he'd known. Mostly divorced women who all looked the same—always a bit on the plump side, with too much makeup on. They dredged their laughter from the depths of their weariness like a pesky hair they plucked from their tongue as they drank the third scotch he'd bought them.

The weather didn't hold. They were caught in a brief rain shower. When he opened his umbrella she threaded her arm through his, natural as anything. Now she was very close. A raindrop made a thin, shimmering line down her powdered face.

Fog rose from the lake, tickled his throat; he tried to suppress a cough. He wanted to avoid anything that would make him seem old. In the lower half of the park there were still bits of leftover snow. A melted snowman, a single glove left on top. They strolled through shifting zones of steam, rain, cold, warmth. He started sweating. She pressed his forearm with her hand to indicate that he should walk slower, acting like it was she who needed a break.

The rain stopped again, and she let go of his arm. Looked with concern at a few dark drops on her silk stockings. He reached for a clean handkerchief and a flyer slipped out of his jacket pocket.

Quickly he bent to pick it up. THINK CHRISTIAN. ACT CHRISTIAN. BUY CHRISTIAN.

"And you? What do you do for a living?" It seemed to cost her a lot of effort. Was it only now becoming clear to her how much older he was?

"I've worked at a print shop for many years. But I've got something new lined up. Technical assistance for a foreign company."

"Oh," she said.

They were drawing closer to the park exit, he could tell from the mounting clamor, the sirens, the car horns, the voices. On 59th Street they fought their way through the crowds, strolled past baroque porticos and old-fashioned carriages that waited outside the grand hotels for tourists. Marble lobbies with men who disappeared completely behind their uniforms and caps. Lauren looked at a store display window. "*The Grapes of Wrath*," she said, reading one title aloud, then another: "*Mein Kampf*." She laughed again, an embarrassed laugh this time. Maybe it had something to do with the look on his face. "Joe, you can't help it that Hitler's on the *New York Times* bestseller list."

Simply to be a person, he thought. *Who eats, breathes, sleeps, works, sometimes flirts with women, so long as they're over thirty. Simply to be.* At some point he had reached the insight that simply being was the most difficult thing. Everyone wanted to make you into something. Even if it was just a German who couldn't help being German.

They went on in silence, walking through empty playgrounds, bright chalk blurred from the rain, what was left of games of hopscotch. Finally she asked where exactly he was from—her family also came from Germany, she said, had immigrated in the mid-nineteenth century. He told her. She was interested, she said then, in Düsseldorf (*Doozledorf*)—what was it like growing up there? But he didn't want to talk about it. It wouldn't be able to measure up to her childhood and adolescence. Maybe she sensed this, because then she asked, "What was it like when you came here?"

He had to be careful when he thought back on that time. He could wade into these feelings like a lake whose waters slowly rose all around him. As if it were not at all long ago, and if he didn't watch out, everything he had achieved for himself could unravel, could turn out to be an illusion, collapse like a house of cards, as if he had achieved nothing at all, just a feather-light existence that was protected from nothing.

"It wasn't so bad. New York made it easy for me. A great city."

"I could lose myself in this city!" Lauren cried excitedly. "Hey, where do you live, Joe?"

"I'll be honest with you, it's not a prestigious address."

He thought of the crowded tenements. Of the bars, the dance clubs, where white people came like they were going on safari in deepest Africa.

"Harlem. East Harlem."

"There's nothing wrong with that. I've read about it." She pulled the New York guide out of her pocket again and flipped through it till she found Harlem. "Look, there's so much going on there. Negro intellectuals like Langston Hughes, jazz—"

"Sure," he interrupted her, "only at this point the bars are all run by Italians who hire Negro step dancers to pander to a white audience."

"Oh really?"

He was happy to know something for once.

Lauren stopped for a moment, pulled a map out of her pocket, all marked up. Carl had had a map once too. He would spread it out on the kitchen table again and again, tracing routes all across New York City. It had been folded and unfolded so many times that the fold in the middle was torn. And then at some point it was gone. Josef had left it somewhere by mistake.

"The New York Historical Society on 77th is open till five. We could go look at old photographs of the city."

He had never been in a museum before. He didn't know how you were supposed to act.

"I'm happy to walk with you there, Lauren. But then I have to go. I've got work."

"What about coffee?"

He was surprised. What did she see in him? Nevertheless he started looking up and down the street. There was a bar, more of a place for men who were built like dockworkers, and an Automat.

"I like Automats," she said.

The restaurant hadn't been reset yet after the midday rush. The chairs stood carelessly pulled back from the tables. He could picture the haste with which the white- and blue-collar workers had scarfed down their food and then gotten right back up again. Lauren wiped a few crumbs away with her fist; he went to hang up her coat.

He came back carrying a tray with two cups of coffee that clattered against each other and a slice of cheesecake to show how thoughtful he was. He was determined to steer the conversation more himself from now on.

"Automats were a big help to me in the beginning. I was afraid to speak."

"Really, Joe?" she asked, smiling and shaking her head.

"I knew maybe fifty words of English. Thick accent. Immigrants weren't exactly well-liked back then either, and as soon as you opened your mouth your cover was blown. You understand?"

He saw the sympathy in her look.

"And then the Automats, these links in a chain across New York.

They made me feel taken care of. The world would put food out for me in little glass windows. Sandwiches, scones, bagels, all waiting for me to decide. Just drop a coin in the slot, that was it."

She seemed to want to say something, but then after taking a breath she reached for her coffee and took a sip.

Bing Crosby sang airily,

> I'm no millionaire,
> but I'm not the type to care.

"Do you like Bing Crosby? We were born the same year, 1903. I know because people have told me I look a bit like him. What do you think?"

His question was a prompt to get her to look at him. She pulled her coffee cup closer.

"I always check the newspapers to see how much ol' Bing is showing his age, and then I compare the two of us."

"And?"

"So far it's a tie." He took his first sip of coffee. He could see that Lauren was looking for something. She tasted the cheesecake, chewed for a long time, swallowed.

> It's my universe,
> even with an empty purse.
> 'Cause I've got a pocketful of dreams.

"Sorry," said Lauren.

"For what?"

"I don't know. Maybe for getting so quiet all of a sudden."

"But you don't have to say anything." And then he added quietly, "And I don't either, actually."

They smiled at each other.

Small, firm breasts. He could see as she stood up and discreetly tucked her blouse into her skirt.

He still didn't have her phone number. He didn't want to ask, for the very reason that he liked her.

IO

NEUSS, JULY 1949

O N SUNDAY THEY ALL GO TO CHURCH: STAND UP, KNEEL, sit, stand up, sing,

Now thank we all our God,
with heart and hands and voices,
who wondrous things has done
in whom this world rejoices.

"Notice anything?" whispers Carl as the priest holds the host in the air, shows it to the congregation, and gives God the chance to transubstantiate. Josef notices a lot of things, but he doesn't know what in particular he's supposed to be looking out for. "The church bells are missing. They donated the metal to the war effort!"

The people are strangers to him. They all wear poorly cut clothes made of old fabric that looks like it would turn to dust if you so much as blew on it. Josef knows that he hardly looks any better, that he, in Carl's ill-fitting brown suit, is one of them. Only when he opens his mouth does anyone notice the difference.

After mass Josef stands in the church square a bit apart from the rest and smokes. By this point the neighbors nod when they see him. They know who he is, know that they don't really know. After Carl and Edith have finished shaking hands, they head for the park—the Sunday stroll. All that remains of the benches are the stone bases. The pond is a greenish-black, metallic brew, dusted with pollen. No ducks in sight, probably killed for food.

Despite the desolate look of it all, Carl wants to take a family photo. He managed to hang on to his Linhof Technika all throughout the war; now he places it on the tripod he brought with him, instructs Edith, Josef, and the children to stand in front of the pond, presses the self-timer, and hurries back. "Don't close your eyes! Look at the camera!" Josef notices that Carl goes up on his tiptoes.

"I'd like one of those myself. That's a real good one."

"You're welcome to borrow mine," says Carl.

"I'll take you up on that. Thanks."

"But what are you going to take pictures of around here? Rubble?"

He just nods.

"Something to remember us by? Before you move on, if you're moving on?"

He shrugs. "I don't know yet."

Is he staying or is he going—they're waiting for his answer. He has the answer—of course he'll be going, and of course they know that—but the limbo in which they all find themselves together gives him something to hold on to, and as soon as he voices his plan aloud he'll find himself in free fall.

He isn't quite there yet.

Back home Edith serves lunch. There are pork chops—three pieces of meat with appetizing crusts of glistening fat. He and Carl each get a whole piece, Edith shares the third with the children. He eats hungrily. As he does he steals looks at Edith. She eats quickly and matter-of-factly. She passes dishes around and always serves herself last.

"Josef liked to run away as a kid. You don't mind my telling them, do you?"

He smiles. He wouldn't call it running away. He doesn't have a word for it and is interested to hear what his brother has to say.

"He just kept on walking, through the different towns, through the forest. How old were you? Six, seven? I was just a little squirt myself, maybe four. I remember all the excitement at home very well."

"And then?" asked Edith.

Josef takes over now. "A farmer found me and brought me back." He doesn't tell them the most important part. That he was happy. He had snuck into a barn and buried himself in the hay. No one knew where he was, only him. He was safe.

"Don't you two get any ideas!" says Carl and raises his finger at the children in warning.

It's the first time that Carl has said anything about their childhood. Up till now he has seemed to focus solely on the present, solely on the things around them that they can see, hear, and touch, as if the rest were a theatrical mire, as if it were something you could drown in—and it's entirely possible that he's right.

He himself is not especially eager to dwell on it. But he'd had time. In Sandstone he walked three kilometers a day in his cell. He paced back and forth and counted how many times he'd paced the three-meter length of the cell. One thousand times.

Edith and Täubchen clear the table, producing a light, airy background music of scraping and clinking.

"Want to join me again tomorrow? I could use some help."

Carl only asks him every couple of days. It's not supposed to become something he takes for granted, their making the rounds of deliveries together.

"Of course, happy to!"

Carl nods and stands up. "Come on, let's play a game of chess."

Right at the outset Carl makes a mistake. In his eagerness to attack Josef's rook he leaves his queen unprotected. It's only the fourth move, and already Josef has taken Carl's queen, giving up only a knight in exchange. Under the table Carl steps on Josef's foot by mistake; he doesn't notice, takes it for a table leg. Josef doesn't pull his foot back.

"Do you want to take the move back? It takes the fun out of it otherwise."

"That would be dishonest."

Carl doesn't say anything more. He stares at the board, concentrating hard. His need to keep a brave face seems to demand his full attention. Josef takes advantage of the opportunity to tell him about his radio hobby.

"Yeah, we had that here too. When the war started it was banned."

"You can overcome any distance, Carl. You hear someone saying something who at that very moment is sitting in Paris."

"And what do you say?"

"You confirm that you can hear the other person. Maybe say a few words about the weather or exchange details about each other's radio equipment."

"That's all?"

"Sure. Sometimes amateur operators help rescue people by accident when they intercept signals of people in distress. One thing you have to know is that sometimes you can only transmit a great distance away. It has to do with the ground waves. The waves are distributed across various elevations. The waves that travel close to the ground get swallowed up by different obstacles in their path. They call that the dead zone. But in the open air there's barely any loss of energy. The waves rise over all obstacles, buildings, forests, bridges, and then they're reflected back down to earth. But it's usually somewhere very far away. That's why, for example, the report of an avalanche in Austria can be picked up in England. From there a message can be sent back to a town near where the avalanche occurred and help can be called in."

"I can't think." Carl gestures at the board.

Carl has lost his major pieces. They play on in silence. Five minutes later Josef has checkmate.

"I'm a bit out of practice."

"We played every now and then on Ellis Island."

"There you go," says Carl.

They played every kind of game—poker, skat—for money, even though it was against the rules. "I might as well do something illegal now," one of the Japanese men had said once, "otherwise I'd be in here for no reason."

II

NEW YORK, FEBRUARY 1939

A T THE LAST MINUTE HE STEPPED OUT OF THE WAY OF A woman leaving the Bremenhaus, laughing as she turned to the person with her. The fur collar of her coat brushed against his cheek. No one noticed but him. Clown noses and masks in the window displays; it was Fat Tuesday.

He found Schmuederrich outside the Schaller & Weber butcher's shop. He was again wearing the military uniform of the German American Bund. The eyes in his chubby-cheeked face were narrow and bleary from lack of sleep. He held one hand out to shake Josef's and clapped him on the shoulder with the other. "Let them do the talking, all right?"

The air in the Old Heidelberg was stale and overheated. It smelled of pot roast, beer, and cigars. Someone had thrown streamers onto the red-checkered tablecloths. They wound around the vases, which held little swastika flags. A small band played German Carnival songs.

For Carnival comes only once a year, Carnival on the Rhine.

Schmuederrich pointed to a table way in the back. From that distance, Josef recognized Dörsam. The men broke off their discussion and leaned back, but none of them stood up. An elegantly dressed gentleman with brilliantined hair said mockingly, "Good heavens, Schmuederrich, you really dressed to the hilt, didn't you! Now I feel like Hitler wearing a raincoat when he met Mussolini."

Schmuederrich laughed, but the man cut him off with a hand gesture. "This guy here? This is the one with the radio?" Schmuederrich made introductions. The man's name was Dr. Ritter. He was in the textiles business. The third man at the table was a normal-looking guy, blond, big boned, baby faced. "Max has just arrived from Hamburg, but he lived in New York for a few years. He's also a radio hobbyist," said Dr. Ritter, looking at Josef with interest.

Josef took a seat next to Dörsam. Dr. Ritter talked about his grand hotel in Times Square, the Taft—"Old world, you know"—and about the luxury cabin on his ship. Whenever someone else was speaking, he drummed softly on the table with his fingers.

A girl in a yellow silk dress, dressed up in Chinese costume, walked among the tables with a basket of roses, flirting. Max kept sniffing, every few seconds. He seemed not to notice it, but at times this wet rasping sound was all Josef could hear.

Josef wasn't part of the conversation. He waited for the food, and when it came, he awkwardly set about eating his stuffed cabbage, like someone who was seated at the same table quite by accident and wasn't actually one of the party. The words "cleaning house" had been uttered; they were talking about Germany. The words sat there on the table between the bread basket and the swastikas. He wondered if he could just take off without anyone noticing. If these were the businesspeople who needed a radio operator, it would hardly be an improvement on his old job.

Just then Dr. Ritter said, "Herr Klein. What is your opinion of the New York melting pot?"

"I don't think I have an opinion of it," he said cautiously.

"Oh, I know Josef," Schmuederrich jumped in. "He likes it here. Every day he gets to feel like he's on a trip around the world."

Laughter. But Dr. Ritter grew serious again. He had been walking around on the Lower East Side, he said, and he could hardly believe how backward life there was, in this day and age, a pure slum in the middle of a global metropolis, as if the poorest regions of Eastern Europe had just been dumped there, every one of them a criminal. It was high time this city started to fight back. Where did he live?

"In Harlem." He always said it as if he were asking a question. Most people's faces went blank when they heard it, tight lipped, especially women.

"You probably can't find space anywhere else, is that it? I mean the city is bursting at the seams, especially with all the refugees from Europe."

Josef loosened his tie and said nothing.

"And the rioting in Harlem doesn't bother you, Herr Klein?"

"Well, nowadays there's rioting all over the place."

"He's right about that," Schmuederrich jumped in again. "Even at Madison Square Garden we had to hear insults from the anti-fascists. Right, Josef? They called you a 'bloody bastard.'"

He was less and less happy with where the conversation was going.

"I like living there. Good food, pretty women, and the best jazz in the world."

A derisive smile in the corner of Dr. Ritter's mouth. Max seemed satisfied. They were competing against each other, Josef realized.

Snow was falling outside, when the door opened he could see each individual snowflake lit up brightly in the glow of the streetlamps. Washington next week, then Chicago, meetings everywhere—the firm was expanding at breakneck pace.

"He's here," said Dörsam softly to Dr. Ritter, and there stood a tall man about sixty years old, his shoulders dusted with snow, good-looking, like a movie star. He walked up to the table and shook everyone's hand, even Josef's. Josef didn't catch the name. At the table there was a kind of awe; it was palpable.

"The radioman," said Schmuederrich, and Josef felt himself sitting up straighter. He was being sized up; it was a test.

"Let's speak in private, Nikolaus." The man had addressed Dr. Ritter, speaking with an accent that Josef had never heard. The two men went to a spot over by the wall that was screened by a curtain, then they disappeared through the wall like something in a magic trick, and he had the feeling that whatever the test was, he hadn't passed.

It was silent at the table. Everyone seemed to know who the man was, just not him.

"That's Duquesne," said Schmuederrich finally, as if that explained everything. Had he missed something?

They drank their beers very slowly. Dr. Ritter's glass was still half full. Max kneaded a piece of bread and hummed along to the music.

> Who hasn't spent a mild summer's night dreaming of delight
> and drinking wine on the Rhine.
> The soul intoxicated . . . The sick heart healed.

A little later a woman appeared, the kind of woman he had only ever seen in the movies, wearing a fur stole and a silk dress, stunningly beautiful. She swept past them and likewise entered the back room. This time he noticed the leather-padded door.

"Tell us a bit more about your radio equipment," Dr. Ritter said when he came back to the table. Josef placed the photo on the table. He didn't show it to women anymore; they imagined nights being left sitting alone on the couch while squeals and strange voices floated through the room. He had never been able to get a woman to share in his excitement at how small the world truly was. The men, however, saw the picture and started asking questions. Yes, of course he knew Morse code. And yes, he could also transmit speech. Headphones, microphone—he had everything. He played it cool, enjoying the attention and the fact that he was finally in a position to answer questions to their satisfaction. He spoke at length of making single-layer solenoidal coils and electrical loads with variable resistors. He confirmed that it was possible to transmit as far as Hamburg and to receive signals from there. "This would speed up the firm's communications enormously, Herr Dr. Ritter," said Schmuederrich assiduously.

But he didn't tell them the most important thing. What it was like to listen at night to the crackle and static as he carefully turned the tuning knob. To send out a signal and wait for someone to respond. Someone in Toronto, Helsinki, or Cairo. He was just a call sign and a voice; they were all just call signs and voices.

Dr. Ritter steered the conversation to war, to mangled arms and legs and charred faces. Russia, 1917. Max had been there, and had been missing two toes ever since. He'd had to amputate them himself. Schmuederrich had also fought the Bolsheviks, in Munich in 1919, and he must have bagged a couple of 'em too, he said. Dörsam had been on the Western Front, in France. That was where Josef's father had been killed; he himself had still been a child then. They all assured one another that they had always kept the faith. *Old comrades.*

Outside everything was white. He headed back to Harlem. They'd told him the job was his. His radio equipment was needed, also his knowledge of Morse code. Max, who when it came to Morse was still a beginner, would like to learn from him; they could work together.

He didn't feel happy about it. He considered whether he should turn the job down.

He went to Club Hot-Cha, bought a ticket, and sat down at a table. The showgirls hopped, stomped, and strutted; with frozen smiles they kicked their legs high in the air. At the table next to his sat a man whose hand sometimes disappeared under the table. Josef was the only one who could see it, and the man didn't seem to care. Then the dancers walked off and a single showgirl appeared. She wore only feather boas and a pair of hot pants; first she danced with the boas, then she pulled the hot pants off and let the boas drop.

He had wound up at a show like this once before. It was after he had just made it through a three-week journey by boat and the old country seemed to be sinking behind him for good. Carl's voice and the voice of his mother would only be in his head from now on, or in his dreams.

12

NEW YORK, JANUARY 1924

H E COULD STILL FEEL HER HAND ON HIS HAIR. SHE'D CUT IT
for him the day before. They probably wouldn't ever see each other
again—if you went to America, you were gone. That's how his mother said
it: if you went to America, you were gone. She had sounded composed.

He had set two alarm clocks, but he couldn't sleep for fear that he
wouldn't hear them and would miss the train and then, just like Carl,
wouldn't be able to go to America.

He was alone for the first time. He lived in a room with lots of people,
but no one knew him. Meals were served three times a day in soft, bend-
able metal dishes.

Only salt water came from the faucets. No one bathed. The men pissed
over the railing. By the third day he was doing it too, pissing with a soft
sigh of relief into this black something of which the world consisted.

There was no longer such a thing as morning or afternoon. He had
bought a winter ticket; it was cheaper. Black smoke hissed down on the
third-class deck. He knew that up in first class they had an orchestra
that played dance music, a smokers' lounge, and a mail room.

Straw leaked out of the mattresses. Leaked down upon him from the snoring man in the bunk above him. His whole body itched. He lay on his stomach and pinned his hands under him, bits of skin caught under his fingernails.

The men in the other bunks played cards late into the night. He heard of the construction boom in New York. He couldn't work construction. He was too weak for a job like that. He heard that the cities were over-crowded. In the coming year America would be putting the brakes on immigration. He would have liked to talk to Carl about it, to ask Carl to reassure him, Carl who now sat in Düsseldorf with a bandage over his eye.

Sometimes he heard prayers. Ever since what had happened to Carl, since he had lost an eye and with it his entry visa, he knew that prayers didn't help.

One morning the city rose before them from up out of the sea. Suitcases, rugs, baskets, feather beds were brought up from the depths of the ship. Solemnly he put on his father's black suit—good prewar quality, thick material, hardly ever worn. By now the ocean liner had sailed so close to the skyscrapers that he could count the windows, which looked down on them like countless eyes. The photos hadn't prepared him for the sight. The grandeur, the majesty—it was the difference between be-ing blind and seeing.

They had to wait—*first class first*. With their cheap tickets they had already made themselves suspect.

Around him crying children and mothers trying to console them. Men who puffed their chests out, thrust their chins forward, as if America would be a cinch. Patches of ice knocked together in the black water, a lazy splinter and crunch. He blew into his hands, trying to warm them.

Finally they let them on land too, and the firm ground under his feet was a blessing. They all wobbled like sailors. At the pier they were herded over to the ferry landing, while the first-class passengers were already on their way to their homes and hotels.

He stood all the way at the back and watched the fluttering train of hungry seagulls that flew in their wake. He didn't dare throw bread to them. He could feel the others' eyes on him, all poor devils like him. They sailed toward a building that stood in the middle of the water, a grand, castle-like edifice. Ellis Island.

He plunged into a loud tumult. Women in bright peasant dress held their bags close; men in uniform shouted instructions in several languages. The crowd was directionless, helpless. He didn't know what to do either. A man put his false teeth in. Around them the stench of sweat and vomit. He found a bathroom. Here there was pushing and shoving, eventually he started shoving back. He shaved, spit blood. His gums hurt. He drank a sip of water; here too it tasted salty.

"No, this way!" They sent him up a staircase. Talk of what this staircase meant had gotten back to Europe. Upstairs, behind a window, stood doctors who looked you over to see if you were fit to be an American. If you breathed heavily, then no. He sprinted upstairs and stood in a giant hall with wooden benches, chandeliers swaying overhead. He seemed to have passed the test. He took a seat, and as he sat he could feel the rocking motion of the ship in his body for a long time.

He tried to read the faces of the inspectors, looking for what they liked to see. He saw how the young women laughed at jokes, summoned all their charm. He saw a woman get a chalk mark on her shoulder and burst into tears.

"You're next!"

He jumped up immediately. A man who didn't look like a doctor told him to show him his hands and stick out his tongue. He sent him on to an inspector: name, age, date of birth. Every time he answered, the inspector checked the answer against his papers. Finally Josef was handed an open Bible. He was supposed to read a passage out loud, in English. He read, without understanding, and nodded, again without understanding, whenever the inspector said something. He was lucky. An officer waved him on, more friendly than before: "Your landing card, mister." They pinned a piece of paper to his lapel. He walked through a kind of fairground: food stalls, a mail kiosk, booths where you could exchange currency, train tickets to California, bulletin boards with ads for English-language courses and offers for migrant workers. He exchanged his money, Reichsmarks to dollars at a rate of 4.2 billion to 1. He received one hundred eighty-one dollars in return.

He had his luggage sent to the Engelking family, 32 Mott Street, Lower East Side. He tried to remember how they were related. Years ago the Engelkings had sent them a photo: the father in a suit with a round black hat—it was called a bowler hat, Carl said. Later they saw this hat on Charlie Chaplin in the movie house on Königsallee. Engelking looked distinguished; he wrote that he had started a business in New York.

A feeling of happiness rippled through his body as they cast off in the dim afternoon light and steered once more toward the southern tip of Manhattan.

He passed through a ravine of gray stone, walking stiffly, concentrating on every step. The city was filled with a constant din. A hammering, pounding, metal on metal. Sirens wailed.

He kept craning his head back. Scrollwork, gables, columns, even way up high. This was what he imagined Rome to be like, or Athens. *Carl, take a look at this.* He closed one eye. Was it the left or the right? A building with tall stone columns, mythological figures adorning the façade: NEW YORK STOCK EXCHANGE. Men in a hurry all around him. He himself seemed invisible; only when he stopped could he hear them chuffing with annoyance.

He lingered a long time in front of a gold-plated door. Through it he could see a lobby with ornate vaulted ceilings, chandeliers, and richly upholstered furniture. WOOLWORTH BUILDING read the letters above the entrance. A doorman gave him a warning look. *Another one from these ships, from poor Europe!*

The black suit smelled of moldy potato sprouts. Whenever he stood still the smell was everywhere, so intense that it horrified him. His mouth was dry, and there was a steady pain weighing down on his forehead. That night he found a boardinghouse for new arrivals. It was a squalid basement. He didn't want to go see the Engelkings yet. He had to know what it was like to have to fend for himself in this city.

The light stayed on the whole night. Under the cardboard boxes and wooden boards the bare concrete floor. The blankets were full of holes. His head on his kit bag, his legs curled up; if he were to stretch them out, they would be in another man's face. His bunk on the ship seemed like a luxury now. His exhaustion was great enough; he would close his eyes and make it through this night, this one night. He would look around for a better place to stay. With that, he fell asleep. With the first light that fell into the basement through the narrow street-level windows, he awoke and sat up, saw men slowly getting up, gathering their things, and trudging off toward the stairs, something ashamed in their movements, each of them wanting to put this experience behind him.

That day he walked the streets up and down, sometimes stopping when he saw a notice. He sensed Carl next to him, Carl giving his opinions. WAITER WANTED. *No, we'll find something better.* He saw churches in between tall apartment buildings. They seemed pinned in, their arms pressed close to their sides. Much different than in Düsseldorf, where the churches stood apart, even on little hills, so that they towered over everything. It all seemed out of proportion, and as a result his small stature seemed to him less tragic here, with the tall, sleek towers sneering down at everything. But he couldn't really gauge how fast to walk, the appropriate distance to allow between himself and others. He found himself surrounded by sighs and curses and angry *excuse-me*s, which meant the opposite. In the aisle at the grocery store a woman ahead of him moved aside to let him pass, and when he stepped back he was in the way of the surly customers behind him. On the stairs leading down to the subway he felt like he was just about to fall on someone. Often he knocked into people's shoulders, hat brims jabbed him in the face, he was jostled, and all the while the hissed curses seemed directed at him, as if he was the one at fault. He began to see himself from high above, a black dot moving through the streets.

He looked up the Engelking family when he started yearning for a bath and could feel the lice in his hair. The family lived on the Lower East Side. He wandered first through half of Chinatown, a neighborhood where all the signs were in Chinese, except for CHOP SUEY, which he guessed was meant to be immediately identifiable to Americans.

The family lived in a single greasy room, their clothes hung on nails on the walls. Five kids—all of them had a cough. The business they'd founded was on the kitchen table: a pile of busted umbrellas.

The worst thing was the noise that filled the space between the apartment buildings: peddlers' cries, the rumble of cars, and the screams from inside the buildings, which sounded like someone was being beaten. Women sat outside in their house dresses. One pushed a breast back under her neckline; it had fallen out. Bare legs with blue bruises. The misery continued as he moved down the street. Shouting women, limping men, dogs mating, peddlers pushing carts. A cat landed on its back at his feet and let out a pitiful yowl. From a window he heard children laughing. There were many languages spoken on the Engelkings' street, everything except English.

He left the family after only one night and this time went to a sailors' hostel. He was a bit relieved. He had discovered what it was to be alone.

He dragged himself through the streets, his hands in the pockets of his ancient suit.

He knew he would eventually have to become somebody, but he still had time for that. He could start fresh—yes, he was starting fresh. He wandered through the streets feeling invincible. Invincible, as if he hadn't been born yet.

He had stopped thinking about Carl.

After a few days, Arthur found him. Josef was lying on his suitcase; Arthur looked him up and down. "German. I can tell by the cigarettes."

Josef sat up. "Hardworking people," he said, pitching himself, and smiled, because Arthur had something trustworthy and kind in his gaze, and he wore a red-blond Charlie Chaplin mustache. Josef gave him his last Bremaria; Arthur offered him a Chesterfield in exchange.

"I've been seeing you walking down Vandam Street for days. I've got my shop there. I'd have a place for you to stay. A couch. What's your name?"

"Josef."

"Give Joe a try."

He ordered himself to trust Arthur. He followed him into the subway, his red-blond hair always in sight, let him lead him around the city, through its countless entrances and exits, its noise. Often he didn't know where the noise was coming from. At some point they were back aboveground. This was the Bronx, Arthur said.

The apartment was right next to an elevated train track, on the sixth floor. Arthur locked the door behind them. Darkness, the smell of wet wool. He could barely see a thing. "You can have the couch. The bathroom is down the hall. Two dollars a week. You can earn it from me at the shop. A print shop."

Everything in this apartment shook whenever a train thundered past. He had never heard such a noise. He lay on his back, and the noise sent vibrations throughout his body. He felt the full extent of it, from the tips of his toes to the top of his head, and realized that for the first time this body belonged to him, as if this city had given him shape, footing, however much it might rattle him.

13

NEW YORK, MARCH 1939

MAX WAS VERY TALL. AS HE STEPPED INSIDE JOSEF'S APART-ment he stooped a little, shoulders slumped, as if ever since he'd gotten his first growth spurt he'd also been bowing apologetically to others. Princess started barking.

"Does he bite?"

"She doesn't bite. She doesn't usually bark either."

Max tossed his wet hat and wet coat on the couch. Rain had been falling in Harlem for hours, blurred light outside the window. "Rough neighborhood. I was afraid I'd wind up with a knife in my back. Before I went back to Germany I lived in Bushwick. It was better there."

He thought about how to respond. "Here we've got the best jazz in the world," he finally countered.

"In Germany that'll land you in jail."

"Oh yeah?"

"Jazzhounds go to jail." Max smiled, and it wasn't clear whether he approved of this rule or was making fun of it.

"Should we start?" asked Josef.

"Easy does it, now. Calm down. The appointment is in half an hour. Can you make some coffee?"

Easy does it, now. Calm down. No one ever said that who was actually calm.

Max used one finger to transmit instead of placing three fingers on the Morse key and using his index finger to press the knob. His code didn't have any rhythm, was downright unmusical. He had a long line of numbers in front of him. Encryption was prohibited for amateurs. Josef didn't know what problem he should point out to Max first. He was sitting there with his mouth all twisted up and sending nonsense out into the ether.

"They're going to send you back a question mark."

"Really?"

"You're not leaving a clear space between signals, no one can understand you. How long have you been sending Morse code?"

"During training in Hamburg they convinced me to use my right hand. I'm left-handed. It's hard with my right hand."

"Was there a test?"

The look on Max's face turned into a sneer; there was no answer. Again the question mark came through to them: *dit-dit-dah-dah-dit-dit.*

"You have to relax your arm more. Look, this is how you do it." Josef pulled the key closer and demonstrated.

"I can't learn it that quickly."

"Then use the microphone."

"They only want Morse code. Can't you take over for today?"

"Encryption is prohibited. If somebody recognizes my handwriting, I'll be in for it."

Max pulled out two ten-dollar bills. Josef rubbed his neck, then he nodded and took the money. "For today. But I'll have to think about whether I can keep doing it in the future."

"You go ahead and think about it."

Again the scornful look. Josef hesitated, then he pulled the row of numbers closer and started transmitting. After ten minutes he received a confirmation. Max sat down on the couch and lit himself a cigarette—Bremaria, from Germany—but only when Josef looked over did he offer him one. Josef took a drag. The taste filled his senses, took him back to Düsseldorf, back to the fields by the Rhine, the sight of ships, back to being young at that time, a youth without a future.

"At one o'clock they're expecting the next transmission, this time on another frequency," Max told him.

"Why are you sending in code?"

"Should just anybody be able to find out who our customers are and what we're selling them?"

"And why aren't we sending everything at once?"

"Security measures. This way they can't track our coordinates."

Max swirled his cold coffee. Next door Mrs. Meeropol was yelling at her kids.

"What is it we're sending?"

"Orders, claims, customer information, new locations. Dr. Ritter has left for Chicago by now."

"How does the encryption work?"

"You use a book. Sometime soon I'll bring somebody with me. He's the one who does it." Max's foot jittered.

"Does the company have that much business?"

"Yes."

Max was tense in a way that seemed to carry over to Josef. He put on Ella Fitzgerald, "Goodnight, My Love," and smoked, trying to fight off the feeling that something wasn't right.

At one o'clock the signal was too weak. Josef went up on the roof, checked the antenna; just as he'd thought, the wire had come loose from its housing. Josef put it back in place. He looked across the roofs, the swaying clotheslines, the forgotten bedsheets blowing in the wind. He thought about Max. Tall people had it easy. By plain virtue of their height they radiated authority and superiority. But in Max's case something seemed to have gone wrong—something about that slightly hunched back of his, like he'd rather be short than tall.

When he came back down, he could hear a howling, buzzing, and crackling coming from the apartment, as if from a large insect. Max was turning the tuning knob aimlessly.

"Turn that thing off for a second."

Max looked up at him and, to his surprise, did as he asked.

"What's this really about?"

"Business. We told you already."

A cold glare, eyes moving restlessly left and right.

He hesitated. "Tell me about Germany. What did you witness there?"

"What did I witness?" Max did an imitation of someone who was meant to sound flustered and hysterical.

"You said jazzhounds are getting arrested."

"Yeah, they'd probably arrest you too." Max laughed, then, seeing that Josef was serious, looked at the clock. "Almost two. Back to work, Herr Klein. Or else I'll have to take the money back."

Josef sent everything in ten minutes and received a confirmation. Max again parked himself on the couch, scratching the panting German shepherd behind the ears.

"These days they hate Germans here," Max complained.

"There are good reasons for that, don't you think?"

"I was gone for two years. And now they look at you like you're the scum of the earth."

"So?" Josef caught sight of Max's hands: wide, frog-like fingertips and soft white skin.

"The problem is," Max went on, "the Germans here are doing it all wrong. I was at the rally at Madison Square Garden myself. And I saw you there."

"I was there for our customers' sake. Not my own."

Max rubbed his chin. "I'm going to let you in on something. Fritz Kuhn isn't authorized."

"What do I care?"

"The party distanced itself from Kuhn years ago. That meant no more parades and rallies in America, no swastikas, no Kuhn. But Kuhn is still at it. He actually thinks Hitler is going to name him top Nazi in charge of all of America someday."

"What about the photo that shows Kuhn and Hitler together?" he asked in spite of himself.

"The photo is from the Olympics in Berlin. That day Hitler was taking photos with anybody who asked."

Josef looked at him, thinking. They shared a sense of outrage about Kuhn, but for completely different reasons. Josef waited till Max had lit his next cigarette and taken a drag.

"Why did you go back to Germany two years ago?"

"Oh, I'd seen the ads. The Reich pays for your passage. Very enticing."

Josef had seen the ads too. Everyone saw them. Including Mrs. Dollings. Somehow he didn't feel like it was him the ads were trying to reach.

"So why are you back, then?"

"I'll tell you some other time."

That night he took the dog for a walk in the darkness on 125th Street. The rain had stopped, but the power had gone out. A woman was holding on to a streetlamp. She bent over and spit blood.

He walked past the auto repair shops, the scrap heap, and the collection facilities for bottles and paper. A cold wind blew in from the river. A man stood motionless, looking at the dark sky and talking to himself. Josef was seeing people like him, disturbed people, more and more often. They seemed like a foretaste or an aftereffect of the street orators, who had taken the idea of talking quietly to oneself a step further, gathering other people around them and shouting the words "world domination" and "injustice" into their faces.

Max had told him that he spent the worst years of the Depression as a window washer. He came in the twenties, with the last big wave of immigrants, and he only ever found bad jobs. Delivery driver, elevator boy, dishwasher. And even these jobs he ended up losing.

Window washer was a job you could always get—nobody wanted it. They would let him out the window twenty floors up with some ropes around him, while the office workers at their desks tried hard not to notice him. He'd dip the window brush in soapy water and wipe it across the glass, and the whole time he felt like he was fighting for his life. A dollar a day. They were the same windows, on Wall Street, that the stockbrokers had jumped out of. He, on the other hand, had survived the big crisis. "If you don't have much, you can't lose much either."

It was the only moment that fit the slumped shoulders, and Josef had felt sorry for him. It was a better feeling than the uneasiness Max made him feel every time he said something about Germany and looked at Josef with that cold gaze of his.

14

NEW YORK, MARCH 1939

As PROMISED, THE NEXT TIME HE CAME, MAX BROUGHT someone with him. The man slunk past him with his eyes lowered, mumbled, "Ludwig," and vanished into a corner.

Poorly shaven, a bright bald spot, wrinkled suit, somewhere around fifty. He seemed determined to act as if he wasn't there at all, but in so doing he drew even more attention to himself. Josef asked if he wouldn't rather come sit with them; the man said no. Josef brought him a chair. The man took a seat, brought out a book wrapped in brown paper, and ran his left index finger down the lines, taking notes with his right hand. This was the guy who did the encryption? When Josef got closer, Ludwig quickly slammed the book shut and smiled. He had the glassy-eyed look of a drunk.

"Where'd you dig him up?" asked Josef as Max followed him into the kitchen.

"Ritter has total confidence in him. Go ahead and ask him yourself."

Ludwig spoke very little, and when he did it was so garbled that Josef soon got tired of having to ask him to repeat himself. After several attempts he was reasonably sure that Ludwig had worked as a bookseller at the Germania bookstore in Yorkville, had lived in America for a few years, and was now glad to have a new job. What had he done when he lived in Germany? Ludwig mumbled something that sounded like "a little of this, a little of that." Leaning back in his chair, Ludwig sometimes closed his eyes. It wasn't clear if this was from sleepiness or concentration. And it was just as easy to imagine that he didn't shut his eyes completely but rather was secretly looking around the room.

Again Josef needed only ten minutes to transmit the columns of numbers. Again he had no idea what he was sending.

When it was time for a break he put on Billie Holiday.

"More jungle music today, huh?" sneered Max and threw two ten-dollar bills onto the table. Josef put the bills in his pocket. The next scheduled transmission was in half an hour. The men had made themselves comfortable on the couch, petting Princess and blowing smoke into the air.

"You got anything to eat? We'll pay extra."

"Why don't we go out?"

Ludwig and Max exchanged glances.

"How about you go pick something up for us?"

"What am I, your nanny?"

"We don't have enough time. Here, two dollars, now go and pick something up for us. Please, please, dear Josef."

He walked with the sun in his eyes and saw only silhouettes. There were strangers in his apartment. He walked quickly to Idrie's and bought four slices of bean pie, then two bagels at the grocery store.

When he was back, he first looked around the room suspiciously, then he threw the bags onto the table. Max took out a bean pie.

"What's this?"

"It's Italian," Josef said.

"They really know what they're doing, those Italians," Max said, chewing, and Josef fought back a smile.

Ludwig pulled apart the rubberlike bagel. "And this here? This Italian too?"

Josef nodded.

"That's a bagel, you idiot," said Max. "Josef here is putting us on."

At night, when he was alone again, he thought of Lauren. Ten days had passed since they'd met, and he hadn't heard anything from her. He wasn't sure what Lauren was looking for, whether it was just a friend in the global ham radio community or a man. And he didn't know which he wanted either. Unlike most women, she didn't seem to have her mind set on anything in particular, or to be inspecting him for positive and negative qualities. This inspection was usually driven by the suspicion that there had to be something wrong with him if he was still unmarried.

Nevertheless there seemed to be something about him that women liked. Arthur called it the James Cagney factor: that crooked grin of his, sloping down toward the right side of his face, a movie-star bad-guy grin. The fact that on top of the dangerous smile he was also short—some women found it downright irresistible.

He mostly hung out by the bar, half standing, half sitting. That way he was always free to make a quick exit. There was a kind of woman who acted like she was just trying to order something but was glad to be pulled into a conversation. He would buy her a drink; the barstool made him look as tall as any other guy. Then he would pay her compliments, one after another, like dropping coins into a jukebox so the music wouldn't stop.

He hadn't paid Lauren a single compliment. He wouldn't even have been able to come up with one. She wasn't pretty, after all. And what it was that actually excited him—how could he put that into words? It had to do with who she was inside. *You've got character. You're smart.*

A man couldn't say something like that to a woman.

He dialed in the frequency he had spoken to Lauren on. He did it in much the same way that he sometimes looked at souvenirs he'd kept from other women: a forgotten pair of sunglasses, a pencil, a candy wrapper. He didn't really expect to hear from her again. But he also wasn't sure if it would be such a good thing if he did, given his unusual work situation. She hadn't called him, though he'd given her his number. She was probably too busy finding a room and a job in New York. Then suddenly he heard her voice.

"W2!" he cried.

She'd been at home with her parents for the past two days, explaining her decision to go to New York. Her parents wouldn't let her leave. She wasn't exactly locked up, it wasn't house arrest, no, but tears and yelling, her mother hysterical, her father calm and sensible as usual, but on her mother's side. It was horrible. Her mother had called her irresponsible, inconsiderate, ungrateful, she had everything here, she could just as easily go to college in Poughkeepsie if she absolutely insisted on going to college, what in heaven's name did she hope to find in New York, that godless city, nothing but noise and violence.

She didn't know, was all she could ever say to her mother. She just knew that she wanted to live in New York.

Tomorrow she was hopping a bus to Manhattan. Next week she was starting a job as a night nurse at Manhattan General—just a training position at first. Definitely not an easy job, but she had to make money somehow, her own money. She talked as if they were alone, but the whole world was listening in. It was against radio etiquette to talk about personal matters, and of course she knew this and kept stammering out apologies—"Sorry, sorry"—which only made her sob even louder.

"Can we see each other?"

He was alarmed. He thought of the men turning up regularly at his apartment of late, and how unpleasant it would be to have to lie to Lauren when she asked about his work, to tell her everything was great. "I have to be out of town for a while, traveling," he said. "I've got this new job."

"Oh." He heard her sniffle. "How long?"

"Two months," he was pained to answer. Emptiness. Static.

"I'll call you in two months, Joe." He heard voices in the background. Someone knocked on the door, then Lauren broke the connection.

He had asked Arthur for a week off. His hopes of being able to quit his job with Arthur as a way of escaping the political tumult of the print shop hadn't really worked out. The new job was no alternative, which, really, he could have guessed. He was mad at himself. He had wanted to prove his abilities as a radio operator and had ignored everything that didn't add up.

He found Arthur in his office, hazy with cigarette smoke, poring over magazines and flyers. It was just nine o'clock in the morning, the shop floor was still quiet. Arthur smoothed out his Chaplin mustache.

"Have a good break?"

"I don't know. I've got two strange characters in my apartment who have commandeered my radio to use for a Hamburg textile company—and pressed me into service too since they can't do anything themselves, not even get their own food, and in exchange for all of it I'm making a pile of money."

Arthur put his cigarette out very slowly.

"Did the job come through Schmuederrich?"

He nodded.

"You know you can go to jail for this, don't you?"

He could see through the frosted-glass door that the ceiling lamps in the shop had come on. Something tightened in his throat. He heard Arthur saying, "I'm not going to claim that my activities with the black Hitler fans aren't without risk. But working for the Germans is extremely reckless."

"I'm not working for the Germans," said Josef quietly.

"Oh yes you are."

Now it had been said aloud. He could barely breathe by this point. The oxygen seemed not to reach his lungs.

Arthur said quietly, "Whatever you do, just don't make a big scene in front of them. If at some point they mention it themselves, act like it had been obvious from the get-go. Which if you ask me, it was. How can you be so naïve?"

"I'll stop."

"Good luck. I know Schmuederrich and his men. He wears that uniform of his for a reason."

Panic flooded his body, brief flashing moments of horror that reached down to his toes. As if his body already knew everything, knew the true magnitude of the situation. He accepted a cigarette from Arthur. They smoked in silence. The machines were clattering loudly by now, they could hear voices.

"Sorry. I can't offer you any reassurances. You're in a heap of shit," said Arthur before he left.

"I suppose I'll need to extend my time off from the print shop a little bit longer," he answered hoarsely.

15

NEUSS, JULY 1949

H E LIES IN HIS ROOM, COMPLETELY ENCASED IN CARL'S LIFE, down to his underwear. But his body seems not to want to let go of American time. His arms and legs are heavy with sleep. He could always sleep more. The sheets are warm and fragrant—he has never slept on such good sheets.

How long has he been here? The heat seems to blur everything together, make it all indistinguishable, like newsprint smudged under his fingertips.

He plays with the tassels of the white curtains. He makes little knots in them, and when he realizes, he undoes them again (but only for Edith's sake). When he stands up the floorboards creak. And so he stays in bed. He wishes the family would forget him. That they would move on with their lives so he could move on with his. But then again, what life?

Here he is, suddenly back in his homeland, but it's in ruins. The streets full of rubble and children playing. He could go to work for Carl, but that's the last thing he feels like doing.

He imitates Carl's voice: "I listened to Radio London. Tell me now, were you, over in America—were you able to educate yourself about what was happening here? No? Why not? Oh, so maybe you did after all?"

He thinks of the curiosity in Edith's voice: "What's it like to walk through New York? I mean, what's it like when the buildings are so tall—isn't it scary?"

There is something delicate, and yet at the same time strong, about Edith. It's as though while Carl keeps ratcheting things up, she keeps dialing them back, lapsing into simple existence, an existence that has her bending down, picking up, passing around, bringing, clearing away, pouring, asking, nodding, with scarcely noticeable resentment.

They talk about everything but say little. "It's like an oven outside," said Edith yesterday.

"I'm only breathing through my mouth, like a dog," he said.

She smiled. Then she asked, "Does it ever get this hot in New York?"

"Yes, and then people go to the air-conditioned department stores."

"Air-conditioned?"

"Cool air from a cooling system."

"That must cost a fortune."

"We Americans will do anything for the customer." *We*—he had actually said "we."

"One of the hens died. Do you know how to butcher a hen, Josef?"

"Unfortunately that's not something I learned in New York."

"I'll take the hen to a neighbor."

"Carl can't do it?"

They looked at each other. He laughed first; she laughed with him. Then she turned around, shamefaced. Pulled the knot of her apron a bit tighter before she bent back over the oven.

He presses his cheek into the pillow. He observes himself as he cries, and doesn't trust himself. And then the words: *I want to go home. I want to go home.* He doesn't trust these words either. There is no home.

Now he hears other voices. From the kitchen. Carl is shouting at his son. It lasts a good long time, then comes silence, and then something else. He recognizes the sound. When he goes to investigate, the boy is already out the door. Carl turns and looks at him, surprised.

The floorboards creak with every breath he takes.

"What did he do this time?"

"Stole a stamp."

"For God's sake, that was me. I wrote a letter."

"Why didn't you ask me?"

He doesn't know how to answer that. He laughs awkwardly.

"Just who were you writing?"

"Someone I knew from New York. He lives in Pulheim now."

"Did he get deported too?"

"A year before me," Josef says, making an effort to keep calm. The scorn in his brother's voice gets to him nonetheless.

"And how did you know each other?"

"Through the German American Bund. A political organization. It was patriotic and was committed to the fight against Communism."

"That sounds like a good thing," says Carl.

Yes, it sounds good. He left out a few details.

Carl steps closer and says, "The Communists now occupy half of Germany. It'll be fun to see how that turns out."

"It sure will."

"Did you ever once have to deal with kids, Josef?"

"My girlfriends were all childless."

"Girlfriends," Carl repeats.

"Girlfriends."

"What's this person's name, this person you're writing?"

"Hans Dörsam."

In the evening, swallows go sailing across the sky. The bench in the garden is a good place to watch them. He shakes a cigarette out of the pack—still American—and suddenly has a feeling, as though he were capable of picking up all the world's news, bad news too, the kind of news that always catches you unprepared, like a shot in the back. He's in just the right mood, the kind of mood one should always be in: open, full of life and feeling. He knows now he'll be moving on.

When he tastes the filter, he puts the cigarette out with his shoe, picks up the butt, and puts it back in the pack. So Carl won't have to make a fuss. As he's standing up he sees the boy in the corner of his eye. He seems to have been standing in the doorway for quite a while now, watching him. Like a spy. He has to laugh. All over the world, everywhere he goes, he is watched.

"Come here for a second," Josef calls out to him. The boy comes closer and stops in front of him.

"Sit down."

The boy doesn't move.

"Care for one?" He offers his cigarettes to the boy. The boy shakes his head.

"You don't smoke?"

"I'm thirteen."

Josef puts the pack back in his pants pocket.

"I took the stamp. Your father knows now. I'm sorry."

He was expecting gratitude, but the boy just shrugs his shoulders. Did he not understand him?

"Soon you'll be grown up, and you'll start fighting back. You're almost as tall as your father already."

The boy says nothing.

"Half a year at the most, then you'll start fighting back."

Silence. What's he doing wrong?

"I'd like to give you something, but I don't have any money. All I've got is empty pockets. In your family I'm like another child."

"Can I go?" asks the boy.

The next day he sees Edith sawing, screwing, sanding, varnishing. She's building a cupboard down in the basement. Edith can do things like that. Carl has gone to Koblenz—business. The children have gone off into the fields with their teacher to look for potato beetles. Restful quiet in the house. He feels like cooking lunch himself for once.

He lingers outside the door for a long time, trying to glean from her movements what kind of mood she's in. Really it's always the same with her. She works. Last night she dropped into an armchair with a sigh and stared at the little glass of turnip schnapps that Carl had handed her. Then, more or less indifferently, she tipped the liquor back.

He understands her. Quite well, in fact.

He himself managed to get away from him.

He could tell Edith what's playing and set her free. In his imagination they're sitting in his apartment in Harlem and listening to jazz.

No, he doesn't think she should run off with him of all people, her no-account brother-in-law. He of all people shouldn't be the one to set her free. On the other hand, men are now scarce in Germany.

"Josef, why are you hanging around like that?" she calls out.

"I can make us some lunch."

This gets a smile from her. She pushes herself up off the floor, screws the top on a can of lacquer, wipes her hands on her apron.

"I can cook, believe me!"

Now she's laughing, as if he'd told a really good joke. "All right, fine. But I'll come with you and show you where everything is."

While she looks on, he opens the doors of the pantry with both hands and feels as though he were taking a woman's dress off. Before him are jars of beans, semolina, flour, a few potatoes, and a bottle of sunflower oil. Not much, but in the garden he saw ripe tomatoes and parsley.

"I'll cook us something Italian!" he declares.

"What exactly do you need?" she asks.

"Tomatoes."

She watches him in the garden, and for every tomato he picks he first has to secure her permission. Finally they pay the hens a visit. He's able to snag two eggs, almost too much for what he has planned: gnocchi. She repeats the word after him, a question in her voice. "They're Italian potato dumplings."

While he chops onions, Edith applies glue to two shards of a broken cup and presses them together.

"What were your days like?" she asks and puts glue on another crack. Before now no one wanted to hear any details about Ellis Island. He grabs a big potato and starts to tell her about it.

"Our life on the island. It was like this. In the beginning they would wake us up at six o'clock in the morning. Then they realized it didn't actually make any sense—what were they getting us up so early for? It's not like we had anything to do. And so they started letting us sleep until eight thirty. Breakfast was served throughout the morning, but after that you had to pay."

He looks over at Edith. She's testing out the mended cup. "How many of you were there?"

"A few hundred. Four or five hundred. The majority were Germans. Then Italians and Japanese."

"And none of them had committed any crimes?"

He puts some water on to boil and drops in the potatoes. The harmless storytelling approach won't work.

"Starting in December 1941 it was enough to be German. In some cases even the wives and children were moved onto the island with the husbands. They thought it was just temporary, but they were held there for years."

He didn't tell her about the other men. Or that on April 20th there was cake for everyone, and on each slice Dörsam wrote *"Heil Adolf"* in chocolate icing.

"But why?"

"Some were interned so that they could be exchanged for American prisoners."

She shakes her head uncertainly.

"It's true, Edith, whole families were torn apart."

"Well, that's awful," she says.

He nods and waits for the next question, but it doesn't come. The potatoes bob in the water; he dices the tomatoes. "But they treated us well." Edith brings out her sewing kit. Her fingers probe the hole in a sock. He tells her about the library, where they could find anything they wanted, including newspapers; about the board games, the card games, and the soccer games in the courtyard. And he tells her about the two rows of barbed wire. That from his window he could see two rows of barbed wire and beyond them Manhattan and often wondered whether he could possibly make it. It was just a half-mile swim to New Jersey. Difficult, but doable. He often went swimming in the ocean in the summer. Coney Island was his favorite beach, but you could also swim in the Harlem River, right where he lived. But she knew that. He'd told her already. The neighborhood with the jazz clubs and the black Americans.

"So it wasn't like being imprisoned here," she said.

"They treated us well, that's true. But that's a good thing, isn't it?" He tries to meet her eye. "Right, Edith?"

"Of course it's a good thing," she says icily. Her slight reserve hurts him. Is she trying to suggest he should have been punished with German methods? Her expression is blank. With one hand she fishes for a ball of yarn in her sewing basket; it's gotten tangled up with another.

The words are still with him. He'll never forget them. *They should stick you Germans in your own camps.*

Whenever he thinks of these words, he thinks of everything else he saw that afternoon. The FBI had picked them up from the island in groups and taken them to the Bureau's offices for a film screening. His face had felt very tense, and he had had to shut his eyes. When he opened them at one point, the men on-screen were just leaving a shed, handkerchiefs pressed to their noses and mouths, dogged looks on their faces. Whispers in the screening room. Someone had called out, *"Heil Hitler."* Laughter had broken out. The American guards ignored both. Dörsam's face was like stone. Later, on the ferry, as they sailed toward the stately buildings on the water in the red twilight, Dörsam said, "And the carpet bombings of our cities? The mountains of corpses in our streets? Of course they don't show us *that!*"

The man could actually find a way to get outraged, even now.

Behind him someone had said, "Now, that's how you run a prison camp!" Josef had turned around and nodded at the GI, assuming there was a measure of understanding between them. But the soldier's eyes were cold: "They should stick you Germans in your own camps."

He had turned his back on the man again, his hand on the railing, the knuckles tense and white.

Now he looks nervously around the kitchen, trying, as he sets the table, to forget the words. He serves Edith gnocchi with tomato sauce: "*Buon appetito*, dear sister-in-law."

"It looks appetizing," she says and tastes carefully.

"Well, how do you like it?"

"It's a nice thing to eat."

"It's a nice thing to eat?"

She smiles. "Carl wouldn't like it."

I believe it, he thinks.

"Carl punishes Paul often, doesn't he?"

Why won't she say anything? Edith knows how to get through to her son. Sometimes she puts her hand on his shoulder. Then even his nervous blinking stops.

And so he goes on: "I wouldn't want to be Carl's child. I wouldn't be surprised if he gets it in his head to punish me next."

"He's a good man, Josef. And don't forget, you weren't here. It was a difficult time in Germany."

"What I'm actually trying to say, Edith, is that Carl makes you unhappy."

She lets go of her fork.

"You deserve a better life," he hears himself saying softly. "Edith, don't put up with so much. Try to find more enjoyment in your life."

"Who do you think you are, Josef?"

She hasn't had much practice in shouting, unlike Carl. She jumps up. He also gets up, reaches for her hand—why? Because he's already lost, he can at least touch her hand just once. To his surprise she doesn't resist. They stand silently across from each other. As if suddenly, despite it all, she understands everything. Everything, everything. Or is she just frozen with shock? *Don't kiss her*, he tells himself. *If you kiss her now, you won't just ruin her life but your own too. And you're world champion at that.*

He lets go of her slender hand.

"Sorry, Edith. I shouldn't intrude. Please forgive me."

They spend the rest of the meal in silence, and when he offers to help her wash up, she sends him outside, like the kids. *Go off and play somewhere*—he can almost hear her saying it.

16

NEW YORK, APRIL 1939

H E TRIED HARD NOT TO GIVE ANYTHING AWAY. HE HAD DIS-
connected an important copper wire from the transmitter; for the
time being the radio was dead. He fumbled around in the back while
they looked on, and as he did so noted that when it came to technical
matters they were both completely clueless. Max stood around helplessly
and kept asking, "Will you be able to fix it?" Finally, when they'd already
missed both transmitting windows, he took the soldering iron and re-
sealed the clipped connection so that everything worked again.

When the two of them had left he felt like a wrung-out sponge, unable to resume its old shape.

They really did need him. That's what he had wanted to know.

The next time he served them drinks, claiming, since it was still early in
the day, that it was his birthday and he wanted to celebrate. Max went
with beer; Ludwig had whiskey. He made sure to keep refilling their
glasses. With Ludwig he had to pour often—he could handle a lot—but
with Max, however, he slowly began to notice him growing gentle and
sleepy and finally starting to hum along to Billie Holiday.

"It's not a textile company. Right?"

"What else is it supposed to be, Josef?"

"It's for the Germans. For Germany."

The two of them looked at each other and laughed quietly, as if he were a child who had said something funny.

"You sure catch on quick," said Max.

"And what is it we're sending?"

"Industry and military figures. Not to worry. A lot of it is completely legal, from trade publications—anyone can access it."

Max's hands were in his pockets; Josef could see they were balled up into fists. He tapped his foot nervously, and not along to the music.

Ludwig sank deep into his chair.

"They send people to prison for this."

"We have to know the state of America's military so that we're not at a disadvantage. Every country acts this way. What's the problem?"

He went on. Josef shouldn't believe everything the Americans said about the Germans. Like that Germany was preparing for war—that was propaganda. The world just couldn't handle the fact that Germany had gotten so strong.

"Theft does come into play, though," Ludwig interjected.

"Thanks to the people who work in the factories, we now have the Norden bombsight. And that's a good thing, Josef, isn't it? The Norden bombsight can hit a pickle jar from a height of six thousand meters! With it you can avoid an inferno like Guernica."

He looked at the two of them wearily.

After they'd put on their coats and hats and were headed out the door, Ludwig turned back to look at him. He was completely plastered. "Sorry, Josef. You're a good guy."

He opened Thoreau and encountered lines that made him angry, that all of a sudden seemed to him as lofty as skyscrapers:

Disobedience is the true foundation of liberty. The obedient must be slaves.

Because he didn't know what else to do, he went to see Schmuederrich. He walked right past the secretary and her shout of "Stop!" with an assertiveness that he possessed only when he was furious.

Schmuederrich got up from behind his desk.

"Figured you'd be coming. Max called me before you got here."

"You could have just asked me."

"Be glad you're getting paid. We could also offer you an autograph from Hitler. No joke. There's a few true patriots here who want nothing else."

Josef didn't return Schmuederrich's smile.

"What?" asked Schmuederrich. "What else do you want?"

"To quit. I'm not working for Germany."

And then Schmuederrich said things that merged with a sudden droning in Josef's ears, a droning as if through gauze, and later, back on 86th Street, he remembered some of them, things like *Now, pull yourself together, you chump, you idiot, you pipsqueak, or else I'll send a few guys round to see you and remind you who calls the shots around here.*

When Max and Ludwig rang the doorbell the next day at the appointed time, he just didn't open the door. They knocked. "It's us, Josef. Open up." He heard them talking to each other. Princess barked.

He left the apartment that night feeling triumphant, his mind on Thoreau. The next thing he knew, Princess's damp breath was above him, her panting and her tongue, and there were faces all around him, lined up against the sky. Two men helped him to his feet and accompanied him up the stairs to his door.

"Thanks," he mumbled and tried to close the door behind him. Then one of them pushed past him into the living room and checked over his equipment, whistling appreciatively. The other came in after him, jumped up on the coffee table, and checked the ceiling lamp. The first checked the wall sockets, the other started pulling out drawers, then they both got down on their knees and checked under the rug. Finally the second man said, "From now on no more funny business." He said it in German. The dog whimpered, and when they were gone she jumped into the chair where Ludwig always sat, working on the encryption and nurturing his buzz.

He slept for a long time. He dreamed he had spiders on his hands, and he woke up when his hands started trying to shake the spiders off.

He dragged himself out of bed, his body leaden. He fed the dog and cooled his chin with a wet shirt. He put some coffee on, took the milk out of the refrigerator, and could tell from the way it moved around inside the carton—more shifting than sloshing—that it had gone bad. He poured it down the drain and washed the clotted white clumps away with water from the faucet.

His chin was mildly swollen. He felt the skin—no, it didn't seem like anything was broken. He knew what a broken bone felt like. He knew it from having had a father who beat him enough to make it last. Every time, when it was over, his mother had said cheerily, "Now, that'll be good for a week at least."

No one had ever beaten him up since then. Not for twenty-five years—a quarter century. On the street, whenever he saw a fight brewing, he immediately turned around and walked away; if someone started getting smart with him at a bar and put his fists up, he apologized at once and got out of there.

He pushed the chest of drawers in front of the apartment door. But over the next few days he didn't hear anything more from them.

Had they given up on him? Could they have realized that he was the wrong man for the job? On the other hand, if they didn't need him anymore, wouldn't that mean he was in real danger now?

He didn't leave the apartment. He called the grocer's, and the boy brought him bread, beer, sandwiches. He wrapped himself in a blanket, pulled it tight, and felt a pain coming on in the darkness of the apartment that was old, much older than what he was dealing with now. Outside, the train rattled by, voices from the street drifted past. He wrapped himself tighter in the feeling that he was falling; he had only to close his eyes and something pulled him out of this world.

When they turned up again a week later he was almost relieved, but he made a point of acting standoffish. "So here you are again, you assholes."

This time Max strutted pompously around the room. He also fiddled with the lampshade and the sockets and ordered Josef to turn Duke Ellington up louder, saying that was the only reason he put up with this jungle music—if someone was listening in on them this music would drown everything out.

Josef kept something in his mouth at all times—a cigarette, a toothpick, gum, later pork dumplings from the Chinese take-out place. He didn't want to talk. Over in the chair, Ludwig took a drink from his flask every few minutes. He sat there and scribbled numbers onto his notepad, on his knees the open book.

Josef went into the kitchen, put water on to boil, and peeled an orange. The acid hurt the nail of his index finger, which he bit sometimes. He ran some water over his hands in the sink, and suddenly Max was standing next to him. "They pulled Ludwig out of a Berlin prison. A pickpocket and crook. He's stolen from me too."

"This keeps getting better and better." Hands still wet, he opened the cabinet door with his pinky to grab himself a cup. "Why would America let a criminal into the country?"

"They made him out to be a refugee. They like signing up people like him. They can do what they want with them and nobody's going to miss them, you understand? They gave him a bit of training, how to use encryption, how to tap somebody's phone, but once he got here he just started hitting the bottle."

"That's not exactly reassuring."

"Duquesne was against bringing you on, by the way."

Now he was paying attention. "Who?"

"Fritz Joubert Duquesne. The elegant gentleman at the Old Heidelberg. You don't have any training as an agent and aren't working voluntarily. But we don't have enough people here who can work a radio. That's why we're taking this risk in dealing with you."

"Risk."

"Sure. Maybe you'll get nervous and run to the FBI."

Josef was silent.

"Duquesne is an old, experienced spymaster," said Max and he took a seat at the kitchen table with a sigh. "He was working for the Germans as far back as the Great War. He's been around."

"Sounds like a great boss."

"He's already past sixty. He's not as gung ho as he used to be, but he needs money. He has a demanding young mistress, and she lives on Central Park."

"I saw her at the Old Heidelberg."

"No, you saw Lily. Lily Stein. She's one of us too. She came here from Germany not long ago. A Jew from Vienna."

"I don't get it."

"We don't either, to be honest."

Max pulled out a box of matches and a magnifying glass. Spoke quietly: "Rubber-lined, self-sealing fuel tanks for aircraft."

Josef hesitated. "That's what we're about to send?"

"Fresh from the docks." He flashed Josef a confident smile. "At least you'll have enough money soon to move to a better neighborhood."

"Not at all interested."

"Don't you want to make something of yourself? Or do you want to be a nobody, is that it?"

"That's exactly right. I want to be a nobody," Josef replied.

17

NEW YORK, APRIL 1939

H E RECOGNIZED THE UNEMPLOYED FROM THE FACT THAT they did everything slowly, as if to prolong the few activities that made up their day.

He was sitting in a café not far from the print shop. A glance at the clock—he was meeting Arthur. He picked up the little metal canister and very slowly poured milk into his coffee. He sprinkled some sugar in, stirred thoroughly, and watched the swirling liquid till it grew still. Then he paused.

He was doing everything slowly too. Someone could look at him and think he didn't have a job either.

But ever since he'd taken time off from the print shop, he had plenty of days off, and almost always had afternoons off, since by then it was already nighttime in Germany. He was drinking strong Italian coffee. Everything he did, he did with a feeling of timelessness. Maybe this was what other people did on vacation. He wasn't sure—he had never taken a vacation.

He had so much time that he did things he felt would meet with Lauren's approval. He went to the New York Historical Society. There he learned a lot about Harlem. About the Dutch settlers in the last century. And on a map of Manhattan he saw that the island was already completely developed by the nineteenth century. But the churches didn't yet have other buildings towering over them like they did today.

He had also gone to Macy's and had his measurements taken in the men's department. He stayed over an hour, indulged in seeking advice and being attended to like a prince. Whenever some question of detail came up, he always chose the most expensive option. In no respect should his suit be inferior to Herr Dr. Ritter's. The suit would be ready next week.

He paged through the *New York Times* and looked for news about Germany.

Arthur took a seat across the table from him.

"Hitler is now having his own beer brewed in Bavaria, with just one percent alcohol," Josef read aloud to him. "And Berlin is flirting with Moscow."

"For purely economic reasons. The Bolsheviks are still the enemy, don't you worry. My business is safe!"

"Good for you," said Josef.

"And how's your work going?" asked Arthur.

"I'm afraid you were right. They don't let a guy off the hook so easily. Plus on top of that these people have zero technical talent."

Arthur slowly shook his head. "Who knows, maybe that's not entirely by accident."

"What do you mean?"

"I don't know. But I can tell when something's fishy. Do you really think they don't have any better people?"

Josef was silent. He glanced at the faces of the people around them. No one was looking at them.

"What is it you're up to, anyway?"

"Operation Sonnenstaub. Solar dust. That's all I know."

"Operation Sonnenstaub."

"I heard it in Max's headphones once. They usually just confirm receipt of the transmission. But once they sent back a demand from Hamburg: 'More Sonnenstaub.'"

Which probably meant *Put a little more effort into it, boys.*

They usually stayed for three or four hours. They filled his apartment with smoke. Ella Fitzgerald sang. April came, then May. The treetops swayed outside his window, their leaves fanned out like divas.

He didn't know what to watch out for. All he knew was that Max was a blowhard. Big things were in the works behind the scenes, he whispered, only unfortunately he wasn't allowed to say anything just yet. The boasting didn't suit him. Sometimes he looked at Max's hands with pity, the wide fingertips and light skin. At these times he felt like he understood something about him, saw him dangling outside the twentieth story of some building washing windows.

"How did you get roped into this thing, anyway?"

"Roped into it?" Max balked. "It's an honor to be permitted to serve the fatherland!"

And then Max told him the real version. In response to the German Reich's advertising campaign intended to bring back German emigrants, he had set out for Germany in 1937. When he got off the ship, two men took him aside and suggested he go through training in Germany so he could travel back to the US as an agent. He was excited by the idea, he said, because actually he really liked it in America, it was just that he was barely able to make any money here.

When traveling back to the US two years later, he cited disappointment with the new Germany as his reason for returning, which the American authorities were happy to hear. He had been trained on an estate in Brandenburg, all very secretive. From the outside no one could tell what was going on there. He even saw the head of military intelligence once, Canaris. It was only briefly, Max said. He had come from Berlin with General Lahousen, the head of the sabotage division. And then he stopped in mid-sentence. He couldn't say anything more. "By the way, though, Canaris is as short as you, Josef."

On another occasion Max made a point of saying how much more colossal everything was in Germany, and how in comparison the German American Bund was just a parody. He made fun of Camp Siegfried on Long Island, where young German Americans imitated the Hitler Youth and the League of German Girls, the girls getting pregnant one after the other. His scorn was often directed at Schmuederrich, who kept up a whole string of love affairs, even though he was a fat ass and was also married to a woman named Else, who was an American by birth—but there were probably women who felt sorry for soft men like him and couldn't bring themselves to turn him down. Still, he said, it was good for espionage. Schmuederrich had already provided valuable information he'd picked up in hotel bars that served an international clientele.

Josef wondered if it was the same for him in his dealings with Schmuederrich. It wasn't a love affair in his case, but he was too willing to indulge him. He thought of their meetings in the Rotesandbar, the alcohol and Schmuederrich's way of talking to you like he'd known you forever. Schmuederrich's body exuded something both intimate and overwhelming that you instinctively wanted to steer clear of, like the odor from inside an apartment that had drifted out onto the landing—and yet, just as instinctively, you admonished yourself to stay and put up with it.

When he was alone again he opened the window and leaned his forehead against the wooden casing. Max had hinted at horrible things: he shouldn't be surprised if he noticed in the coming days that he was being followed. It was for his own good, a kind of protection. They were making sure he wasn't being followed by the wrong people.

In his head he kept track of the other people on the street. He was on the lookout for men until it became clear to him that the people watching him could also be women. But then again, white women didn't come to Harlem. And so he only watched for white men. Would they stop, would they actually look up at him, standing in the window, would they be waiting somewhere, would they wait in a car? Would particular men start popping up again and again, maybe even faces he knew from somewhere else? If they actually wanted to stay on his heels, they would have to keep watch outside, otherwise it wouldn't work. He never noticed anything.

He waited. He smoked. Then he took the dog for a walk across the glass- and tin-can-strewn field by the river, headed for the bridge abutment, which he hid himself behind for a while; he could no longer take a single normal step. He watched for movement in the area around the river—they must have given up by now. He took sudden detours. He avoided his usual routes, walked over the bridge straight into the Bronx. He stuck close to the brownstones, and once, when a Negro couple stepped out of a building and the door stayed open a crack, he slipped inside. Music playing on the radio behind every apartment door, and still his heartbeat was louder. He went all the way up to the roof, the strange building under his feet like an animal he'd bagged on a hunt.

He had to do something. It wouldn't take much to express his defiance, his resistance, but it was just a fly knocking against a windowpane—vain effort. He felt exhausted after these wanderings, which had no other purpose than to throw off the people following him. They mustn't get to know his habits, mustn't find out anything about him, mustn't think they understood him. For the first time he felt a sense of protectiveness where his life was concerned—no one had the right to cheat their way to gaining knowledge of him. He had lived invisibly, and it should stay that way.

One rainy day a delivery truck drove up in front of the building. A man jumped out of the cab and helped the driver park. The rain fell down his shirt and ran off his flat cap, but the man didn't seem to mind.

It was Ludwig. And the man now climbing out of the delivery truck was Max.

Max had gotten his old job back making beverage deliveries. As a cover, he told him when he got upstairs. From then on there was always a white delivery truck parked outside the building, with the words THIRST QUENCHER written on the side.

Max drove the truck to Red Hook and chatted up the dockworkers. Who would suspect a cigarette-smoking delivery truck driver hauling lemonade and soda? Sometimes he sold them a few bottles under the table for cheap. Then they got even more talkative.

"You could easily do it yourself and make some extra cash," said Max. "You've got kind of a Heinz Rühmann look—the likable regular guy, the working stiff."

"Heinz Rühmann?"

"He's an actor. About your age. Also short. You look a bit like him."

Seemed as though there were a lot of people he was supposed to look like.

But Josef had other plans. He didn't want to take on more work under any circumstances. Instead he was thinking about how he could do less and, above all, how he could rid himself of Max and Ludwig. He missed the quiet and the vital sense of being able to disappear. To disappear and, at the same time, summon voices into his apartment, whenever he felt like it.

He felt as if the war between the nations had broken out within reach of his couch, where he usually just dozed, thought about things, and scratched Princess behind the ears.

They always had to limit each transmission to just a few minutes; after fifteen minutes someone could locate their signal. And even still they were in no way secure. Josef thought about it a lot, talking quietly to himself, and the dog pricked up her ears, hearing his conversations with himself.

Now when he left the house with the dog he didn't look at the river or the sky anymore but rather at something inside himself: his fear. Sometimes the fear made his throat tighten. Sometimes it filled his chest with what felt like liquid ice. Sometimes it sat in his stomach. He became aware of how, depending on what form it took that day, the fear could exercise total control over his thoughts.

Then he had an idea. A radio that fit inside a suitcase would make them mobile, much less easy to track down—and he would finally get the two of them out of his apartment. The delivery truck was perfect for it.

He saw various places in his mind. Brighton Beach, the street right by the boardwalk, good for transmitting, no obstacles. No. Coney Island was too busy. The parking lot in the Bronx outside the nationalists' headquarters. Red Hook in Brooklyn. These thoughts reassured him, blotted out the fear for a time.

Treason. Electric chair. He had read an article in the newspaper about the victims' eyes bursting, about them wearing diapers because they would shit themselves when the thousand volts were sent surging through their bodies.

18

NEW YORK, MAY 1939

IT WAS THE FIRST DAY WHEN THE AIR OUTSIDE WAS WARMER than the air inside. When he opened the door to leave his building, he felt summer pouring over him and winter at his back. He took the subway downtown, got out a stop early, walked down 96th Street to the East River and then south along the Rhinelander Reef to Carl Schurz Park. He had a date with Lauren.

Lauren had called him. "I figured you would have to be back in New York by now, and look at that, I was right. You answered the phone. I'm talking to you."

Confident laughter.

He joined in, laughing quietly. He had never been gone. He had been living in a state of numbness for two months. Over time he had gotten used to it.

Carl Schurz Park stretched from the entrance at East 86th Street over a hill and down to the shore promenade. The evening was bright. A warm, salty wind blew in from the East River and played in the clothes of the dog walkers, sailors, and couples.

Yorkville had been Lauren's idea. Maybe to prove that his German origins didn't bother her. Not wanting to argue, he had said yes to Lauren on the phone in an almost drunkenly overexuberant tone of voice: "Yes, my dear. Yes. Yorkville. If you wish to see some krauts, yes."

Max had warned him about Yorkville. The GIs had started to set their sights on the neighborhood, he said. It had to do with that movie. *Confessions of a Nazi Spy* had started playing at the Strand Theatre on Broadway a short while back. Josef had read an article about it. The wind had shifted: Before, he read, Hollywood had been careful not to run afoul of the German market; they had even removed Jewish names from the credits. But now that the situation in Germany had worsened and war was in the air, Hollywood was choosing confrontation for the first time. The film was based on a true story: a German spy ring in New York had been uncovered last year.

He felt like he'd been living on the far side of the moon.

He had put an exclamation point next to the showtimes, torn the page out, and taken it home with him.

He wore his new suit and felt a confidence that seemed to pass directly from the expensive material to his skin. On a bench sat a young woman pushing a stroller back and forth, in her free hand a cigarette. He took a deep breath and waited. Ships sailed past, leaving long bright trails of wake behind them like the train of a wedding gown. Every time he saw ships he thought of Europe, thought of home, a home that didn't exist anymore, was only preserved in his dreams.

"Hello, W4, I've tracked down your coordinates!"

He turned around. Lauren was walking toward him, beaming. She wore a dark dress with white polka dots, espadrille pumps. This time her blond hair flowed down in an Olympia roll under the small hat that she wore cocked sharply to one side. She had just rubbed moisturizer on her hands; he felt a greasy moist layer on his. In her small handbag was a New York travel guide. He tapped it with his finger. "Who was Carl Schurz?" he asked in a mock teacher's voice.

She laughed. "A German revolutionary. Came to New York in the middle of the last century, campaigned for Lincoln, and became the first German senator. His wife founded the first kindergarten in America."

"Excellent, Miss W2."

They walked to the park entrance and then down 86th Street toward Park Avenue. He could barely follow the conversation at first. She spoke at a frantic pace, telling him all about her stressful night shifts. She had the hardest job in New York, she said—talk about backbreaking labor. There was a note of amusement in her voice, as if, on the other hand, she didn't take any of it seriously. They passed the Rathskeller, Café Hindenburg, and Der Schwarze Adler. He would have liked to find her pretty, but she wasn't today either. She had an inharmonious face with a small, short chin and slightly bulging gray eyes. But he liked her voice. He felt himself putting on his crooked grifter's smile, which women said made him look attractive. That's how he knew that he wanted her to like him.

How was his trip? Where did he go? He waved his hand dismissively and gave a brief shake of his head. "I'll tell you later." Was everything all right? she asked. Her directness shook him. He froze, his throat tight. Then he took a deep breath, told himself she had no idea what she was asking. She was young. She was simply trying everything out, just like her backbreaking job and just like this city. She was trying him out.

They went past the Berlin Bar and the Old Heidelberg. The antifascists' protests were having an effect; only occasionally could a defiant little swastika flag be seen in one of the shop windows.

Lauren told him that she had applied for a spot in a scholarship program and had been rejected. Just what was it she wanted to study? "American history and literature."

"And why these particular subjects?" he asked, unsure of himself, and as they passed another restaurant he peered in the open door. From inside came the smell of roasted meat.

"I actually want to be a journalist," she said quietly.

"A journalist?" he said.

In response, she went down a list of famous women journalists: Frances Sweeney, Nellie Bly, Dorothy Day, Dorothy Thompson. All names he had never heard. She seemed to take note. Thompson had interviewed Hitler in Germany years ago, she told him. And now she was collecting money for refugees at different charity events in New York. A fantastic person. He nodded agreement and tried to come up with a response. His mouth was dry.

"No rain this time," he said finally and noted her look of bewilderment.

They went past the Yorkville cinema. Lauren read off the German titles with great effort and the wrong pronunciation. *"Fünf Millionen suchen einen Erben."* He said it properly for her—*Five Million Look for an Heir*—and also *"Olympia, Fest der Völker"*—*Olympia, Festival of Nations*—by Leni Riefenstahl.

He took a closer look at the poster. So that was Heinz Rühmann, the regular-guy type that he was supposed to resemble?

They passed a large construction fence behind which a building was being torn down to make room for a taller one, then a bookstore that boasted of carrying books that were banned in Germany. On the corner of Park Avenue was the genteel Amalfi. He held the door open for Lauren. "Here?" she asked, astounded, and he nodded quite casually. Inside, it smelled of lobster, of cocktails and perfume. The air hit his face like a spray. White-tiled walls, chandeliers, and real silver. He saw with equal parts terror and triumphant bliss that only the wealthy upper crust dined here.

A white-gloved waiter blocked their way. "Good evening. What name, please?"

"What name?" Josef repeated the question, trying to win time, like he used to do when he didn't understand something.

"Do you not have a reservation?"

"Reservation?"

"You need a reservation."

"But there are a few empty tables over there."

"They're reserved."

Now he could feel Lauren's hand on his arm. The hand was pulling him away.

"There are so many restaurants around here, Joe. We'll find something," she said when they were back outside. Her eyes were already scanning the different signs with dishes advertised in chalk: *Schnitzel*, *Kalbsbraten*, *Klöße*, and *Rotkohl*. "I'd much rather eat German food anyway," she said as a waiter in knee-length lederhosen stepped outside a restaurant.

Why he didn't want to go to the first restaurant she pointed out, and no, not to the Old Heidelberg or the Berlin Bar either, this he couldn't explain to Lauren, who by now had gone quiet in a mix of disappointment and unease. He said no to every place, acting as though he was very concerned about quality. Finally he pulled Lauren into a pastry shop. There he bought a small bag of *Windbeutel*—cream puffs.

"So this is my dinner?"

He laughed. The golden dough crumbled onto her dress. At this moment the sun was shining red in the street. A look of relief spread across Lauren's face, a relief that he also felt the moment he tasted the cream filling.

"Now I'm full."

"Then I guess this evening was a bargain for me," he said.

The next moment she grabbed his arm and tried to pull him away.

"What's wrong, Lauren?"

"Ignore it, please."

Now he heard it. "Kraut!" The shout was coming from behind them. "Hey, you Nazi! Stop right there!"

He turned around. Thank God Schmuederrich wasn't wearing the Bund's military uniform today. "I know that guy. He's just someone I know who likes to mess with me." Schmuederrich caught up with them. Now here he stood before them in all his girth and with his mouth open.

"I find such jokes tasteless," Lauren told Schmuederrich.

"Thank you for bringing that to my attention, miss. I'll make a note of it."

He shook her hand and held it, Josef thought, far too long. "Your idea isn't bad," he said to Josef in German. "We're just waiting for the green light. Then you can get started."

Schmuederrich meant the mobile radio. Josef had finally told Max his idea, but now he regretted it. Regretted that he was handing them good ideas now too.

"What an unpleasant person," said Lauren after Schmuederrich had walked off into the crowd. He told her he agreed, and he was happy—apparently Schmuederrich's special charm didn't work on women like Lauren, and that spoke in her favor.

He had never taken a woman back to Harlem with him. They usually wanted to go out in brutal Times Square, or to see a show on Broadway. The shows in Harlem didn't appeal to them. They flashed defensive smiles when he told them that the rich white people who lived on Park Avenue had been driving up to the Cotton Club in their limousines for years, a club where Negroes worked as waiters or as performers but weren't allowed in as patrons. What he meant, however, was the normal Harlem in which he lived, where in summer people set up tables on the sidewalk and played chess. Maybe the women he went out with feared that they themselves were in some way part of the exoticness when the appeal continued to escape them. Better to go to Times Square. To Coney Island. To Broadway.

The streets were packed, a taxi would take too long. He decided to take Lauren on the subway. There he looked at her without inhibition, almost as though she were his possession. For four stops this possession pitched and swayed back and forth before his eyes. She smiled at him, and for a second time he noticed the age difference, her smile impossible for him to read—was it bold or just friendly?

Back aboveground on 116th Street she called out a bit too loudly, "Oh, how beautiful it is here!" People turned and looked at them, smiling. The street was lined with stately brownstones. Once more he felt how some muscle within him relaxed whenever he returned to Harlem from the window-display glamour of Midtown.

"The Dutch used to live here. Then the subway was built, and it was easier for them to get downtown, and once they started going often enough they finally decided to pick up and move down there for good. They left their buildings here." He knew all of this from the museum.

She looked at him attentively. He went on. "But did you know, Lauren, that the rents for Negroes are higher than they are for the few white people here? It's because they can't find apartments anywhere else. The landlords take advantage."

Harlem in the last light of day. A veil descended, steadily draining all the color from the streets. He now saw everything through Lauren's eyes, as if in a kind of double vision, but it seemed to go over well with her. The Abyssinian Baptist Church and the Harlem Alhambra got a favorable look; a red neon sign announced a film, *Paradise in Harlem*,

featuring an all-black cast. They passed by a shop advertising fur coat
storage, photo stores, cafés, barbershops, newsstands, food carts selling bacon, eggs, hot dogs. Suits with padded shoulders. Knit ties. The
signs advertising the prices usually larger than the item for sale. More
and more people on the street, always more than anywhere else. From
the buildings came the hum of sewing machines. Floral-print dresses
drying on clotheslines. They walked next to each other as if their des-
tination were clear. Soon they had reached his building.

"Should we go to the Savoy Ballroom? I can't dance very well, but they
have the best orchestras around. Duke Ellington, Louis Armstrong,
Chick Webb!"

"Couldn't we go to your place instead? I'd really like to see your radio
setup," said Lauren.

He did a walk-through of the apartment in his head. No, everything
was put away. Just as Max had instructed him. He had thrown away the
pamphlets from the print shop. He always hid the tables of call numbers
and frequencies behind the radio equipment. He took a deep breath,
then he let her up.

19

NEW YORK, MAY 1939

SHE DIDN'T SEEM THE LEAST BIT SELF-CONSCIOUS. HE ASKED himself if that bothered him, if he didn't prefer a little female nervousness. Or was this really only about the radio? His street was plain—boring redbrick tenements, a tire shop, an auto repair shop— but here too Lauren directed her keen, alert gaze at all of it. He thought of her home: A hotel with many rooms. Forty rooms. Five suites and two cottages in the garden. He saw Lauren going in and out, laughing and making conversation with families, with married couples, with honeymooners. She saw pajamas wrinkled with sleep, toothbrushes with crooked bristles. She saw the traces of strangers' love lives; she said hello and goodbye and thank you; she spoke her friendly lines as daughter of the house. Was this the reason she could follow a man she barely knew into the lobby of his building and act like it was the most natural thing in the world? Meanwhile he was looking around to see which of the neighbors were at their windows, ready to poke fun.

On the top step he asked her to wait for a moment. Her face vanished as the light in the stairwell went out, but he could still see her nod. Since the two German agents had started coming around, the apartment was tidy in a way it had never been before. He always got rid of everything, even the cigarette butts, and washed the cups and glasses. The only exception was his bed, which was unmade, the imprint of his body visible on the sheet. He closed the door. It was unlikely that Lauren would enter this room today.

"You can come in. The coast is clear."

She kept a firm grip on herself, her hands crossed on her shoulders, while she inspected the apartment. Princess sniffed at her legs.

"This is unbelievable!" she cried every now and then. "The way you live! I've never seen anything like it!"

A girl. No, a woman. A young woman, who, after she'd taken off her shoes, was the same height as he.

She looked around, clearly intent on trying to understand something about him based on his apartment. "You live very simply," she said finally. "You don't even have pictures on the walls. How come you don't have any books?"

He pulled Thoreau out from under a stack of amateur radio magazines and heard a long sigh. He didn't dare ask what it meant—appreciation?

"My mother idolizes him."

"There was a time when he was very important to me," he said, attempting to play down the fact that he actually had nothing here but Thoreau.

"Gandhi got his ideas from Thoreau," Lauren said pensively. And then shook her head. "That might work in India maybe."

"Isn't Gandhi in prison?"

"Not at the moment. But he was just fasting again. With success. Then they do everything he wants."

"You don't seem to like him."

"He suggested to the Jews in Germany that they should practice nonviolent resistance. Some people think their idea of reality is more real than reality itself."

He showed her another book, *Der Radio-Amateur* by Dr. Eugen Nesper. "This book was published fifteen years ago in Berlin. Back then amateur broadcasting was just starting to take off. People thought it was a miracle!"

She flipped through the book, smiling. Stopped on a page with a drawing of a log cabin in the mountains. A man stood outside, with headphones on, a cable ran from the headphones back into the cabin.

"Could you translate this for me?" Lauren asked and pointed at the caption.

"'With arms outstretched, his gaze directed at the stars, he receives, in the dark of night, far from the cultural centers of man, the news of the world, as if it were the music of the spheres.'"

"That's like me in the Catskills. Completely cut off from any kind of culture. And what's this here?"

He was certain that she had more culture there than most people in New York City, who were so caught up in the daily struggle to survive that they couldn't look left or right. His eye fell on an issue of *Social Justice*, and he pushed the paper under the coffee table with his foot as he continued to translate.

"'At this point the printed newspaper has become widely established as a medium for conveying information. Its disadvantage, however, is the impossibility of disseminating information immediately, in statu nascendi so to speak; it can only ever do so with a certain temporal delay. Thus, in actuality, a newspaper is never completely current.'"

"Newspapers will die out at some point because the radio is faster."

"Not if you become a journalist. Then the newspapers will hang on a bit longer!"

She gave him a faintly scornful look. "Your attempt to soften the blow is far too transparent."

He felt his face turning red.

By way of conciliation she said, "And what's this here?"

"Here the functions of the radio are described."

"I see. And just what are the functions of the radio, Mr. Klein?"

"'The dissemination of economic news; the broadcasting of sermons and prayers; the broadcasting of music, such as opera (without coughing and sneezing); issuing weather reports, storm warnings; the broadcasting of music for factory floors, mines, hospitals; the broadcasting of political speeches; promotion of understanding between nations.'"

"Music without coughing and sneezing—yeah, back in 1924 that probably was a sensation."

She smiled, and he decided to smile back this time.

"May I?"

She turned on the transceiver and turned the tuning knob. Broken skin around her fingernails. Like his mother, who had worked for years in a tavern kitchen. Every night she took a brush and tried to get out everything that had gotten caught under her fingernails. Did Lauren have to scrub her hands like that at the hospital?

"If there's a war, we won't be allowed to transmit outside the country anymore," she said.

"There's not going to be a war." The words slipped out of him. "That's just anti-German propaganda." Max said it all the time, then Josef argued, or thought he did at least, and now he was saying it himself.

Lauren tilted her head, as if to get a better look at him, this idiot sitting across from her. "And the arms buildup?"

He hesitated. "I couldn't say. I haven't been there for many years."

"What difference does that make?"

"None," he said grudgingly. "Whiskey? Scotch?" he asked.

"Water."

He went to pour himself a whiskey—Macy's Old Musket, aged ten years, on sale for $2.49—took a sip as he walked back and immediately felt the heaviness setting in, all the way down to his fingertips. He regretted pouring himself a drink while this young woman, his W2, sipped water and began almost to crawl inside the radio, as if she were going to disappear; while she, headphones on, went off somewhere else—a trance. He knew it himself. The static and squealing alone were enough to send a wave of euphoria flooding through him.

"Switzerland." Now she was filling him in. "The man is talking about a dog that went missing in Grenoble. Gray and white." She played the cheerful explorer on the tuning knob. Everything, just not a man and a woman in an apartment together, at night, in May.

"How old are you, W2?"

She took off the headphones and turned around to face him. "Twenty-four. Why?"

"Aren't I too old for you?"

"Too old for what?"

He went quiet, embarrassed.

She had an amused look on her face. "Aren't you a bit direct, Joe Klein, or is that just how one acts at your age?"

"Of course. One doesn't want to lose any time. One has less of it, after all."

She laughed and turned back to the radio, but she had gone red.

"I'll make us some spaghetti," he announced and went off into the kitchen, looking among old onions with green shoots for one he could use. He had an eggplant and a few tomatoes. He'd be able to whip something together.

She stood in the doorframe and held up the page he'd torn from the *New York Times*.

"Will you take me with you?"

He froze. Sauce dripped from the spoon to his shoe.

"You circled the movie," she said.

He still didn't say anything.

"Sorry, Joe, the paper was just sitting there on the couch."

"I'd rather go see *Paradise in Harlem*," he joked. "Or"—he took the paper from her hand and read—"*Only Angels Have Wings* with Cary Grant."

"Why?"

He took a step closer. And now was standing very close. Her breath in his face. "This is why," he said. "A Nazi movie isn't as good for this kind of thing."

"What?" she asked quietly.

He was standing so close to her now that she might well have guessed. She didn't step back.

He could still feel her lips on his when he was back standing at the stove. He congratulated himself on his clever offensive. He had wanted to kiss Lauren anyway, on this their second time seeing each other, and it had happened at the right moment. Lauren had laughed quietly, a laugh that gave him credit for the smooth move and that was at the same time a bit delighted. He wasn't the first person to have kissed her—that too was clear now. She seemed not at all unsure of herself.

He poured the noodles into a colander, mixed them with the sauce, handed her a plate.

"So long as it's not the eight a.m. screening on Sunday morning, then let's go."

"How about the one at eight p.m.?"

"I'll get the tickets."

After they'd finished eating she sat down next to him on the couch, petting Princess, who sat in front of them, her hand drawing long lines down her back. He decided not to make any more advances today—first they had to get through this movie. While Lauren talked about her work at the hospital, he realized how much he liked her. She told him about a ditzy coworker; he lost himself in her voice. Then he realized that Lauren was talking about something else now, about men who were brought in at night with a knife in their stomach, and about screaming wives she had to calm down, about kids with chicken bones stuck in their throats, about drunk drivers who ran into trees, about people who'd been beaten up. She had to take care of the patients until the doctor had time to see them. Lauren lit a cigarette and said, "The German American Bund beat up two people the other day, two protesters."

"That's no good."

"This lunatic in Germany is a menace to the whole world. These days you have to pick a side. That's what these two men did. It was the right thing to do."

He nodded thoughtfully and knew she was right.

"Did you hear about the attacks in Washington Heights, Joe? The victims landed in our emergency room. One shopkeeper recognized his assailant from back in Berlin."

She looked at him, challenging him. *Now it's your turn*, she seemed to be saying.

"Does this have anything to do with me?"

Lauren hesitated. "You've got friends in Yorkville, don't you?"

"Well, sure. I wouldn't call them friends. And there's lots of things in Yorkville: athletic clubs, reading groups, choirs, baking clubs, and of course also a mini version of Hitler's Germany."

He got up and went into the kitchen. His voice still echoed in his ear. He poured himself some more whiskey and came back just as she was saying something about Isadore Greenbaum. He immediately saw the suit pants pulled down around his ankles, and the article in the *New York Times* two days later. "A hero!"

He muttered agreement and felt the back of his neck getting hot, as if he were blushing with shame. The feeling spread down his back. He'd been there, after all. He had seen Greenbaum with his own eyes. And he himself had been as far from jumping up and protesting as could be.

Without thinking he pushed the standing lamp away so that the light wasn't shining on him. Lauren slid a bit closer; she had misunderstood him. The lamp now shone on the QSL cards on the wall. XiAY, a man with a sombrero who lived somewhere in Mexico. Josef squinted; his tongue followed, forming the words: Avenida Ixtaccihuatl 27.

"It's getting pretty late," said Lauren quietly.

"You're right. I'll walk you to the subway."

The wind blew a smattering of raindrops out on the street; maybe that's why Lauren walked so quickly. At the top of the stairs of the subway station on Lexington she assured him that he could leave her alone now, it wasn't dangerous.

"But what about all the beatings and assaults all over New York?"

She looked at him with surprise, searched his eyes.

"Sorry, Lauren, that was a dumb joke."

Suddenly he wasn't sure if their date on Sunday was going to happen. But he would be there.

20

NEUSS, JULY 1949

Dörsam answers the phone saying his name is Meer-busch. Josef recognizes his voice right away.

He says his own name, "Josef Klein," then adds, "Joe," then, "from the old days at the Old Heidelberg," and is about to say *Ellis Island* when finally Dörsam interrupts him.

"Right, I know who you are." Josef, his heart beating in his throat, makes an effort to hear goodwill in the voice. But then Dörsam asks cuttingly, "Where did you get my number?"

"From Schmuederrich."

"Oh, him."

"Can we meet?"

There's a pause. Dörsam seems to be thinking.

"Tomorrow morning at eleven o'clock in Cologne. Can you manage that?"

"Of course," says Josef. He'll find some way to manage it.

"Come to the Kunibert monastery, behind the train station. Stand by the entrance and wait."

He hears the click of the receiver landing back on the hook.

He keeps an eye on Carl throughout the evening, and when finally his brother opens his newspaper and leans back contentedly in his chair, he informs him that he'd like to go to Cologne tomorrow. He feels like a little kid who has to ask permission. Because he doesn't want to lie, he also doesn't have an explanation for why he'd like to go to Cologne, and so when Carl asks, "Oh yeah? What do you want to go there for?" he says he just has to get out of Neuss for a bit, which isn't untrue. "Maybe I'll take a few photos with the Linhof."

"Go ahead, then. You've got money."

He does have money. Carl gave him ten marks, "for helping out."

The next morning he sets out early, swallows sailing across the royal-blue sky, under which every other impression of the city seems to dissipate. The camera is heavy; it weighs his shoulder down, but it also reassures him, makes him feel as though he really is taking a harmless day trip.

He buys a ticket at the train station, leaves an hour later. It's a short journey, and as the cathedral begins to soar up ahead of him, so venerable and dark, cracked, rough looking, damaged in a few places, but unmistakably the cathedral, he feels such sadness that he stares out the window and simply lets the tears flow.

The train pulls into a giant station that he once saw forty years ago with his father, his mother, and Carl, a Sunday trip. He remembers the suit Carl had to wear, too big for him; his timid, unhappy mother on the Rhine promenade among people much better off than they. His father didn't make much money. A sign painter who hoped he could switch careers and become an electrician. The government had promised a promotion to those who enlisted in the first days of the war.

The front hall has also survived the war, an overly ornate, gloomy edifice. Outside, his eyes wander over many barren lots, over a few one-story buildings that had been built quickly on top of old leftover foundations, over piles of rubble that were already overgrown with weeds. He has some time still and walks in the direction of the old city. He sees individual buildings here and there propping each other up like drunks. On a wooden fence the words OUT WITH THE NAZI PLAGUE. On a wall, between two bullet holes: HITLER KAPUT.

At a makeshift wooden kiosk he buys a coffee. A one-legged man who seems to be working with a blind organ grinder holds out his hat.

On Ellis Island he had always given Dörsam a wide berth. He didn't want to be seen with him too often. As the Americans saw it, Dörsam was bad news. Should he call him Herr Meerbusch? He mustn't make any mistakes.

At half past ten, he starts heading back to the train station, first down Domstraße and then Machabäerstraße. He turns onto Kunibertsklostergasse, which is nothing but empty windows and staircases with no buildings surrounding them. He doesn't have to wait long. Dörsam is also early.

"Heil Hitler! Come with me!"

Josef quickens his gait to match Dörsam's, which is brisk, but not hurried, and already he has the impression that he's a pesky fly that Dörsam is trying to brush off.

"All this here isn't going to stay like this. The last word has yet to be spoken."

Josef nods politely.

Dörsam keeps talking: "Germans long for what was here years ago, believe me. They don't want democracy and they certainly don't want any occupation powers. In South America they're preparing something, a coup." And then he looks at Josef, who has been nodding politely this whole time, and recoils in shock. "I thought you were someone else. You're not Josef Wolpensinger. Now I remember. You're the one with the radio. I don't have a good memory for names, or for faces. You look like him, the other Josef."

Josef wonders whether Dörsam might have just told him too much, and also if Dörsam has a screw loose. Overthrow Adenauer? Good luck with that.

"I look like a lot of people," says Josef. They've reached the Rhine now. The silvery gray water is choppy from the wind. He doesn't recognize any of it, although he knows he was here, his parents, Carl, and him, in a former life.

"But now I remember you. Now I remember!"

Josef walks a foot or two behind Dörsam. As hard as he tries, he can't keep up with him; whenever he catches up to him, Dörsam just starts walking faster. Dörsam walks with his torso pitched stiffly forward, as if he were trying to walk off a stomachache.

"You didn't exactly do much for us. Did you?"

Josef hesitates. As of late the fact that he didn't do much has been a point in his favor. But he had done too much. And on the other hand, yes, too little.

"You're the one who built a radio. You kept repeating that over and over again in court."

"I was told that if I was deported help would be waiting for me." He hurries after Dörsam now, in Carl's baggy suit.

"For the big fish. You're a small fry."

Josef says nothing. He would like to light a cigarette, his last one from America, but the wind on the bank of the Rhine is so strong it would be a waste. Dörsam stops and looks at a bridge. "This is new. All the bridges were bombed by the Americans."

It's not true. The Waffen-SS blew up the bridges as the Americans were marching in; Carl told him. But if he wants something from Dörsam it wouldn't be wise to contradict him.

"Schmuederrich is in Buenos Aires. He was a friend of yours?"

Josef nods. Schmuederrich, sure, sure, a friend.

"So you want to go to South America too, huh? That's why you wanted to meet with me?"

"I don't have a future here. Maybe I can make myself useful in Buenos Aires?"

"Just what did you do for us anyway?"

He hesitates. Then he decides to bet it all on the one card he has.

"I did a lot for you. Operation Sonnenstaub."

Dörsam's face lights up. "Operation Sonnenstaub!"

Josef quickly changes the subject. "I don't have any papers."

"Come back to Cologne in four weeks. Do you have money?"

"No."

"That's not good." Dörsam keeps walking, unfazed.

"What does that mean, that's not good?"

"You can get a job, can't you? Or sell that camera you've got in your pocket? What kind is it?"

"A Linhof."

"Sell it."

"I can't. It's my brother's. Just how much money do I need?"

"Depends. If you can do without a lot of comfort, a little money is enough. Maybe five hundred dollars. First you cross the border at Aachen. Hitchhike to Eupen and take the regional train to Herbesthal. There's a train that goes from Herbesthal to Brussels. From there you take a train to Paris. You actually need a visa for Belgium, but you're from England, you didn't know anything about it—that will get you through. In Paris you take a train to Le Havre. Plan on it taking a day. From Le Havre the ship to Dakar, with a stop in Casablanca. Can you remember all this?"

"I don't know." Dörsam waits till he's written down all the different stages of the journey on the back of his train ticket.

"You can apply for a visa in Bonn." Dörsam looks at his watch. "A little late for it today."

Eupen, Herbesthal, Brussels, Paris, Le Havre, Casablanca, Dakar, he's got it all down. "The ticket for the ship?"

"In Le Havre. You need the money for bribes. It's not as bad as it sounds. All of Europe is on the move. Use the chaos to your advantage. Maybe you can sign on as a sailor, then they'll give you free passage. And once you get to Buenos Aires, get in touch with Schmuederrich. Restaurant ABC. I'll send a telegraph. You can make yourself useful there. I'll be coming later, when I've finished my work here."

He sees that Dörsam keeps looking around nervously, his way of signaling that the meeting is over. Josef summons his courage and asks, "What ever became of Dr. Ritter?"

"Dr. Ritter? He's an exporter in Hamburg now. Why do you ask?"

"And General Lahousen?"

"Why would you bring him up? A traitor!"

"I'm just interested in what becomes of a person like that."

"The Americans gave him a fat pension after he sold everybody out and sent them to their deaths. Lives somewhere in Tirol now. Innsbruck, I think."

A few minutes later he's alone again. Dörsam is walking up toward the cathedral, and Josef would also like to head that way but opts not to and continues walking along the Rhine.

The water is blue and sparkling, not a cloud in the sky. The black trail of smoke left by a steamship hovers over the river. While the ship's paddle wheel struggles against the current, he searches in vain for the feeling of peace that the Harlem River always brought him. The conversation is still running through his head. It makes him uneasy. Will he be able to steer clear of the Germans once he gets to Buenos Aires? Maybe, somehow, he can even keep going. He could cross the border in Mexico—America is his true homeland after all.

Back in Neuss he notices that Edith has started avoiding his gaze. Yesterday it was happening as well. He hasn't given it too much thought. But now it seems to him as though she were making an extra show of being busy and that there was a mild fury in everything she did. All the tasks she performed around the house, which he so liked to watch, that were so calming—she now carries them out with more severity, more loudly. As if she wanted to drive him off.

When Carl goes into the parlor, where of late he's been playing chess against himself ("And soon I'll be able to beat you, my dear man"), he goes up to Edith. She looks up from the dishes. "Please," he says. "At least when Carl's around. He's going to think I've done something awful to you!"

She looks hurt. It occurs to him that maybe that's the reason she's so angry? That there wasn't much, and there will be even less?

"You're going to leave," she says, and he can sense that it's not a request, but an accusation. There's a bitterness to it. *You're leaving. We're staying. I'm staying. Everything is going to stay just as it is.*

21

NEW YORK, MAY 1939

HE KNEW THE COMPONENTS. HE HAD WRITTEN EVERYTHING down. He wanted to start by building the coil and the capacitor. Save the Audion, the antenna, and the amplifier for the next phase of work. He just wanted to buy what would fit in his leather briefcase, to make several trips. This way he could keep things under control—the device mustn't get too big or too heavy. He also needed to stock up on wires, switches, clips, and a new soldering iron. His plan was to not buy anything prefabricated; instead he would have something tailor-made, handcrafted almost. That way it would be harder to trace the source. The whole thing capable of being stowed in two suitcases max.

He left the dog at home. She whined as he left like she did every time he closed the door on her wet nose. He fished a letter from Carl out of the mailbox—airmail. He opened it outside as he walked.

Dear Josef,

He skipped straight to the last page—that's where Carl always put the most important news.

Our daughter will soon be a year old. Our son three years old. The two of them are a great joy to us! Don't you want to marry and bring children into the world yourself someday? It truly is the greatest happiness in life.

How's work? Are you getting along better with your boss, have you gotten past your differences of opinion? A man should always make sure he's on good terms with his superiors. I hope you don't mind the advice.

By the way, my business was declared essential to the war effort. So you don't have to worry about us if it does come to war. Also I'm considered unfit for military service—one eye isn't enough for the front. What's that saying? A blessing in disguise.

Warm greetings from your brother Carl, Edith, and the kids

At the newsstand Josef bought the *New York Times*. He went over the list again on the train. Memories came flooding back to him: the different steps, the focus, handing wire and cables back and forth, Arthur's voice. "You have to bend little feet at the ends of the wire. Look, like this." Maybe Arthur would help him if he got stuck.

He had a hundred seventy dollars on him. He held his briefcase close as the subway rattled downtown. "Only the best materials," Max had said. "We've got the green light from Hamburg!"

He searched for some small feeling of triumph. His ideas were being taken seriously. But he felt only apprehension.

Delancey Street. Foley Square. Fulton Street. He opened up the newspaper. Today he found the name on page three. A private airport was now being built for him, an hour from Berchtesgaden. A Catholic priest had been sentenced to sixteen months in prison for speaking ill of him.

Trinity Church. He had gone a stop too far. He was now in the Syrian Quarter, signs in Arabic all around him. From Liberty Street down to Battery Park, everything here west of Broadway was in Arabic script. He walked past tables with men playing chess and smoking water pipes, handcarts with exotic fruit. It smelled of coffee and cardamom. LITTLE SYRIA. SON OF THE SHEIKH, SYRIAN COOKING. He would bring Lauren here, assuming she was still interested in him. "Why should she be interested in you *at all?* What can you offer her, you good-for-nothing?" Arthur had been ribbing him. "Yeah, the FBI must have sent her after me," he'd answered.

He stepped inside a Syrian church, maybe just because he read its name, Saint Joseph's Maronite Church. A silence enveloped him, as if he'd plunged his head underwater. He said a prayer. He prayed for Carl, prayed that Carl really wouldn't be sent to the front.

He unfolded the letter and learned that Carl had bought a house. Not incentivized:

> The deplorable has become common practice around here—no, the proper, normal way. Edith doesn't much care for the house, it's old and it's got some things wrong with it, but you can't have everything—a clean conscience and luxury. At least not in these times!

A photo was enclosed. The family in the park. It was an older photo: Carl, posing proudly with one foot forward, showing off the family. Thick wool coats and fur collars, snow in the background.

He crossed himself and stepped back outside. The cool, fruity air of the water pipes drifted through the street. He crossed Liberty Street and soon reached Cortland Street, Radio Row. The radio components glittered in the heat. A whole street crammed with replacement parts; the technology was developing at such a rapid pace that the stores kept

having to make room for the newest items. Steel and aluminum casings, speakers, and tubes were piled up on the sidewalks. A crowd of
buyers threaded its way among it all, browsing. A few were gathered
in little groups—experts talking shop. In the sun it smelled of burnt
rubber, lubricating oil, and metal. Music drifted out of the shops, jazz
mixing with classical. It lent rhythm to the shimmering metal. He
saw old Radiolas and old Stromberg Treasure Chests with beautifully
crafted wooden casings. They once went for three hundred dollars;
now they were practically giving them away, but without any guarantee
that they would work.

He felt the wooden surface of a Philco Midget, an obsolete model
from 1931 that was shaped like a cathedral. "You got a car?" He jumped.
"We install radios. Make an appointment." The man was dressed like
a mechanic. He handed him a business card. Cars were parked on the
curb, the doors wide open. Curious passersby stopped to take a look.

In the shop windows hung seashells from the South Seas and dried
fish, souvenirs from the sailors who came here to stock up on radio
gear. East Radio Store. Superior Equipment and Repair. He decided
on Ammon's Radio Store.

He walked in and pulled out his list. The salesman looked at it for
a long time. "A quarz with a transmitting range of over three thousand
miles. What are you planning on using it for, anyway?"

"It's not for me, it's for someone I know." He lapsed back into his
German accent, as he always did when he was nervous.

"Do you use a radio yourself?"

"Yes, I'm an amateur operator."

The list was now sitting on the display table between them. He wanted
to just grab it and leave the store.

"But the quarz is supposed to have a range of over three thousand
miles?"

"That's not illegal."

"Not yet."

The salesman was eyeing him suspiciously and made no attempt to hide it.

"I don't have a quarz like that in stock right now."

"All right. I'll be going, then." And he took the piece of paper.

"Hold on now. I can get you the other parts."

The salesman went down the shelves, grabbing some wire here, clips and rubber components there. Josef had hoped this would give him some time to think. But the salesman drew him into a conversation. He had shellac on the list—what did he need that for? Probably for isolation purposes, right? He'd advise against that. Paraffin or insulating varnish was better.

"All right."

"Do you have tinfoil at home?"

"No."

"Oh, but you'll need it. You have to use it to cover the back of the panel, but don't forget to leave room for the leads."

He nodded absently.

He was still alone with the salesman. Should he just go? There was something about the way the man looked at him every time he put an item on the table, and the way he loudly announced what it was.

Then he took a receipt pad, warped from the humidity, and began to write down each item.

"You're German?"

"I've lived here for fifteen years." Josef picked up a clip, inspecting it, as if he hadn't decided yet.

"But you're from Germany?"

"I should think you can hear it."

The salesman nodded. "Comes out to a hundred fifty dollars. And I'll need your name and address."

He hesitated.

"Better yet, just show me your ID. Then you won't have to spell out that German name for me."

"It's not complicated—Joe Klein."

The salesman looked up.

"How about that. That is easy. And where do you live, Joe?"

Something wasn't right. But he told him, as if out of spite, his address.

"May I see your ID?" asked the salesman.

"No."

"Then I can't sell you these items."

"That's my real address, that's my real name too," snorted Josef, no longer able to keep his voice down.

"I can't sell you the equipment. Sorry."

He reached into his jacket pocket, took out his ID, and slammed it down on the table. The salesman took a quick look at it.

"Thanks a lot. Now, what exactly was the problem?"

"There is no problem. That was the problem."

"Sometimes I just don't get you Germans."

"I'm not German. I'm a citizen."

"You'll always be a German."

He didn't wait for the salesman to pack the items up. He just threw everything into his briefcase. A copper clamp fell to the ground. He picked it up and hurried out of the shop.

22

NEW YORK, MAY 1939

WHEN HE DIDN'T SEE LAUREN IN THE LOBBY, HE GOT UN-easy. He was a bit late. He bought two tickets, waited five minutes, then joined the line outside the theatre. There was text printed on the back of his ticket: IF HITLER MOVES INTO THE WHITE HOUSE, EVERY PERSON WHO SEES THIS FILM WILL BE ARRESTED. Very funny. But every now and then he heard someone laughing.

The theatre was under guard—two cops standing on either side of the door. He'd worked his way up to the entrance when, behind him, he heard Lauren calling his name. She was holding popcorn and soda. "Can't watch Nazis without popcorn."

They sat in the second-to-last row; all the way in the back sat the perverts, even if they couldn't expect much inspiration from this movie. He sank into the plushy embrace of the theatre seat. They didn't talk. First previews, then the movie: the Warner Bros. fanfare sounded, then ominous strings. *Confessions of a Nazi Spy* flickered over the screen.

A silhouetted figure told of an espionage case in New York; the confessions of the agents were "stranger than fiction."

A meeting hall in New York. Swastikas on the wall and a banner: NUR EINER SCHAFFT'S: DER FÜHRER! HALTE IHM DIE TREUE! *Only one man can get it done: the Führer! Keep the faith with him!*

Stiff-walking Germans—they had a hard time with the English but it was all the easier for them to lift their arms in salute. *"Toomorrow ze verld iss auers. Heil Hitler!"* They all seemed thoroughly foolish. The audience laughed. Why the hell did he pick this of all movies to take Lauren to?

Nazis dropping flyers out of a stunt plane flying over New York: THE PRESIDENT IS A COMMUNIST! And: HITLER WANTS PEACE!

In the back room of a Yorkville restaurant—wasn't that the Old Heidelberg?—a frightened man who wants to stop working for the German spy network is being put through the wringer by burly Gestapo men. "Have you ever heard of an organization known as the Gestapo? We'll forget it this time."

Even this seemed ridiculous, but he didn't feel like laughing. Lauren leaned over and whispered, "He should just go to the FBI."

"They'd arrest him immediately."

"Not if he testifies against the others."

What did she know about it?

"Ze Tcherman desstiny off Amerika," said someone on-screen. The chuckling in the theatre was getting more and more on his nerves, the cozy comfort of shared feeling. Even Lauren was laughing quietly, and when he turned to her she said, "No, it's just funny is all. The way you talk is different. You can barely tell that you're . . ." She didn't say anything more. Only when Hitler appeared did the giggling in the theatre cease. Not an actor, the real thing. Hitler raving before the Reichstag, Hitler proudly surveying a regiment. The silence in the theatre was more frightening than everything that came before, which of course had merely been ridiculous.

Lauren leaned over again and whispered, "They couldn't find an actor who was willing to play Hitler. They were all too afraid. There were death threats against the director! That's why they're using original footage."

"I know."

His voice sounded icy. Lauren's hands now lay folded together in her lap. A German immigrant by the name of Kurt Schneider tried to procure blank passports for the spy ring. He went about it so ineptly that the FBI was soon on his trail. While Kurt Schneider raced through the streets, running straight into the hands of his pursuers, Josef took a sip of soda and looked over at Lauren, her face lit up in the silver glow, working hard to glean some valuable bit of insight from the movie.

He thought of his own stupid behavior at the radio store a few days ago. But no one had explained anything to him. No one had given him instructions. They just told him to go ahead.

On the screen Germany was busy preparing the way for the global Germanic empire. With wax writing. With disappearing ink. With hollow walking sticks. They had only sent twenty lines of code to Hamburg in the last week. Max complained that there was barely any information coming in of late. Ships' cooks, housemaids, factory workers—they weren't delivering. He asked Max if these kinds of people were the only ones working for German intelligence but got no answer.

Kurt Schneider was arrested. A confession was easy to coax out of him; he'd been so pleased to have spent time running around as a Nazi.

Lauren whispered, "Hard to believe they'd recruit such saps."

"Oh, they do," he said quietly.

Lauren gave him a searching look. He felt her eyes on him but said nothing.

"The movie is so contradictory, Joe. The Germans are presented as dopes, and yet we're supposed to believe that they're about to reduce New York to rubble and ash."

"And how do you know they're not going to do just that?"

Lauren looked at him again. Then she said, "You're right. We don't know."

Later, in the lobby, he was silent as Lauren talked. He suspected that after so much ridiculed German he wouldn't have his accent under control. He stared at the film poster: YOUR GERMAN NEIGHBOR— WHERE ARE HIS ORDERS COMING FROM? WHO'S HE REPORTING TO?

He heard Lauren saying that the movie had won a prize, it had beaten *The Wizard of Oz* in a contest. "Granted, it's a propaganda film. Still, though, the issue of how frustrated immigrants are easy to manipulate is well presented, don't you think?"

She was still mid-sentence when he grabbed her by the elbow and led her outside.

It was dark by now. The air on Broadway smelled of dust and gas fumes. He liked this smell. They threaded their way among the people and neon signs. SCHAEFER BEER, PEPSI COLA—gold and red letters glowing against the night sky.

They walked in silence, side by side, strangely lost and yet, because of this, oddly connected. He took her hand, caressed the palm with his thumb, and felt reminded of another woman; he tried to remember which.

"Don't expect so much of me," she said quietly.

"What do you mean?" he asked and let go of her hand.

She was silent.

"What a joke," he said. And finally: "It's late. I'll get you a taxi and take you home."

"No, that's not necessary."

"Yes, it is, Lauren."

He knew that he had to take her home, and suddenly he felt like God, all-knowing. He grandly hailed a cab, though he didn't even know where Lauren lived. She looked at him quizzically, a bit hostile, but this too he just let slide right off him. He held the door open for her. She got in on the other side.

"Lauren, I'm taking you home. I'll need your address."

She leaned forward and told her street and house number to the back of the driver's head. It was an address in Brooklyn, a long ride.

They turned off Frankfort Street and onto the Brooklyn Bridge. Lauren looked out the window, her face turned away from him. Lauren's instincts were working. After all, he was keeping something secret from her, something essential.

It had started raining; a pedestrian opened up a newspaper and held it over his hat.

Suddenly Lauren exhaled loudly and looked at him: "Really, it's unbelievable how the Germans here act."

He agreed with her, but said, "They haven't been back home for many years. Maybe they're homesick."

"For Germany?"

"Yes. For the country as they remember it."

"But they're supporting today's Germany."

"Maybe they're confusing homesickness with patriotism."

"But patriotism isn't any better, Joe!" she said. She was getting worked up now.

He didn't say anything. The driver was starting to cast glances at them in the rearview mirror.

"Do you think patriotism is something harmless?" She wouldn't let it go.

He felt a twinge of anger but made an effort to keep his voice calm. "I don't know, Lauren. I, for example, like America. What's wrong with that?"

"Joe, in the name of patriotism they want to establish authoritarian regimes like Germany's all over the world."

"So Communism isn't authoritarian?"

She sighed, and when no answer came he said, "The danger is just as real, Lauren. There's a Communist threat. Surely you don't deny it, do you? The Jew Trotsky is sitting there in Mexico and planning an attack on America. Just to mention one example."

"He's there in exile, Joe. His being Jewish caused big problems for him in Russia." She emphasized every word, like she was talking to a deaf person. Then she turned and looked out the window and seemed not to want to continue the conversation. Her profile was sharply defined. He saw her pointed chin, there was something touching about it, and even though he was furious at Lauren, he would have liked to take her in his arms and press her to him. What in God's name were they talking about anyway? They passed by a large cemetery and he had no idea where they were. He knew Brooklyn only from his trips to Coney Island. Every now and then they'd made deliveries to a politically engaged women's group in Bushwick that called itself Women Against Communism.

The taxi stopped. Josef could see the lights of a freighter down a side street, which meant they were on a street running parallel to the shore.

Lauren got out. Standing in the rain, she knocked on his window. He rolled it down. "I think you've gotten Thoreau all wrong. Thoreau's individualism isn't a license to reshape the world as you see fit."

He watched her walk up to a two-story house with a small front yard. When the light went on inside, he told the driver to take him to the nearest subway.

"You shouldn't talk to women about politics," said the driver as he paid.

He turned up his collar and ran off. The rain beat against his face, each drop a little fist.

23

NEUSS, JULY 1949

THE LINHOF'S LENS BOARD SCREWS OFF EASILY, THE RING nut gives way, the locking nut rolls into his hand. The lens is easy to pop out as well. He runs his finger over the glass—Zeiss, good quality. The leather bellows that the lens was attached to is quite long. He moves it this way and that, testing it, then stretches it out as far as it will go; there doesn't seem to be any anchoring. Next up before he takes apart the housing is the flashbulb. The screws clatter as they drop out, one by one—that was easy.

It's been a long time since he last got to work on some piece of gadgetry. On Ellis Island there were no machines or electrical devices, no tools, and no work either. Only books, board games, a few soccer balls (mostly for the younger inmates), newspapers. Every day he waited for the paper. It would be a week old, and sometimes there were pages missing. This made him suspicious, and he would use the article previews on the first page to try to reconstruct whatever it was they were hiding from him this time.

The first time it happened was at Sandstone. Reading the newspaper and being staggered and horrified. Later it became a sign to him that he was onto something. Something that possibly no one else knew about.

The first article that gave him pause appeared in the summer of 1942. He had been in prison for just over half a year. Eight Germans had landed on the beach at Amagansett. A German U-boat had dropped them just off the coast of Long Island; they paddled toward the shore in rubber boats in the gray of dawn. They were just able to bury their waterproof crates of explosives and timed fuses before they were seen by a shore guard. They offered him money and hurried off, then the guard contacted the police. The wet sand showed where the crates were hidden; cigarette butts of German origin were scattered everywhere. Not hard to guess who they were dealing with: German spies. On top of that, they accidentally left important documents on the train to New York. *Look at that*, he thought. *More dopes working behind enemy lines for the German Reich.*

Their objectives: blow up industrial facilities and infrastructure like aluminum plants, bridges, and train tracks; plunge America into chaos. Operation Pastorius.

The bellows isn't quite as easy to dismount. Josef spends a while trying to jimmy it loose with the screwdriver from an awkward angle until finally something gives way. He finds clumps of dust on the inside and blows them away. Carl's photos in the city park were slightly overexposed, so he checks the folds but can't find any tears anywhere—though they might just be too tiny.

He can hear Carl in the kitchen. Must have just gotten home. Carl is yelling at his son. Actually it's more of a nagging, like the women on the Lower East Side, as if the voice had a life of its own and was seizing hold of Carl's body. It made Josef feel sorry for him.

At first he had wanted to go up to his brother and tell him to calm down, tell him everything's fine. But at this point he just wants to belt him one.

But at least Carl's story has been a smooth one. Not his. His is crooked and warped.

In prison he sometimes thought of Gandhi. For Gandhi things had moved forward, toward something, despite his being in prison, whereas in his case things moved backward, his life got smaller and smaller, contained less and less.

He has cleaned the bellows, and now he takes a little oil to grease the joints. Then he turns the pivot plate. Screw after screw comes out, the mounts come loose.

Normally he makes himself scarce right before Carl comes back in the early afternoon, exhausted from his delivery route. He takes his lonely walks through town, through streets with caved-in roofs and charred walls, and on his way back he prepares a few harmless topics that make for easy conversation: *Did you see that Maikelowski is selling beer now?*

Not today. Taking the camera apart is too much fun. By now there's a pile of metal spread out on the table in front of him. He looks at the handle of the cable release. There are a few cracks in the rubber coating. Carl has taken a lot of photos with the shutter release, starting with his honeymoon, and relatively few of his surroundings—no buildings, hardly any other people, always just himself, himself alone and himself with Edith, then later with the kids.

Ever since their gnocchi lunch, Edith has stopped tidying up in his room. Carl mustn't know this. Josef makes his bed every morning, and whatever he uses he puts away immediately. When Carl or the children are around, Edith acts friendly toward him. If they're alone, she's distant.

He inspects the baseboard and focus cam. What brilliant precision workmanship! He touches the screwdriver to the casing, takes off the mount for the tripod. Screw after screw, they roll toward him. Carl stomps around the bedroom. He can hear him speaking with Edith but can't understand a word.

A few weeks after the first article on Pastorius, he read that a few of the agents on the beach in Amagansett had gotten drunk in a bar in

Brittany the night before the U-boat was set to depart and blabbed out their whole plan. At a much later date, he read that one of the agents had gone to the FBI after their arrival and ratted out all the others. He was in the middle of reading about this when suddenly there stood Schmuederrich behind him. He was sitting upstairs in the gallery with a view of the Statue of Liberty.

"What are you reading?"

"Newspaper." A sigh. Fidgeting behind him. Then Schmuederrich ripped the paper out of his hands. "Ugh, this Lahousen. A traitor! A swine! Just wants to save his own ass. Now that the war's over anybody can claim whatever he wants!"

Ellis Island. The windowpanes foggy and opaque. But in there the Third Reich still hadn't fallen.

When time started to drag, he tried to be a monk, tried to be someone who could focus all his attention and become fascinated by the smallest things—it was all God's creation, after all: the honeycomb-shaped white floor tiles, the water pitcher on the table, the two columns in the room, the tiles on the walls, veined with tiny cracks and missing in a few places, the *Heil Hitler* that echoed through the hallways like a ghost.

Stay on the margins till it's all over. It could happen any day.

When they had to leave they called out, "Till next time in Buenos Aires."

And now Buenos Aires seems like the only option for him too.

"What are you doing? Are you crazy?"

"I'll put it right back together again, Carl. I just wanted to get a look at the mechanics of it."

"You'll put it back together now, immediately! For God's sake! Do you know what that thing cost?"

He knows. He gets right to work. Even though he would have liked to have a bit more time to check out the inner workings. But Carl stands behind him and waits, stern and silent, until eventually he says, "Right, you have to concentrate, maybe I'm in your way," and leaves.

Piece by piece, screw by screw. In an hour the Linhof is back in one piece. Except for one screw. It's leftover.

Should he hide it? No. He decides to come clean. To his amazement Carl just laughs. "That one's yours, kid. There's no doubt you've got a screw loose!"

Four weeks later the eight agents went before a military tribunal, and then that same day to the electric chair. Except for two: the ones who had turned themselves in to the FBI and betrayed their comrades only got prison sentences. But that too Josef only read about years later. Back then it was supposed to look like Hoover and his clever men at the FBI had done it all on their own, without the help of any defecting agents.

Another article. He'd felt a bit sick after reading this one. Three American sailors and one British sailor offered to shoot the condemned agents to spare the US government the cost of the electricity needed for the execution. But the government wasn't about to let this opportunity get away.

24

NEW YORK, JULY 1939

HE STOOD IN FOLEY SQUARE, AND LIKE A SHIP IN A ROUGH sea he was buffeted by the people surging past him, while the stock-still buildings seemed to accept him as one of their own. Before him stood the white, broad courthouse building with columns and stairs leading up it—a grand majestic temple. The FBI had its offices here. He tried to seem like a tourist, opened up a map, looked at the small park just north of the square, folded the map up again.

His life too could be folded up like a piece of paper and tucked into someone's pocket, some officer, some agent. He had decided he would come down here, but this time it was only to look, no pressure. As a result he was very calm. He took breaths, felt the sun on his nose. He would start working for Arthur again next week, would get to print things like AMERICA FOR WHITE PEOPLE again. He did, after all, need a job that the IRS considered legit—manning a radio terminal for German intelligence didn't fit that bill.

He turned his gaze toward the entrance. Imagined himself climbing the wide front steps, being intercepted by a doorman.

How can I help you?

I'd like to report something to the FBI.

He didn't want to think any further than that. He turned away from the building. No, he thought. Not today.

He started walking south through flickering sunlight. Extravagant summer hats floated past, the smell of perfume and suntan lotion. He walked over the Brooklyn Bridge, feeling its heavy vibrations, while below him a sailboat plowed through the water. Arthur had spoken once of secret offices just north of Red Hook. He had mentioned names, but Josef couldn't remember them. They could set you up with new papers. A new name and everything. He left the bridge and turned down Old Fulton Street, past rows of identical brownstones.

He walked along the shore, gazing at the Manhattan skyline under a blue sky. When he reached wide Atlantic Avenue he realized he was hungry. At a diner he ordered roasted potatoes and herring, drank a soda and then a coffee. It was already evening, though still bright out. He kept trying to remember the address as he walked. He went through several intersections: Pacific Street, Baltic Street, Degraw Street. In a park he sat on a bench and a short while later was lying on his back, asleep. When he opened his eyes there was a policeman staring down at him; in his dream he had felt him grab hold of his arm and start shaking him. Josef walked to the park entrance. It was almost dark now.

He made it to Red Hook, a waterfront neighborhood of squat red-brick houses that reminded him of Düsseldorf. Past the houses were piers and seedy red warehouses that opened up to the boat landings. Large, crooked cranes like dying insects. He was greeted by the smell of oil, the palpable sense of frenzied activity, of men running this way and that. They were stacking wooden crates, brief, throaty shouts and orders flying back and forth. Workers stood under the awning of a loading platform, their shoes stained with the juice of crushed red berries. One stuck a cigarette in his mouth, then a strawberry. He looked at him, and Josef promptly stumbled over a few iron rods.

In a loud sailors' bar he treated himself to a drink, and another soon after the first. All around him were faces reddened by salt, wind, and drink. A drunk chatter filled the air. He knew the contacts hung around here. He just wanted to have a look, he told himself. A life that wasn't meant for him anyway and that he would soon leave behind— but after his third drink, that was his steadfast conviction: yes, he wanted a new life. The bartender had gotten into an argument with two sailors. One hand resting on his hip, the other on the beer tap, he claimed that America wouldn't take part in the coming war, no way, not this time. Europe would have to work things out on its own. The sailors disagreed. Outside, men were shouting at each other. A line of ants crawled across the wooden bar. He paid.

The street was now bathed in yellow light, and the smell of decay drifted in from the harbor. He stumbled over the iron bars again. He caught himself and realized now that he was drunk. The realization made him feel sorry for himself, and for the first time in days he thought of Lauren, now with tearful affection. He hadn't heard anything from her since the movie, and he hadn't dared contact her. At first he had tried to tell himself that it wouldn't bother him one bit if he never heard from Lauren again. But all the time he was waiting for her call. He even, in case she wrote him—he saw her addressing a few earnest and forbearing lines to him, apologizing for her caustic remarks and at the same time politely questioning his understanding of politics—he even checked the mailbox several times a day, reaching his hand in to make sure no letters had gotten stuck. The reach had become a habit, a familiar pain. He stuck his hand into the mailbox and pulled it out empty every time, or at most with a handful of bills. Even his walk to the FBI office was a secret way of visiting Lauren: he did things that she would approve of if she knew who he really was. But instead of turning himself in, he was now going about trying to prepare his escape.

He walked north on Columbia Street, saw offices with greasy windows, saw a sign that read JABLINSKI, ATTORNEY AT LAW. Suddenly he was convinced that this was the name that Arthur had told him. He stepped into a dark rear courtyard, walked up an iron spiral staircase to the rear building, illuminated only by the dim glow of a bare lightbulb. Behind the doors the sound of footsteps and children coughing, the smell of burnt milk pudding. The door upstairs opened very quickly, as if he was on the right track. A heavyset man, his suspenders off and hanging from his waist, seated in front of an overstuffed filing cabinet, asked what he could do for him. It was as if he were in a dream and, realizing that he was dreaming, suddenly couldn't speak. He ran into the tough, rubberlike walls of his dream cocoon, and even though he was awake he couldn't find his way out.

"Can't you talk?"

"I was sent here," he said very slowly, "though it could also be a mistake."

"You'll have to tell me what you want!"

Was that a sign? "I heard you help people."

"I'm a lawyer," the man snapped. "That's my job."

"Do you also help people out with papers?" Josef asked.

"Get lost." The man closed the door.

"Where do I have to go? Tell me!" But his voice was drowned out by music coming suddenly from a radio.

He felt completely sober now, and a horrible anxiousness took hold of him. When, after walking a few hundred feet, he saw the flickering green light of a bar, he went inside, joined the few patrons sitting at the bar, and ordered an Old Musket, which shone golden and soothing in his glass. Let it all be blotted out, the whole day and, if possible, the days to come—but the drink had hardly any effect, as if his state of wakefulness were now permanent. The bartender read the newspaper. When Josef asked, he shared a few pages with him, and Josef looked, as he often had of late, for furnished rooms outside the city, where nobody wanted to live. ASBURY, LIGHT, SUNNY, WELL-HEATED ROOM, $5 WEEKLY, GENTLEMEN 0244. He just had to call, go out there, put down money— but what was he supposed to live off of in these backwaters? Was he supposed to tend cows like he did back when he was a boy?

Only now did Josef notice him. He might have been there the whole time. He'd kept his hat on and pulled it low over his forehead. But Josef recognized him. It was Duquesne. No doubt about it. He had a face that had seen everything: wars, prisons, presidents, African steppe. And something else too: a stately, dignified quality. Josef tried to make eye contact; the man seemed to turn away a little. Carefully, very gingerly, Josef reached for his glass, lifted it up, and drank.

Then he went off toward the bathroom, but took a few steps back into the room.

"Mr. Duquesne?" he spoke to the man's back. "I'm Josef Klein, Joe. We met at the Old Heidelberg a few months ago. Do you mind?"

"You must be mistaken." The man didn't even turn around. But Josef had recognized the peculiar accent. When he came back from the bathroom, he saw that the man was already on the other side of the street. He threw a dollar on the bar, grabbed his hat, and followed him at a distance of about a hundred feet. The street was empty, his pursuit was obvious, and the thought occurred to him that it might make more sense to just run and catch up with him. But something held him back. He watched with interest as Duquesne varied his speed, one minute strolling along and staring into the windows of parked cars, the next walking with great haste. Sometimes the street was so dark that Duquesne was swallowed up completely until he resurfaced in the light of the next streetlamp. But then he vanished for good. In the doorway where he'd lost Duquesne a few bodies lay sleeping, buried under a pile of blankets, a few bare feet poking out. It was one o'clock in the morning. Too late for the subway.

He would have to make it back to Manhattan on foot and then look for a taxi.

"Is there something you want to tell me?"

Duquesne suddenly stepped toward him out of the darkness.

"Herr Duquesne?"

"Will you quit saying my name?"

He felt stupid and helpless. He could see the whites of Duquesne's eyes, they were staring right at him, waiting, as if he were counting the seconds. Josef reached for his collar, as if it were too tight.

"No, I don't have anything to tell you. I want to know what all this is about, what we're doing. I've been pulled into something that could have unwelcome consequences. I want to know if we're in danger. I'm, I want . . ." He stopped talking. Duquesne had given a surly, involuntary jerk, as if he had no sympathy for him, or at least wasn't prepared to offer any fatherly guidance, and in the echo of his stammered words he realized that he sounded tearful and confused.

"Do you know what the problem is? You! People like you are going to ruin everything for us!"

"I don't understand."

"No, you don't! You don't understand a thing!"

He saw Duquesne cross the dark street, but now with a careless, shuffling gait that he hadn't had before. Josef stood frozen. Only when Duquesne was out of sight did he start moving.

By the time he reached the Brooklyn Bridge, the city lay beneath an apricot-brown sky.

25

NEW YORK, JULY 1939

Nothing. they didn't show up. he waited in vain for them on Sunday—not that he missed Max and Ludwig, but their absence, without any explanation, was unsettling. Had something happened to them?

The next morning his sheets were tangled and untucked. When he got up he went through his routine fearfully, taking the utmost care with everything—feeding the dog, putting on coffee—as if this way he could counteract last night's tossing and turning.

Shortly before eight o'clock he took Princess out. The July sun rose festively over Harlem. The children all tried to pet Princess's head. She reacted cheerfully at first and then, as the hands started coming from all sides, with mounting uneasiness. He came to her rescue with a whistle. On the weedy vacant lot he threw her a little ball. She leapt after it, nudged it playfully with her snout, and wagged her tail.

Then she trotted over to the water's edge and looked back at him, waiting for his permission. He threw a stick, and she plowed excitedly through the water. Finally she was swimming; from the bank he saw a dog's head bobbing on the pale green surface.

He undressed and followed her into the cold water in his underwear.

Worse than the cold was the soft, slimy silt of the riverbed that surged up between his toes. He dove under and enjoyed the firm embrace of the water. He swam a few strokes, saw the shimmering surface above him and below him a murky gray. When he came back to the surface, he was far from the bank, ducks swimming around him, self-contained in their smooth plumage, like little boats.

Princess barked. He could sense her fear. He swam over to her, and together they went back to the shore. He didn't have a towel with him, and so he dried himself off with his shirt and buttoned his suit jacket over his bare chest. Let people think what they wanted about him.

Back at the apartment he turned the radio on, smoked a Bremaria Brinkmann that Max had left behind while Glenn Miller's "Oh, Baby" played, and enjoyed the feel of the salt water on his body, the smell of algae and oil, of silt and earth. Crumbling bits of dirt were spread out on the wooden floor; he had left his shoes on. Work at the print shop didn't start until noon, so now he folded open the *New York Times*, searched for the name, read that *Die Meistersinger von Nürnberg* was his favorite opera and that he expected international Jewry to bear all costs for the emigration of their own people from Germany. In an article on the same page he read that both Cuba and Florida had refused a ship with over nine hundred refugees and sent it back to Germany. He put the paper away and stared into space.

Now the radio was playing Emily Post, speaking about "America and its etiquette": A man was to take his hat off when a woman stepped into the elevator with him, because the elevator was the equivalent of a room. In the hallway however, which was more like a street, he might put his hat back on. He turned to the next station to hear more music.

The buzzer rang. He quickly put on a T-shirt and answered.

Someone was coming up the stairs, slower than usual. It was Schmueder-rich. Panting, he stomped past him into the living room and looked around. Beads of sweat on his forehead.

"What's this, you're alone? Figured I'd meet your little girlfriend here. You're still together, aren't you? Will you make me some coffee?"

Schmuederrich's body seemed to take up the whole room. His broad neck and the black chest hairs curling out from his collar took up Josef's entire field of vision. He went into the kitchen, put some water on to boil, and tried to understand the situation. "Milk?" he called out.

"And sugar," Schmuederrich called back.

Back in the living room Josef placed the cup in his hand directly so Schmuederrich wouldn't sit down anywhere.

"What brings you here, Hans?"

"Did you know that up until very recently the United States was the only country in the world that didn't have a decent counterintelligence operation?"

"No, I didn't know that."

"Every other country is happy to put its spies here. Up to now the FBI's hands were tied, they were more responsible for domestic matters. Which didn't exactly make them popular. But last year Hoover and his men finally landed a big success. It's showing at the movies now—we can all go watch. It's like this: we have to work harder. The FBI has been granted broader powers. Things are getting dicey. The Japanese are good spies. Better than us."

Schmuederrich nodded, letting his words sink in. Josef tried to keep the unimpressed look on his face. Schmuederrich put his cup down on the table in front of the radio.

"Stop trailing our own people, Josef."

"I didn't trail anybody."

"And don't ever think about going to the FBI again."

This time he didn't say anything in response. He immediately felt a heavy weight on his chest, pressing all the way up to his throat.

"What do you think you're doing, little man?" Schmuederrich took a deep breath, in and out. "Life's been good to you. Just look at the weather today. Beautiful. And that swell girlfriend of yours. But we can't afford to make any mistakes. Amateurs are too dangerous in the long run."

Josef looked over toward the door; the bits of muck leading that way were now completely crumbled. Could he get past Schmuederrich? Princess lay on her side, her tail wagged nervously up and down.

"You're done. Where's the radio you built for us?"

Had he heard right? Or was it a trick—was he about to get beat up?

"Show it to me."

He went into the bedroom and pulled the box out from under the bed. Thought for a second about locking the door from the inside. He didn't trust Schmuederrich.

"Where are you? Do you need some help?"

It didn't sound like a threat. Schmuederrich had slid back into his chummy voice, like they were wallpapering a room together.

His hands were shaking all the same when, a moment later, he laid the parts out on the table. Princess was standing in between them by now, her ears turning in all directions.

"Do you have someone who can finish building it for you?"

"That's none of your goddamn concern. And once Germany has conquered the world, don't think there'll be a job waiting for you."

"No, of course not, Hans."

Schmuederrich threw everything into a bag—it was made of thin fabric; the parts made bulges and sharp outlines in the material—and off he went toward the door, just like that, like a character in the propaganda movie.

"Stay," whispered Josef. The dog had politely started following Schmuederrich to the door.

"Not a word to anybody."

"Of course not, Hans."

"Including that girlfriend of yours. And by the way, we know where your brother lives."

"You're trying to scare me, is that it?"

"You just leave his letters lying around out in the open," said Schmueder-rich angrily.

After Schmuederrich had left, he washed the river water from his body, then he left the apartment and headed for the print shop. On the way he imagined telling Arthur everything immediately, relieved that it was over, and outraged that Schmuederrich would threaten him.

But when he arrived, he just nodded to Arthur and got right to work. The clatter of the machines in his ears was more pleasant than ever, the familiar hand motions calmed him down, as if time had been turned back, as if he'd woken up from a nightmare. They were gone. He would write Lauren a postcard; he would apologize and send flowers. Flowers were good.

26

NEW YORK, JULY 1939

LAUREN WAS LATE. "SORRY, THE SUBWAY, THE MISERABLE packed subway on a rainy day!" she said, but it sounded like she was blaming him. He helped her out of her coat; it was heavy with rain. "That's actually his job," she said with a glance at the waiter, who was running back and forth between patrons, visibly overwhelmed, his face glowing red.

"But I'm happy to do it," he said quietly.

He led her to their table by the window, which he had asked for specifically on account of the view, but the glass was fogged up; you could only see the blurry glow of headlights and neon signs.

"It's rather warm and loud in here."

"I'm very happy that you're here, Lauren," he said stiffly.

She nodded mercifully. With a touch of self-pity she looked over at some more people who were just coming in. "Now it's going to get even louder in here!"

"Should we go someplace else, Lauren? You did say you wanted to go to Amalfi, since we couldn't get a table last time."

"That's true." She looked him in the eye, for the first time since she'd arrived.

He had written her a card:

> Sorry for the disagreement the other day. Please let me take you out to dinner to make up for it.

"Thank you for the card," she had said on the phone. Nothing about the flowers. Clearly the words weren't enough, not these words.

Lauren's gaze followed a newly arrived couple as if they were criminal intruders.

"Is something bothering you?"

"What do you mean?"

He gave up and signaled the waiter.

She studied the menu very closely. She kept flipping between pages. Meanwhile he was trying to find pizza and instead found a lot of Italian words he didn't understand. When the waiter stepped up to the table, Lauren resurfaced.

"We'll start with antipasti," she announced. "Genoa salami, Sicilian olives, pickled eggplant, squid with saffron sauce."

"A very good selection," the waiter said appreciatively. "And for your second course?"

"The chicken soup with egg, fennel, and artichoke hearts," she continued. "And for the main course the monkfish."

"Dessert?"

"We'll decide later." The waiter gave a bow and hurried off. Lauren had an intimidating air about her. Josef had to clear his throat before he could get himself to speak.

"Are the flowers still blooming? The courier promised to deliver them immediately. It was a very hot day."

"I got rid of the yellow asters. The color clashed with the red roses and the bluebells."

The mix of colors was the thing he'd liked most. He'd put the arrangement together himself.

"Sorry, Joe. I didn't mean it like that."

"You know what you remind me of?" he asked.

"No, what?"

"A cat. First it comes trotting up to you, and then once it gets a few feet away it stops and starts frantically cleaning itself."

"That's cruel."

"You're nervous. Are you afraid of me?"

She shook her head and held tight to her napkin.

They didn't say a word until the wine and appetizers came. The waiter placed the little dishes closer to Lauren's plate than to his, as if she were a goddess who had to be appeased. Lauren tasted a slice of salami, her fingers splayed.

He raised his glass. She calmly dabbed at her lips, then she raised hers.

"So, when we're done are you going to pay for all this with the Third Reich's money? I'm not stupid, Joe."

"No, you are not."

He saw red lipstick on the napkin, the impression of the mouth that had just said these words to him.

"Joe?"

He raised his eyes. "What?"

"I'm glad you aren't trying to deny it."

"Since when," he hesitated, "since when have you thought this about me?"

The waiter came and took the appetizers away. Lauren lit a cigarette, and when they were alone again she said, "Since the movie. It was obvious you knew what you were talking about." She paused for a moment and looked straight at him. It was hard for him to hold her gaze.

"And?" he asked. "What now?"

"You don't want to be in the wrong, but you know that you are, and you're trying to keep it a secret from yourself."

He was amazed how much she knew about him. He purposely blew smoke over the chicken soup that now sat on the table before them. He was teetering between the urge to go ahead and fully confide in Lauren and the stronger impulse to make a run for it.

"Please trust me, Joe. I think you've stumbled into something and now you can't find your way out of it!"

"I told them I quit," he said gruffly.

Her face remained just as kindly and approving, as if this were exactly how she'd imagined this conversation would go. "Good. That's a start."

Then she put her cigarette out and started eating her chicken soup.

27

NEUSS, AUGUST 1949

AN EVENING LIKE MOST ANY OTHER: THEY SIT IN THE kitchen, Carl writes invoices, Edith darns socks, the children read. He has the newspaper spread out in front of him, smoothing it out with his hand every now and then, while his eyes scan the articles. A club wishing to put on a party can apply for exemption from the entertainment tax. New information about the allocation of land for small garden plots in Rommerskirchen and Otzenrath.

He's searching. He's searching for news that could apply to him. You have to keep your eyes open. You need patience. This is what he can do.

The last important piece of news he read was four years ago. December 1945: General Lahousen, head of sabotage for German military intelligence, gave an interview to the international press in Nuremberg.

He glances over at Carl. Sometimes when he's concentrating his brother will push his tongue out between his lips and forget it's there.

"Paul?" It takes a few seconds for the boy to look up at him. "Paul? What's the tallest building in New York?"

"I don't know."

"The Empire State Building."

"How tall is it?"

"Four hundred forty-three meters—that's including the antenna," Josef tells him.

"That's tall."

"Are there a lot of suicides in New York?" asks Täubchen.

"What could possibly make you think of such a thing?" asks Edith, stunned.

"Since the buildings are so tall. It makes it easy."

"Makes a whole heap of work for the people down below, though," Josef says with a wink.

Täubchen laughs. Carl looks up briefly from his invoices and exchanges glances with Edith.

Edith has started tidying up in his room again. This too is something between him and her: no one knows that she stopped, and no one, only he, knows that she started again.

"Time for bed," Edith says to the children. And stands up herself, says something needs taking care of, something to do with the laundry.

To be left alone with Carl all of a sudden is always jarring, like when a half-full box of rice is tipped over and the contents shift to one side. Without Carl having to say anything, he senses that his brother's heart, like his, is beating faster.

Carl no longer says outright when something is bothering him. His face says it all. Josef starts to wonder what he could have done wrong this time. Was it that he walked barefoot through the kitchen? That he scratched his ear at dinner? That he found a station that plays jazz and cranked the volume? When Carl asked, "What is that?" he only answered, "Music." Carl gave him a look, drained and disappointed. He clearly felt he'd been misunderstood, and turned away.

Carl has now been staring at his papers for a while without writing anything.

"Got all the invoices done?" asks Josef.

And Carl answers, "Tell me. Now. Or else you have to go."

"What?"

"Whatever it is you're hiding."

Josef looks to the left and right, as if there were other people around. The next moment he feels like he did back then, when they came into his apartment, pushed him up against the wall, and put sharp handcuffs on him. Which nevertheless he barely felt—it was only when thinking back on it, because his wrists were bruised and hurting for days afterward. And suddenly it's very easy. He just says what he said in court.

"I built a portable radio."

"And what's illegal about that?"

"For German military intelligence."

When describing what happened, only say what everyone can agree on. Whatever else happened, and whatever you might think about it, omit at all costs.

"And what made you do it? How did it start?"

"With a lie. At first it was supposed to be about business. And then there was no getting out of it."

"What's that supposed to mean?"

"They turned up the pressure."

"So you went along with it out of fear?"

"If you want to put it like that, sure."

Carl holds his empty beer glass at an angle, pondering this. "Fear. I was afraid too. But there are more important things."

Josef nods. He can live with this result. And of course he hasn't told him everything yet. He has something else up his sleeve, and that gives him a good feeling.

"But why didn't you tell me this long ago?" Carl keeps probing; he too can sense that they're not done yet.

"Fear."

He ran out of cigarettes long ago. He sure could use one right now. They're very expensive.

"Fear again? Come now, my dear man. What could I do to you?"

Anything you wanted, he thinks. "Throw me out."

"Oh, forget about that. One more time, why did it take you so long to tell me?"

"I don't know. Gandhi was shot last year. Bad things are happening all the time."

"You're comparing yourself to Gandhi?"

"He sat in jail a long time too."

He sees a vein start to swell on Carl's forehead. "I'm trying to have a rational conversation here, man to man, brother to brother."

"The victor decides what's right and what's wrong. Or don't they? A few miles away the Russians are in charge."

"Those who are in power aren't automatically in the right, Josef. We were able to learn that lesson all too well over the past few years."

He feels a fire in his chest, tearing him in every direction at once.

"You weren't even at the front, Carl."

His brother looks at him in disbelief. "Have you ever tried to sleep when there are bombs falling on you night after night? When you're in a bunker with water up to your waist and you have to hold your kids in your arms?"

His brother is shouting.

And he hasn't even said everything he wants to say yet. Now he has to be quick, no doubt about it: "Just because you listened to Radio London doesn't make you a resistance fighter."

And Carl screams, "Who do you think you are? What are you getting at? Why would you say such a thing?"

And he hears Edith's footsteps coming closer and then quickly moving away again. He stands up. Carl gets up too. Dishes clatter. He feels his heart pumping and suddenly a barrier has come down.

"You always were an idiot," he hears Carl saying.

And now he rears back and slugs him. Just like long ago when Carl was a little squirt and easy to beat up—two years are a huge difference at that age. But not anymore. And yet Carl doesn't hit back now, and he doesn't shout either. No, Carl reaches up and touches his eye for a second, seems to be checking something, and Josef skulks over to the door and out onto the landing and almost falls down the stairs in shame. Yes, he seems to be stepping into shame, to be sinking into it, and he's surprised, when he gets outside, in the pitch-black street, that there's still anything left of him. He feels his face glowing red, his heart hammering in his throat. It's painful, what kind of an idiot is he, but he doesn't dare go back, not yet, and so he walks down the street, which mercifully swallows him up. Postwar Germany is saving energy. The darkness does him good.

Then he starts to run. He's panting, running over the bridge, over the Rhine, then to the old buildings on the opposite bank in Düsseldorf. They stand there like they've been glued to each other, the ones he knows from his childhood, the ones that have survived and that now remind him of the buildings in the Bronx, which at the time reminded him of the buildings in Düsseldorf, and now he's out in the fields, where the air embraces him, humid and warm. He drops onto some hay in a barn, and when he wakes up in the morning he gets up immediately, knocks the dust off his suit, and heads back.

He gets back to Sternstraße around noon, sweaty, sunburned, thirsty, and hungry. The boy opens the door, looks back at his mother. Edith sets down a basket of laundry, smooths the front of her blouse. "Sit. I'll make you an omelette."

From the far corner of the living room he hears Carl's thundering footsteps. A knot immediately forms in his stomach. But Carl is already calling from the hallway: "I'm sorry, Josef. Come on, let's make peace." He turns around and throws his arms around his brother's neck.

28

NEW YORK, NOVEMBER 1939

SHE GOT UP OUT OF BED, HER SHORT NYLON NIGHTIE CLING-
ing to her thighs, charged with static electricity. She had very white
legs. He liked her white legs. She opened the window; cool air and the
smell of burning leaves breezed inside. At this time of year small piles of
them were swept together on the curb and lit on fire.

Frost on the dormer windowpanes, fog from the ocean. Europe was at
war. Germany had invaded Poland.

Lauren walked around the room on her tiptoes.

"Why are you doing that?"

"So I don't disturb anyone."

"But there's nobody here."

"Habit."

The landlady had broken her leg and was in the hospital, which was
why he could spend the night at Lauren's. For the first time. For him
there was something slightly momentous about it.

The view from Lauren's bed was of the sky, against which the delicate
leaves of the evergreens spread out like fans. The trees made him think of
Asia somehow. A neighborhood of single-family homes with front yards,
barely any immigrants.

Lauren ran water in the tub, took some soap, and went to work on her underwear. "Primitive." She laughed. Lauren had taught him that you must only eat soft-boiled eggs with a plastic spoon; to his amazement, any kind of metal, even silver, was all wrong. Once Lauren told him that, as a girl, she had attached wings to her shoulders—an image he could no longer get out of his head.

A wasp came reeling into the room, exhausted from the summer. He watched it with patient sympathy.

"Come back to bed," he said.

She got back in bed and lay by his side so they could look at each other. She had a crooked line to the right of her nose in the morning because she slept on her side; by around noon the line would be gone.

"Don't you want to go back to your comfortable life in the Catskills?"

She ignored the question. "Tell me again what it was like back then."

She always seemed moved when he told her that starting when he was a very young boy he had tended cows in exchange for milk and butter. That's what things were like. Then at fourteen he was taken out of school, and after that working for the farmer was all he did. He turned over in bed, slipped down to her feet, and started massaging them. He knew she liked that.

"Yes, I know how to milk a cow. Does that make me attractive?"

She laughed. He bit her calf. He crawled over her, his foot in her face. She put up with it—he waited for her to knock his foot away, but she put up with him. Yes, she even started giggling. Now he could feel her nose with his big toe.

"And your childhood, Lauren?"

She crawled out from under him and lay down beside him.

"I was an odd kid," she said. "My parents told me, they said, 'You're an odd kid,' but they said it lovingly and proudly. I went through a phase

where I couldn't explain anything with words. I'd say I could explain
it better if I draw it, it's simpler that way. They didn't understand that.
Because of course drawing is much harder. But it was true in a way. Back
then I had the sense that words weren't enough."

He thought about this. Even more unusual, he thought, than the
drawing or Lauren's difficulty explaining certain things was the idea that
Lauren told her parents anything at all.

The nights were different now. As soon as the war started all amateur
operators had to silence their radios. On the other hand, now Lauren
was in his life. As if she had walked in through a revolving door, and the
radio had gone out the other side.

She recommended books for him to read.

A tall bookshelf on the one straight wall of the attic room was filled
with books. Organized into sections, one of them novels by and about
immigrants. He read the titles: *Jews Without Money, Call It Sleep, Christ
in Concrete*. He wondered if Lauren had owned the books before—that
is, before they'd met—or had bought them for the express purpose of
trying to understand him. He couldn't bring himself to ask.

There were always at least three open books on the night table, spines
pointed at the ceiling like wounded birds. She read everything all at once.
Currently it was a lot about American history. She was applying for another scholarship and getting ready for the next exam—she wanted to
start at Columbia next spring at the latest.

At night, in bed, when Lauren was tired and thinking about something, she squinted a little.

He worried about her sometimes. She seemed to him like a lamp that
burned both day and night. He asked himself whether the hard work
at Manhattan General might get to be too much for her. She claimed
everything was fine. Said she had a better understanding of life now that

she was seeing the world from the gritty streets of New York and not from the lofty perch of a mountain resort.

But of course, thanks to her family, she always had a safety net beneath her. She could go back home at any time. That was the difference between her and him.

She went regularly to charity events at the big hotels, like the Waldorf Astoria or the Plaza. She gave blood ("Don't you want to, Joe?" "No, thanks." "German blood!" "Very funny."). She went to demonstrations against Hitler's Germany. There were two factions: intervene or stay out of it.

Lauren spoke out in favor of intervention. He argued, "That's exactly why the Germans in America are so demonized. It's a way of mobilizing the population so that soon the US can start sending American troops to Europe."

"Don't you realize what's happening in Europe right now? Germany is invading other countries, plundering and murdering."

He nodded. Yes, of course he knew that. And it troubled him. But couldn't what he was saying also be true? "Not all Germans are like that," he said quietly. "And yet you still see these posters around the city, DON'T BUY FROM GERMANS."

She grew pensive. "Maybe that's just how it's got to be, Joe. Maybe there's no other way."

She snored at night. He didn't know if he should tell her or not. Men were allowed to snore, not women.

He sometimes felt a shadow over his right shoulder. Someone would come creeping up suddenly and do awful things; they'd throw a bag over his head and start working him over. He could feel it in every sinew of his body. He felt the punches, hooks to the chin, kicks in the stomach, in the head, he lay on the ground, couldn't breathe anymore, his nose swollen, blood in his throat, the pain so bad he was losing his mind, and yet he didn't lose consciousness; that relief still wouldn't come. Every image of violence he had ever seen in his life came flooding back to him, things he'd seen in movies and at night, on dark side streets. The images assailed him.

Lauren sometimes shook him gently as he slept. "You were screaming."

He hadn't heard anything from Carl since the war began.

He had started dreaming of his father from time to time. His father going off to war. One minute he's standing there and looking different than usual: in uniform, ready to become someone else. A vise on his heart. It's uncomfortable for him how his father tries to say goodbye and doesn't know how—a clap on the shoulder, that's all. A few days later his father is dead. Shot in France. They're moving with a cart to the next rundown flat, his mother, Carl, and him.

The father who beat him and Carl once a week. He didn't miss his father. He was happy he wasn't around anymore. But Carl cried a lot. Carl was just nine, after all. While he, at eleven, suddenly felt like he'd grown up in the span of a day. And really, not much had changed since then.

She got out of bed and went looking for the blow-dryer. Spent many long minutes blowing warm air on her legs, stomach, and face and made quite a lot of noise. She'd said at one point that the hot air helped her relax. Sometimes she even brought her blow-dryer with her to his place.

"You're a spoiled rich girl," he shouted over the noise.

"Let's go to Coney Island," she shouted back. "The weather's beautiful."

A sky of azure blue—a perfect sky. The sun shining low, touching everything with devotion, and drawing out the colors that lay hidden within.

They took the train to Brighton Beach, from there they would walk along the beach to the heart of Coney Island. To the left and right, under the copper-green elevated train tracks, were shops selling Russian goods—caviar, sweets, furs. Lauren looked at the displays with interest.

"So have they still not tried to contact you?" she asked, looking at a white fur coat. But it was his face she was looking at, reflected in the windowpane.

"I would tell you right away."

"Yes, you would."

He was working full-time for Arthur again, but the pay was less, because there were fewer jobs. Arthur had sent the Hitlerites packing. "If I don't the FBI will shut me down." Mrs. Dollings was outraged over Hitler, the prince of peace, and had resigned as head of the Park Avenue Patriots.

The Bund had quieted down; its leader, Fritz Kuhn, was behind bars for tax evasion. When he was arrested he was falling-down drunk.

His deal with Lauren was that he would go to the FBI immediately as soon as his old friends tried to contact him. She was certain they would try to contact him. The war was on, and they needed him.

Down a narrow side street they saw a bright strip of yellow sand and above it the ink-blue Atlantic. The boardwalk was almost empty—just a few doormen out walking dogs. Seagulls hovered over the ocean, wings outspread. In the distance a tight group of structures soared into the sky: the roller coaster, its track twisting through the air like a spinal column;

the large Ferris wheel rising up out of the yellow-blue emptiness. Everything was closed for the winter. He carefully put his arm around Lauren. She could react indignantly at times, try to shake his arm off, but here on the beach she allowed it.

He had been on the Ferris wheel with his girlfriends a few times. They all wanted to get married and have kids. Because of this he never said things like "I love you"; he had always been afraid of seeming invested. He acted casually, and when the women left, their leaving was just as casual, no fuss, no ceremony.

Lauren sat down on the wooden steps leading down to the beach. He sat down beside her. They watched the layers of surf rolling one on top of the other. White foam at the edges, armies of white bubbles crawling forward, churning. A hiss and roar, and farther out to sea a crash and thunder. A rug of glass, many feet wide, was rolled out and then pulled back, again and again, leaving crinkled patches on the hard, smooth sand.

"Europe's over there," she said.

"You can't see it."

"But it's still there."

"I love you, Lauren."

She gave him a kiss. He didn't know if that was supposed to mean the same thing.

29

NEUSS–BUENOS AIRES, SEPTEMBER–OCTOBER 1949

THE HEADLIGHTS OF AN ONCOMING CAR BOUNCE UP AND down, like a friendly nod. The road is bumpy. Gravel knocks against metal.

Fields and small groups of trees along the length of the road. In the distance a dark strip rising on the horizon. The country road takes a sharp turn. Carl keeps an even distance from the edge of the wood as he drives, his eyes searching.

"Anywhere," says Josef.

They stop. He gets out, slaps the hood. "Carl, drive!"

Clouds fly across the night sky. The moonlight shines in the truck's metal finish. Carl is standing next to him. "Well, you're off to a good start. Here, your bag."

Josef laughs. Then they embrace again. They know this is the last time they'll see each other; granted, they thought the same thing twenty-five years ago, but this time it really will be. For a small-time businessman from the Rhineland there's no reason to ever go on vacation in South America.

"Write us along the way whenever you can. Promise?"

"I promise."

He can feel an intensity of emotion and has to shut himself off to it, or else he'll start blubbering again. "Now drive!" says Josef and starts walking across a field. The crop has been harvested. The soil is black, rich; it stinks a little. "This thing's not going to end well," Carl calls after him. "Bad seeds grow tall," Josef calls back, looking ahead toward the woods, tears in his eyes. *This is crazy*, he tells himself. *You wanted out of Neuss, out of the little Klein family prison. And now you're crying. Because now you're free.*

He turns around. Carl is still standing there; he raises his hand and waves. Josef raises his hand and waves back.

Then he plunges into the wood. Quiet envelops him; he hears only the snapping of twigs under his feet. The gap in the border, the smuggler route, runs along here. They bent over the map, shoulder to shoulder, like they once had as young men over the map of Manhattan. This time drawing a line through Aachen, rural roads, the forest, and on the other side Belgium, Eupen the closest town. If he keeps going straight, he'll be in Belgium in half an hour. He doesn't have a visa for Belgium. "Not a chance. They'll be able to tell in an instant that your passport's a fake," Dörsam had said. But he does have one for Argentina. "That you can risk."

It's eight o'clock. Faint light falls through the treetops; he can hardly see a thing. An autumn wood. He smells the peaty earth and something like gunpowder, lubricating oil, iron. He trudges over roots and tree trunks, panting, but doesn't give himself any time to stop and rest. He's afraid of what he'll hear, sounds that are more than the echo of his own and that could turn his legs leaden with fear.

He's relieved when the forest opens up to fields. Now he's in Belgium. A needling rain has started to fall. He turns up his coat collar, pulls his hat down lower over his forehead. The lights of a town glow on the horizon. The Belgian guards seem to have been watching him for some time. They step into the road and plant themselves in front of him. "Papers?"

He shows them his new papers.

"Joe Klein, born in New York," one border guard reads to the other.

"Wanted to see Aachen," he says, putting on a strong American accent.

"Then you're pretty far off track. Germany is in the other direction." One of them raises his arm toward Germany, ready to help. Waits. Josef also waits. The two of them—this much is certain—have seen all kinds of strange ducks come out of the woods by this point and are always glad to encounter a new variety.

"I'm actually trying to get to Brussels."

"But you need a visa for Belgium."

They stare at each other. Should he make them an offer?

"Let's see your bag. Cigarettes, change of clothes, seems like you're planning on going away for a while."

"Care for one?" He holds out a pack of American cigarettes. Dörsam thought of everything.

"Gee, that's nice of you."

He can't tell if they're making fun of him. "I might also have five dollars," he says carefully.

The border guard takes the bill and the cigarettes from his hand. "Let's leave something for the others. You've got a long trip ahead of you, right?"

He nods. A car approaches. The guard steps in front of it. "Going to Eupen? Take our friend here with you. He's an American."

He whistles Josef over, claps him on the shoulder. "Good luck. Have a nice life."

The buildings are dark. The driver doesn't speak, only nods whenever Josef makes an attempt at conversation. Is it because he was introduced to him as an American? Josef clenches the handle of his bag till his fingers hurt. In Eupen the man drops him off at the train station. Josef checks the timetables for trains to Herbesthal. The next one doesn't leave until morning.

He picks the most run-down hotel in the square, the Hotel Boston, and pays in advance. An old man takes him to a small room with no windows and damp walls, and when he lies down the bedsprings howl and squeak. The wet coat he draped over the radiator waits like his loyal servant and double.

He embraced Edith in front of the rest of the family. He breathed in the smell of her, which flooded into him like the words that she would never be able to find. What she said was something different. "You're making the right decision. There's no way of knowing if Germany will ever get back on its feet."

And Carl agreed with her: "It could take decades!"

In the morning he drinks grain coffee in the breakfast room, spreads margarine and marmalade over the roll a surly young woman has brought him.

"You're no American," she says as he's headed for the door.

"How's that?"

"They don't stay here. They can afford someplace better."

At eight o'clock he takes the regional train to Herbesthal, easily catches the Copenhagen-Brussels Express at nine, and at eleven reaches the Brussels-North train station. The train to Paris doesn't leave until the next morning. He wanders the streets, trying to keep his head down; around noon he checks into a somewhat nicer hotel, where he stays, or rather hides out, until tomorrow. He is able to smooth over his lack of a visa with American cigarettes. Carl sold his Linhof and gave him five hundred marks, which he exchanged for dollars at a bank in Cologne when he was there for his last meeting with Dörsam. A lot of money, but it won't be enough for the whole trip. Dörsam advised him to sign on as a sailor on the ship to Buenos Aires.

In the morning he takes the overcrowded train to Paris. French soldiers stand in the aisles. He sits by the window and watches the villages and fields fly past, all for the last time, his last days in Europe, his homeland—but it means nothing to him. Carl and Edith, and also Täubchen and little Paul, they're what matters to him.

Shortly before they reach the border a conductor starts to question him about his missing visa. Josef doesn't dare offer him cigarettes—there are too many eyes on them. Instead he says he came from London; nobody mentioned anything about a visa. The conductor nods. "Next time, then." He can sense the tension leaving his fellow passengers as they go back to their newspapers and books with a little sigh.

The French border guard doesn't speak any English and simply stamps his ticket.

That evening, Paris, Gare du Nord. An unfriendly hustle and bustle, masses of people, a sea of suitcases, wrinkled suits, hundreds of languages.

He buys his ticket for Le Havre, then a postcard with the Eiffel Tower on it. He addresses it to Edith and limits himself to writing,

All the best from Paris.

But at least it's something. He spends the night at a small overpriced inn. He's been on the road for two days at this point, and as he sips weak coffee in the morning he peers into faces just as exhausted and poorly shaven as his. And still there is something that he scarcely wants to admit to himself: a feeling of euphoria and an almost religious sense of comfort and protection. But he's not quite ready to trust this condition.

He knows it from New York. For years he deluded himself into thinking he was in that city's care, like Thoreau in the woods, and in the end all it gave him was a kick in the ass.

Any number of things can go wrong still, even if his papers look good, a little worn, even. They cost fifty marks. Carl was against it. He spoke of the law: "It's just not right. Let's go to the records office in Düsseldorf. Your birth certificate is bound to be there." But he wanted to be Joe Klein, born in New York. He's putting one over on Judge Byers, putting one over on America.

Because that's the plan: South America is the first stop, then back to the USA.

Cursing and shoving on the train to Le Havre. After five hours they reach the port city—really more of a rubble-strewn wasteland on the English Channel. Sailors from all over the world loiter in the streets. The hotels are few and expensive. At the shipping company's office he pays for passage to Dakar, with a short stop in Casablanca. The names fill him with excitement, as if what awaits him there is something wonderful, momentous, beautiful beyond belief. Africa!

That night he is still skulking around horrible Le Havre, past construction fences, mounds of rubble, and backhoes. Finally he gives in to the overtures of an old prostitute, pays a thousand francs just for the privilege of lying in her bed till morning. The woman could be his mother—he really does just want to sleep. In her tiny room the old woman slides toward him on the mattress, starts rubbing herself against him. He says wearily, "For all that money you could at least give me some peace."

She laughs. "You and your comrades destroyed our city—*that's* what you're paying for, you pig."

She figured out he was German too. Alarmed, he asks how.

"Your underwear's got a German tag."

"Were you a spy in the war?" he asks jokingly, and she says in the same tone, "Yes—for the Germans."

He knows she's telling the truth.

In the morning she wakes him by smacking him in the head. "Your time is up." Out by the harbor there's an old workhorse pulling a giant tree trunk. Josef can't look away until finally the horse is out of sight. Giant white ocean liners are moored in the water, belching out black clouds of smoke. Again this feeling of happiness.

Before he boards the ship he buys Gitanes, chewing gum, and a post-card that he addresses to Carl:

> You can send my luggage now like we discussed: general delivery, Buenos Aires. The next card will come from Casablanca in Africa!

Feeling proud, he tosses it into a mailbox.

The ship is overcrowded. Third-class passengers, like him, have been moved to the cold-storage rooms and the original third-class cabins rebranded as first class. He makes friends with his bunkmates, an Englishman and a Frenchman. They all get seasick immediately. The seas in the English Channel are rough; a strong wind is blowing. The ship turns into a hospital ship. Only when they pass through the Bay of Biscay does the sea grow calm, and off the coast of Spain they start to cruise through the warm, velvety salt air of the Atlantic. It gets warmer almost by the hour, and when, passing Portugal, he finds he's back in fit condition, he goes out walking on deck, feeling reborn, and sees that all of Europe is on this ship—Italians, Germans, Austrians, Eastern

Europeans—just like twenty-five years ago, when he was on his way to
the New World.

"They're fleeing," the Englishman explains.

"Fleeing?"

"Still." The Frenchman nods. "They're still being persecuted in
Eastern Europe, even today. It's only in Germany that they're not.
Ironic, no?"

"How do you know all of this?"

"They tell me."

"You talk to them?"

"Of course."

He would never dare. What if they ask who he is? What he did? Why
he's on this ship?

His new friends take him for an American, or maybe they just act like
they do. They grumble about the Germans onboard. Their assessments
are not good: they find them to be arrogant, to be shirking responsibility,
to be cowardly and without remorse.

"They're not exactly popular in New York either," he is able to add.

Two days later they're approaching Casablanca. The sea is calm and
the air hot. They have six hours before the ship leaves. The Frenchman
acts as their guide, tells them that the city is divided into two sections,
the new section and the medina, the old city, which one shouldn't
venture into alone. Wide streets, horse-drawn carriages, everything
bathed in white light. A boulevard runs along the ocean, past a grand
hotel with Arab women sunbathing in bikinis outside. Tall, skinny
palm trees line the streets. It's the first city he's seen in a long time
that's still intact. He's captivated by the white townhouses with French
balconies and the light that seems to come straight from the Atlantic.

He tries to stamp it all on his memory, every detail, like an image he will later have to paint.

As they near the equator the ship is covered with a white canvas. The sun beats down; the Atlantic glitters. They sail past the Canary Islands. Two days later they reach Dakar. He goes onto shore, sees pith helmets, sees black men in flowing garments, strolling through the streets and speaking French.

And yet it's all familiar to him, as if he were peering behind a curtain that artificially screened off his life in New York. At the museum in New York he had read about Dakar, had read that for three centuries slaves were sent to America from here.

The tips of his shoes are covered in dust, no matter how often he cleans them.

The money he has left isn't enough for passage to Buenos Aires. He has someone show him the way to the shipping company's offices and asks to sign on as a sailor. They laugh at him. "What do we want with a pip-squeak like you?" Then someone takes pity on him and they hire him for a job in the kitchen. Passage and lodging included; no wages. It's fine with him. The next ship leaves in two days. He checks into a rooming house. Spiderwebs cling to the windows; the mattress lies on the stone floor. Outside, a network of yellow dirt alleyways. Lying down, he says aloud to himself, "Dakar, Dakar," and feels content. He feels the periodic call to prayer trickle through his body, lies there and listens to the garlands of words, which, because he doesn't understand a thing, take him to a place beyond all language, a place where he feels an almost physical connection with everything. He thinks of Idrie's bean pies.

This time he writes the whole family.

Even the cemeteries have palm trees here!

He draws a little palm next to the words and tosses the card into a mailbox on the way to the harbor.

––––––––––

The work in the kitchen usually lasts all day. Peeling potatoes, chopping onions, running off to the storeroom, taking orders from a Spaniard who calls him José, even when Josef protests. "My name's Joe."

"José. Get used to it."

José it is, then.

Despite it all he feels a rapture that he can't explain. He is free. For the first time in years. Truly free. He's not young anymore, true, but he's not old yet either. He can make a fresh start, and that's exactly what he plans to do.

The weedy Italian who works alongside him is always friendly but says only gloomy things. "Don't get any illusions," he says often and without any context.

"He's going to meet up with his family," the Spaniard tells him. "His wife and daughter made it out before the war."

At night the sky is black and full of stars. He has never seen such a clear night sky, not in energy-saving Neuss and definitely not in New York, where the night sky glowed red.

The Italian tosses his cigarette butt overboard and says, "Tell me your story, Josef."

Smooth black water beneath them.

"I don't know my story yet," says Josef. "I'm still in the middle of it."

He's glad when, soon afterward, the Spaniard sends him to clean the giant pots, scraping the burnt remnants of thick soups off the bottom, an unpopular job. When the Italian comes around he tries to act invisible and not to breathe.

"Josef? José? Joe? Which is your real name?"

His tongue feels thick, his throat tight. He manages a smile, one that is no longer crooked like a grifter's. Not since Neuss, not anymore.

30

NEW YORK, JUNE–JULY 1940

TIMES SQUARE. THE CALLER HAD ALMOST WHISPERED IT— "The entrance to the Apollo Theater"—and then hung up.

Josef went back to the printing machine, weaving a garland of red roses through black calligraphy. The Christian Front had been disbanded. Yet another important client gone. More greeting cards and wedding invitations since then.

At half past two he headed out, walking purposefully, but not hurrying. The newsboys waved photographs of tanks and steel helmets. In Times Square the news ticker wrapped around the Times Building. Paris had fallen last week. The passersby stared at the moving text.

He loosened his tie. He felt an itch in his throat and a feverish sensation rising from his legs up to his shoulders. If he hadn't emigrated, he might be stalking through the forests of France right now. The thought triggered anxiety. He had almost forgotten this feeling, even though it had been with him constantly in the last year, when the two Germans had taken over his apartment—feelings were something to be forgotten and only remembered when they came back.

Things had been going well for him. Lauren was in his life. Sometimes Lauren showed him newspaper articles that she thought were especially important; even that made him happy.

He still made an effort to look and act his best around her. He always made sure his shoes were shined, took care shaving and put on expensive aftershave, even thought about what he would say when he first greeted her. He always had time for her. If she called while he was busy tinkering with something, he didn't even mention it. On evenings when he expected her to call, he didn't leave the apartment so that she wouldn't have to call more than once. He suspected she wouldn't appreciate that.

He bought a paper off a newsboy. The swastika flag was flying from the Eiffel Tower. The streets deserted, the Parisians had fled.

A sharp pain sat just beneath his skull. He smoked and hoped it would help, waited for the numbness to set in. Two office girls were standing in the entrance of the Apollo Theater, sharing a cigarette. They looked over at him; he ignored them.

He knew that he was looking for a tall figure with slumped shoulders—for Max. He hadn't heard anything from either him or Ludwig since Schmuederrich had fired him. He had wanted to believe the Germans weren't interested in him anymore—after all, in a free country like the US, in a democracy, they couldn't force anyone to do anything.

He finished his second cigarette, and as he was about to stamp it out with his foot, there was Max, standing in front of him. He pulled him over to the wall of film posters and placed his hand on Josef's shoulder, which caught the attention of the two girls. "A new agent has come over from Germany. His name's Sebold and his orders are to expand the network in New York. Every contact is needed now. You have to finish building the radio for us."

"I don't work for you people anymore. That's all I came here to tell you."

Max laughed. "You're still just as stupid as you were last year."

There was something else he was itching to say, but it seemed more wise not to antagonize Max any further. He walked into the flood of pedestrians on Seventh Avenue and realized after a few feet that Max was following him.

He stopped and raised both hands, palms out, posing a question. Max also stopped. They looked at each other. Max followed him for another few hundred feet before he finally gave it up. Max too was just as stupid as he was last year. *Germany wants peace. That's what you said last year, and now there's a war on*—that's what he'd wanted to say to him.

That evening he met Lauren at a diner near Manhattan General before her shift started. She hadn't gotten the scholarship this time either. The reason, she thought, was that she came from a wealthy family. He had offered her another reason, his German background, but she thought that was nonsense.

Now Lauren was simply working more—she was going to pay for college herself. He didn't understand her. If he were her he would go back to her parents, back to the nice hotel with the swimming pool and the dance orchestra, but he didn't tell her that. He had just bitten into something that felt wrong and tasted wrong. It reminded him of childhood somehow, of sunny afternoons in the forest and in the field. Turning his face away, he spit the lettuce leaf he'd been chewing into his napkin. He didn't want to look any closer, but he recognized the crushed shell of a beetle. And Lauren saw it too. "We have to tell the waiter!"

"No, Lauren. Leave it."

"But the kitchen messed up."

"No, they didn't. This was intentional."

She gave him a skeptical look.

Amiably he said, "I might do it too. Yell at Germans. Spit in their food."

"Don't talk like that, Joe."

"Like what?"

"Like you're not taking it seriously."

He wanted to tell her now, tell her about Max, as a further way of proving to her how seriously he was taking things. But as soon as he started speaking he knew it was a mistake.

Her face darkened. "You have to report it. Do you hear me? They're not going to let up."

"Let's just wait a bit, Lauren."

"But you promised."

"Nothing's happened yet, not a thing," he said angrily and thought of the movie. He pictured FBI men and heard the fanfare blowing.

Lauren just looked at him.

He looked over at the wall. He felt sick.

She laid her hand on the table, palm up, an invitation to place his in hers. He didn't take it. He caught the eye of the waiter, ordered a soda, and said, "To America."

"To world peace," she said.

A week later he was walking down a small side street near the Manhattan Bridge. Max and Ludwig were sitting in the white delivery truck with THIRST QUENCHER written on it in blue lettering. They handed him the half-finished radio.

Ludwig called out from the passenger seat, "We took Paris!"

The door slammed shut. He heard the car rumble off and looked carefully at the bag in his hand. He knew he had to get rid of the device. He started walking toward the river, but after a few steps he turned around. Better to wait till dawn.

Back home he put on "After Hours." The slow, lazy blues and Avery Parrish plonking away on the piano like he's bored and how the horn section only came in right at the end—*Great*, he thought, and played it again. He could feel the walls and all the objects in the room, and he could feel himself in it. This here was his life.

A thin copper wire was sticking out of the bag at his feet. He looked at it, and then he looked away. He hesitated, then he gave it a tug, and when he held the wire in his hands he started to make little feet at the end, while Avery Parrish hacked away at his piano. When he was finished, he pushed the bag under the table a bit. He tried to remember the circuit he'd built last year. Finally he pulled it out and had to smile. It was primitive: a simple press key with a contact, in between a spring-loaded washer, but just a slight movement pushed the coil to the desired contact—it worked. He tried it out a few times, back and forth, back and forth. Then he stopped. Yes, early tomorrow morning, before dawn, he would throw it all into the river.

He looked at the leads. They were much too long. They would cause whistling noises by allowing for too much oscillation. Carl. If he sent the radio to Carl, they could talk. He hadn't heard his brother's voice in sixteen years. But Carl had no idea how to use a radio. And the device would be confiscated anyway, or it wouldn't arrive in the first place. He had read in the *New York Times* recently that in Germany you could get a death sentence for listening to an enemy radio station. He could hardly believe it. What had happened to his homeland?

He clipped a wire that was too long in half. Then he searched his toolbox for a soldering iron, soldering tin, flat-nose pliers, tweezers, a fine-tipped screwdriver, alligator clips—he'll just practice a bit of soldering. He had always liked soldering in midair. It took a steady hand, but he didn't have that today; his hands were shaking. He went into the kitchen, poured himself a large glass of Old Musket, enjoyed the melting feeling in his stomach, a calm extending all the way into his limbs. He nodded along to Duke Ellington, muttering, "Soldering tin, soldering tin, soldering tin, I'm at it again." He felt the resin that he'd bought at a musical instrument shop, brown-black cubes with a glass-like sheen, thought now of forests, forests full of men, men running and running away, falling, dying. With the wire cutters he removed the rubber from the ends of the cables, twisted the now-exposed wires together, got them ready for soldering. Princess ran around him. Her claws clicked on the wood floor. Every now and then she barked.

At the front they used mobile radios that they carried in backpacks—he had read about it. He would like to get a look at such a compact piece of equipment. What he was building here was too bulky, you couldn't carry it for long. Or maybe you could. He had never been in battle, and didn't know anything about the limits of what soldiers were capable of doing or whether he would be able to keep up in the heat of things, whole nights spent marching in the rain, in wet clothing, with swollen feet and fever. After Germany's defeat in the Great War they had done away with compulsory military service. And then he had emigrated to America. He closed his eyes. Saw a deciduous forest. Saw faces, jaws clenched under steel helmets. He didn't know anything about war. He was sitting on a couch in an apartment in Harlem. It was all connected, and for the first time he could feel this.

He heated the ends of the wires with the soldering iron. Then he took the tweezers, let a few tiny crumbs of resin melt onto the contacts, and quickly added soldering tin. It melted immediately, coated the leads, and connected them. He had never done it so well. It didn't matter. He would throw the radio in the river tomorrow morning. He imagined Max's and Ludwig's faces when he told them.

He tested the durability by tugging on the ends, then he trimmed the tubing and pulled it over the spot. This was his favorite moment: held above a tiny flame, the melting rubber collapsed in on itself and closed around the wires. Would he fight against the Germans if they invaded America? Yes. Would he also fight against the Germans on German soil?

He put on Fats Waller. Lauren had given him the record.

Yes, your feet's too big.

They had laughed like mad and danced together.

Don't want ya 'cause ya feet's too big.

He danced a few steps, now holding an imaginary Lauren in his arms, found his way back to the kitchen with a fresh glass of Old Musket, sang, "I'll throw it out the window, no, in the river, tomorrow morning." He knew he would need an explanation for Max. He would think of something. From below someone knocked on the ceiling with a broom handle; it was already two o'clock. He turned the music down, then he got busy soldering more wires together. On he went, casually soldering and screwing like the brilliantly lackadaisical piano playing of Avery Parrish until the first light of dawn came in through the window.

He was dreaming of a foxhole when he awoke. Now he lay on the floor between the couch and the coffee table, a haze of smoke in the air, but only from the soldering and all the cigarettes.

At noon Lindbergh came on the radio at the print shop. Suddenly the men were making less noise. They even turned the machines off so they could better hear the world-famous aviator warning the US not to enter the war. Lindbergh was a member of a committee that called itself America First.

Josef kept working, even though today he felt like he couldn't do anything right, not even brushing his teeth in the morning. It was nothing but half measures; he did it all in a haze. He kept looking for ways to take a break—a smoke break and a piss break and a coffee break. America should not try to police the world, Lindbergh said. The men applauded. Someone called out, *Sieg Heil!* Laughter. He looked over at Arthur, who also stood applauding. Arthur finally looked back and shrugged his shoulders.

"Don't get so worked up, Joe. It'll all take care of itself soon enough. Hitler doesn't stand a chance in the long run, and the Germans know it. At some point the military will probably oust him. Then we won't even need to intervene."

Arthur smiled—which got him even more worked up. "Maybe it'd be better if I went looking for another job."

"Go ahead. But who's going to hire a German now?"

In August Trotsky was murdered in Mexico, by the Stalinists. Lauren showed him the article. "I guess your idea that Trotsky was in Mexico planning a Communist takeover of America wasn't so off base, huh?"

"But what can you believe these days, anyway? Can you trust the Hitler-Stalin Pact, for example?"

She looked at him. Sometimes she managed to look at him in such a way that he immediately felt dumb.

"Lauren?" he asked.

"Ugh." She sighed.

"Ugh?"

"Sorry," she said. "You're right."

She had never apologized before. Never admitted he was right. Tonight, her night off, she rummaged nervously in her purse, then she put more lipstick on and said, "We can go."

Something wasn't right. Something was going on with her. She seemed pensive and hesitant, kept looking at the door, then at him.

"What?"

"You should go to the FBI, Joe."

"We've had this conversation already."

"You have to."

"I have to?"

She looked past him. He touched her shoulder.

"They're expecting you."

"Why are they expecting me?"

"Because I was there already myself."

"Did they bring you in?"

"No. I went voluntarily. Because I knew that you wouldn't."

He took a step back, as if he had been struck.

"I did it for you. To put an end to it! The FBI can help you. They told me they could!"

"To put an end to it?"

She nodded. There was something in her eyes. Fear. Not for him.

"We had a deal, Joe. You promised!"

"Don't you trust me?" he asked quietly.

She went into the bedroom. He knew what she was doing, knew it immediately. He heard the bed squeak, and then she came back with the case with the radio inside.

"And this here? What am I supposed to make of this? Is this your idea of trust?"

"Lauren. That's a misunderstanding."

"A misunderstanding?" Now she was shouting.

"I was going to throw the radio away. I took it so it wouldn't do any damage."

He could hear how implausible that sounded. True, he kept putting

Max off, telling him he needed more time. He had hoped for some other solution to present itself, something other than having to destroy his own handiwork.

She grabbed the radio with both hands, lifted it up in the air, and let it drop. Nothing happened. Good soldering work. She kicked it. It flipped up on its side and tipped back over. He pulled Lauren away. "Stop it. I'll go to the FBI tomorrow morning."

They didn't go out that night. He could tell that Lauren would have preferred to just go back to her room in Brooklyn. She dutifully kept him company, drank whiskey with him, they listened to Duke Ellington, but it all just seemed lost and alien to him. He would almost have felt better in a bare prison cell.

He was furious at Lauren.

"Did you tell them we were together?"

She sat reading on the couch, her legs drawn up beneath her, and nodded. What could one person ever know about another? Nothing. But still, she was ashamed. He could see it in her very narrow shoulders, her feet that pointed back toward her—every part of her seemed to shrink from his gaze.

That night he lay next to her, unable to sleep. All the effort he made to lie still, to suppress every impulse to move so as not to wake Lauren, brought time to a standstill. Time—it struck him full in the face, crashed into him like a wave, became something combative and adversarial, and everything became crushing and intense, as if this were the longest night of his life.

Once, as if from a great distance at first, and then suddenly, rapidly, he felt the touch, growing more and more clear, of her hand on his hip—he must have fallen asleep after all but then was thrown immediately back into wakefulness.

That morning he awoke with a headache. Lauren was already up. She was getting dressed with her back to him. Skinny shoulders, narrow hips, everything he'd found enchanting before, now he saw it with sober eyes. He was hurt, but he didn't trust the feeling—he couldn't even trust his own pain.

They reeled past each other, between the bathroom and the kitchen and the little tasks of the morning, putting coffee on, brushing teeth, getting the paper. He had to remind himself how to do everything. He did it all as if for the first or last time. Shirt, pants, tie, shoes, coat, hat. Grab his ID. Lauren sat at the kitchen table, rustled the newspaper, immersed in the articles. He felt a sharp pain in his ribs when he breathed.

Lauren looked up. "I'll take care of Princess."

He was trembling.

"So you think they're going to arrest me?"

"I don't know what to think. Maybe I made a mistake."

They hugged—no kiss. Not like usual. Soon afterward he stepped out onto 126th Street and wondered if he would ever come back—if he would ever be able to come back.

31

NEW YORK, AUGUST 1940

He WAS STANDING STILL; EVERYTHING AROUND HIM WAS moving. He saw filing cabinets, typewriters, scuffed hardwood floors. The agent pressed the phone to his ear and nodded in response to what the voice on the other end was saying. Josef had said who he was, why he'd come, and now he stood still and waited. It hurt to breathe. Each shallow breath seemed to glue his ribs together.

He tried to calm himself down, telling himself he was still a free man, they hadn't immediately arrested him after Lauren's tip-off. Clearly they weren't thinking of him as a criminal. She had mentioned "contacts," nothing more, thank God. He heard hurried steps coming down the hallway, and his heart started racing again.

"Joe Klein?"

A man with a white mustache had appeared in the doorway. He gestured with his hand, and Josef followed him into a room down the hall. It wasn't a cell, wasn't an interrogation room, just a friendly looking office with a couch by the window.

The agent turned around to face him, and now he saw a man around fifty years old, facial features sagging from the eyebrows down, like a face made of melted wax. The smile that lifted the features lent him a gentle and wise air. "Agent Ettinger." He shook Josef's hand, gestured toward the couch, and offered him a cigarette.

"Thank you. That's very kind of you," said Josef.

"*Wir sind nicht die Gestapo*," Ettinger said. *We're not the Gestapo.* He smiled. Josef gave a tentative smile back.

Ettinger switched back to English. "All right, so tell me. When did they first contact you?" His legs were crossed. A notebook rested on his knee. He pulled out a fountain pen.

Josef hesitated. Was this a trap? Did he need a lawyer? He continued not to say anything, until finally Ettinger said, "Listen, Joe, we've known about you for about a year. Ever since you went shopping at the electronics store on Cortland Street."

Ettinger took a drag on his cigarette and watched him. His heart started pounding, and he tried not to let it show. "I'm not one of them. I was forced into it."

"You asked for a quarz with enough transmitting range to reach Europe. Did no one tell you how to go about it a bit less obviously?"

"I need a lawyer, don't I?"

"No, just go ahead and tell me what happened," Ettinger repeated.

He felt dizzy, and his mouth was dry. He spoke haltingly; every word could be a mistake. He talked about the meeting at the Old Heidelberg. He named names: Schmuederrich, Dr. Ritter, Dörsam, Duquesne, Max, Ludwig. He wasn't sure if Ettinger's nodding with the mention of each name meant that they were already known to them. Ettinger didn't write anything down. He just looked at him. Then he put out his cigarette and said, "Max was trained in Germany. He was tasked with recruiting junior agents in New York. You're probably one of them."

"You know more than I do," said Josef.

"That we're not sure of. You can speak openly with me. Tell me what you know. What are they up to?"

Josef took a drag on his cigarette. Now he felt angry. "I was fired last year. I've got nothing to do with them now."

"And what about the radio that you just built?"

Lauren had told them about the radio?

"I took the radio so it wouldn't do any harm. I was going to destroy it. But then I couldn't"—he hesitated and said quietly—"bring myself to."

Ettinger laughed. "Oh, is that so? You're working against the Nazis? So why does your girlfriend go and report you to us?"

"It was a misunderstanding."

Ettinger hesitated a moment, then he shook a new cigarette out of his pack. "Is the radio functional?"

"No. It's missing a quarz. They're hard to come by these days, as you know."

"Take the quarz from your own radio. Get the device working so that it can transmit and receive, and then hand it over to the Germans."

"Why should I do that?"

Ettinger stood up and gave his shoulder a squeeze. "Wait here."

The noise from the street came in from the open window. He stared at the tips of his shoes. He wasn't going to take advantage of the opportunity to look around the room undisturbed, maybe even look at Ettinger's notes. The ash on his cigarette grew ever longer. He couldn't move, couldn't bend over to reach the ashtray.

Ettinger came back with a young woman who brought a tray into the room. She poured him a cup of coffee and asked how he took it. He said milk, he said sugar, as if he were sitting in a café; meanwhile his life was at stake here. When they were alone again, Ettinger took a deep breath.

"Why don't you tell me what information you sent last year."

Although he felt nauseated, he took a sip of coffee, which immediately made the nausea even worse.

"I don't know. They were just columns of numbers."

"You never asked?"

"They told me it was all information that was available in American trade magazines and newspapers."

Ettinger made a note for the first time. Then he looked up and stared at him for a long time. "Did you really believe that?"

Josef thought about it. He no longer knew what he believed last year. He had tried to get through it somehow, that he remembered. "I don't know anymore what I believed last year."

"I can help jog your memory. You attended Nazi rallies. You're a member of the Christian Front. And you printed inflammatory materials."

There was a pounding at his temples. A droning sound issued from the high white walls, as if they were pressing in on him. The tastes of coffee and nicotine on his tongue, each intensifying the other. He felt like he was going to throw up.

"Why aren't you arresting me?"

"Then others will step up to take your place. It's better we keep an eye on the situation and keep it under control. That's why we'd like you to deliver the radio."

Josef nodded.

"And we want you to keep working with them."

"I don't understand. Why keep working?"

"No matter what happens. Maintain contact with them. Inform us of anything new that comes up. You can do that, can't you?"

"I don't know. Can I think about it?"

Ettinger sighed, handed him a card. "If you help us, you can start to make up for what you've done. Make the right decision."

He said goodbye and shook Josef's hand. A colleague escorted Josef out of the building. He would have preferred to have been led to a cell. To somewhere dark. Deep. No thoughts. Nothing more.

In the subway he took the wrong train. He noticed it after two stops. He got out and took the train to Brooklyn. He felt deeply exhausted. Not even the concern that someone could have seen him going to the FBI had any effect on him. An hour later he was ringing Lauren's doorbell. Standing in a well-tended front garden with rose bushes and a pergola covered with creeper vines.

An old woman with labored breathing, Lauren's landlady, opened the door and nodded toward the stairs.

Lauren was sitting in her room. She plucked at her neckerchief, seemed to be maintaining a respectful period of silence, as if her status were no longer clear. He put his arms around her, but more like how one would comfort a child. Then he sat down on the bed and lit a cigarette.

"Please, tell me about it," she said.

He looked out the window, but he didn't see anything, just sank ever deeper into himself.

Tell her about it? That wasn't him at all. He wasn't that man, the man who sat here and had to tell her about the FBI.

"So no arrest," she said softly.

"No arrest."

"And instead?"

"Keep my spot so that nobody steps up to replace me."

"You don't have to do anything else?"

He hesitated. Held his cigarette in the corner of his mouth for a while without taking a drag. Should he tell Lauren that the FBI had known about him for a while already, which meant she hadn't betrayed him?

"You told them about the radio. Why?"

She plucked again at her neckerchief. She had turned red. Then she shook her head gently, as if responding to a thought, and looked him in the eyes. "I was worried, Joe. I didn't know who you were anymore. Forgive me. Joe, please trust me again."

He felt like he understood something. The problem was, he had always trusted too much. He needed more mistrust.

He stood up and put his arms around Lauren again.

A few days later he decided to do as Ettinger had told him. He called Max and set up a meeting. Not long after that he was sitting among clinking bottle crates. Ludwig stank of booze and held a Superman comic in his lap. Max shouted back from the driver's seat, "The Reich propaganda minister has banned Superman—I'll have to report you!" and laughed at his own joke. The car lurched from side to side. "Get a grip will you?" Josef shouted. "If we get stopped, it's all over. Or how else do you want to explain why you're driving around Manhattan with a radio?" Immediately it got quiet.

Two weeks later Ettinger summoned him for a meeting. He gave him instructions on the phone beforehand on how he could shake off anyone who might be following him.

The front car was almost empty when the train came to a stop. He got on, and as the door was closing, he propped it open with his hands and leapt out. He took the next train, got out at Grand Central, ran through the crowds, and then disappeared down another subway tunnel. He rode to Whitehall Terminal and from there went on foot to the Williamsburg Ferry landing.

Ettinger stood on the upper deck, seagulls circling overhead. Josef joined him, stared at the churning water, and waited for Ettinger to start talking.

"Have you found out what's behind Operation Sonnenstaub?"

"No. Max acts like he knows. But Max likes to show off."

He looked Ettinger in the eye. Ettinger let out a breath.

"He doesn't trust you. Tell him you want to do something for the fatherland. You've been convinced by all the things Hitler has managed to accomplish in Europe. You want to start transmitting again."

The buildings of Williamsburg grew closer; in a few minutes they would reach the shore. He would get off here. Ettinger would ride back. They saw kids jumping into the East River, then getting out and lying down on the hot rocks on the shore. Their lives in that moment consisted only of summer and water and heat.

"Anything else new?"

"The new agent from Germany has a large office in the Newsweek Building on 42nd Street. It's listed under some company as cover. He orders every agent to come there alone. Me included."

"We know about Sebold. You'd do better not to go."

"I'm happy to skip it. But why?"

"Stay away from Sebold."

The sunburned deckhand was already holding the rope ready.

"How do I know I can trust you?"

Ettinger gave him a disapproving look. "We could just deport you, you know. Then once you got back home you'd go straight to the front."

"So I am going to be arrested, then?"

Ettinger nodded. "Of course."

"When?"

"When the time comes."

"And will you offer me a deal?"

"I'll put in a good word for you."

32

NEW YORK, SEPTEMBER 1940

H E DID THE DISHES, LISTENED TO THE RADIO, AND WON-
dered why he owned only two of everything—two plates, two
mugs, two glasses. They all saw a lot of use, though, especially when
Lauren was over, and so the dishes never piled up. Josef gave himself
over to the thought that it now made even less sense to buy more dishes.
He counted the days, days that all felt the same, like they were all
a single, drawn-out day, and he didn't even know what he was waiting
for—for them all to get arrested? For America to start dropping bombs
on Germany? For Hitler to come marching into America? In any case
for something big and final that would make it possible to have a new
beginning, instead of this tangible sense that he was headed toward the
end. Lindbergh was on the radio warning the US about getting mixed
up in the "European conflict" when Lauren came into the kitchen with
her hair dripping.

"The blow-dryer is broken." Her eyes leapt over to the radio. He
immediately turned the volume down. "It's unbelievable that they keep
letting him speak!"

"Apparently Lindbergh Drive in Buffalo is going to be renamed soon,"
he said.

She nodded and sat down at the kitchen table with a book.

"Do you think if there were a Joe Klein Street it would have to be renamed too?" His desperate jokes didn't play well with her. She just grimaced. He set a cup down in front of her and poured her some coffee.

She buried herself in her book. She disappeared completely, crawled right into the pages. Lauren's face always looked different depending on what angle he was looking from. When he thought of her, he saw several faces; none had emerged as the one sole face.

"Why haven't you left me?" he asked.

She smiled teasingly and laid her hand on his. "Because then you'd be alone."

The question was meant to be playful, but something dangerously serious had now crept in, and he tried to break it up: "You snore, by the way."

She laughed, taken aback. "Excuse me?"

"You snore pretty much all night long, babe."

She took him with her everywhere she went. Charity events, rallies, demonstrations. It wasn't always easy. He noticed that as soon as he stepped into a room, the mood shifted. Was it because they could tell he was from Germany? Lauren always disputed it afterward: "There are enough Germans in New York who are against Nazi Germany—everybody knows that."

"But why do they look at me like that, then?"

"Maybe because you're so much older than me." She was embarrassed.

That night they went to an exiles' reading at a German bookstore. There she envied him for being able to understand the pieces the exiled writers were reading from, but he felt out of place. The smile on his face as stiff as cardboard. Toward the end he struck up a conversation with a man named Heinz, a German who had emigrated in the twenties and who was also an amateur radio operator. Pretzels were being served; when the tray came by them Heinz took the last pretzel and split it in half.

"Does it taste like the ones back home?" asked Lauren, who had suddenly reappeared at his side.

"We didn't have pretzels. Not in the Rhineland."

"What's wrong with you?"

"I don't like gatherings, just in general," he whispered. "It doesn't matter who's doing the gathering."

"You don't like people."

"I like individual people, just not lots of people. I like you."

It wasn't true. He didn't like Lauren anymore.

That night he stubbed his pinky toe against the bedpost. For two seconds there was no pain, then it shot emphatically into his consciousness. Back in bed he pressed himself close against Lauren's back. Sometimes that's all he was: a body holding another body in the night. It wasn't desperation exactly, more like this was now his one connection to the world.

In the morning Lauren pushed the newspaper toward him. "So that was the earthquake we felt yesterday!"

He read the headline: 27 DEAD, 25 MISSING, 200 HURT IN BLAST AT JERSEY PLANT.

Lauren tapped her finger on an article beneath. It mentioned the Black Tom attack of 1916, carried out by German agents. His throat tightened.

"No, Lauren. No."

"No what?"

"The Germans aren't capable of something like this. At least not the Germans in America."

He stood up, knocked against his coffee cup, and was just able to stop it from tipping over. The sudden movement made Princess start barking.

"Hitler is capable of far worse in Europe, Joe."

The barking. It wouldn't stop.

"You have to leave now," he told Lauren roughly.

"I have to leave?"

She seemed to be waiting for some gesture of affection, but he didn't move. She took her handbag, tossed her reading glasses into it, gave a quick look around the room, making sure not to meet his eye, and walked resolutely to the door. He saw that when she got there she hesitated once more—his last chance. Then the door opened. He heard the rustle of her clothing.

He rushed over to the telephone, called Max, and asked to meet.

"Sure. We have something to celebrate."

"Down by the riverbank, right now."

He found him next to a bridge abutment, legs planted wide, hat pulled down over his forehead, a cigarette in his mouth. Princess merrily jumped up on him. Josef called her back with a stern shout.

"So now you know what Operation Sonnenstaub is."

"You and the others are behind this?"

"I don't owe you any information. You're just a radioman."

A thought flashed up in his mind: he would tell him if he could.

"This attack took you completely by surprise. Admit it."

Max tossed his cigarette butt away. "Whose side are you on, anyway, Josef? I'd watch what you say. You wouldn't want it to get around to the others."

Down on the southern tip of Manhattan, smoke, dust, and ash hung in the air. At the print shop the explosion was all anyone talked about.

The radio was reporting that the death toll had risen to fifty. By now it seemed an established fact that the Germans were behind it.

He heard his name, then Arthur tapped him on the shoulder. "Call for you. Unknown."

In Arthur's office he nodded along to Ettinger's instructions: "Three o'clock on the Hudson."

He hung up, and Arthur stood in his way.

"Now I know what's going on here. I've always said there was something fishy about the whole thing."

"Don't worry so much, Arthur." He had no interest whatsoever in hearing any of Arthur's theories and slipped past him, his hand already on the doorknob. But Arthur kept talking, caught up in the dangerous excitement of revelation; nothing would stand in its way.

"The idea was to fool everybody. To distract everybody with amateurs. Secretly everybody figures the German agents are a bunch of chumps and the situation is under control. Meanwhile, in the background, attacks are being planned, this time by the real agents. You and your buddies' job was always just to distract the FBI. And you don't know it yourselves; that's part of the plan. I mean, who would willingly say to them, 'Sure, I'll play the Nazi sap for you.' No, they want real commitment. Pretty ingenious. Seems like the Nazis."

"That's absurd."

He knew it wasn't absurd. And if Arthur could come to that conclusion, then so could Ettinger, who wanted to meet with him on the Hudson in an hour.

Shortly before three he walked down Vandam Street, heading toward the river. The newsboys thrust the headlines in his face. He looked up at the sky that opened up beyond the canyon of buildings.

Two men were standing next to the wooden bench. One of them was

Ettinger. The other, a chubby younger agent who turned eagerly to face Josef, with alert eyes and moist lips. But Ettinger grabbed his arm to hold him back and whispered something to him.

They walked along the water, one on either side of him. The friendliness was gone. No more cigarettes either. Ettinger seemed to look at him differently now. As if Josef had been putting on an act, while in truth he had always been one step ahead of him.

"The number of dead has gone up to fifty by now. There's something you're not telling us, Joe. Start talking."

"Maybe it's got something to do with this Sebold?"

"It most definitely does not have anything to do with Sebold. You have to get more out of Max."

He looked at Ettinger, shaken, tried to connect back to what it had been like before, them smoking and looking at the skyline together. A certain trust. An understanding. In Ettinger's eyes there was nothing.

———

In December he followed the light, how it pushed its way into the room a bit later every morning, and how the twilight began a little earlier every evening, pressing down on the afternoon and shortening it. The trees had lost their leaves early. New York faded into an all-pervasive gray, into cold, into white clouds of vapor in front of his nose, shapes swelling and then collapsing in on themselves; he watched them when he stood with Ettinger. He concentrated on the fog of Ettinger's breath, which mixed with cigarette smoke. Ever more often now he thought, *Arrest me already, you asshole.* This voice in his head, *Arrest me, you asshole,* and clouds of vapor; these meetings consisted of nothing else.

He now drove the delivery truck for Max. Ludwig had been arrested for shoplifting. He had slid some expensive cigars from their case at

Macy's and then pocketed them; Ettinger told him. Max still didn't know why Ludwig had disappeared. Max, who by this point had improved his Morse code skills, sat with his mouth twisted up among the drink crates. Josef steered the truck through Brooklyn, keeping his eyes open for traffic cops. Ettinger let him know beforehand which routes were safe. Sometimes he noticed Ettinger in a car behind them. He knew that they listened in on Max's transmissions.

Today, a leaden gray afternoon in Central Park, Ettinger arrived a few minutes late. He held a bag of roasted chestnuts in his hand, offering Josef some. To be polite, he fished one out. Josef almost thought he heard a hissing sound when he touched it—they were piping hot.

"The Hercules explosion was an accident, Joe."

"Then please arrest me now." He said it in German: "*Verhaften Sie mich.*"

"How come?" said Ettinger, also in German.

"Because now's the time when my innocence is most apparent."

Ettinger shook his head sadly. "We're not quite there yet."

The next day it was in the newspapers. DOUBTS SABOTAGE IN HER-CULES BLAST—FBI IS MYSTIFIED AS TO CAUSE OF EXPLOSION AT KENVIL, NJ.

Lauren, who in the last few weeks had treated him as though he were personally responsible for what by now were fifty-two deaths, who at the kitchen table pushed newspaper articles his way discussing warships, uniforms, maps, and tanks, grew milder.

He felt weary and drained. But it was with a certain relief that he climbed into the truck with Max the next day.

"So it wasn't an attack, then."

"You idiot!" said Max.

"What?"

"That's a lie the American government is spreading. To prevent panic from spreading among the population!"

Josef started the engine. It was a cold December day, the streets slick. The accumulated smell of gasoline, cigarettes, and acrid sweat hung in the air inside the truck.

"There was no attack, you hear?" Josef simply said it a second time.

"You stupid oaf, you'll believe anything! Sonnenstaub equals Hercules. End of conversation."

"There was no attack!" He was shouting now.

"Calm down, little man."

On Flushing Avenue he noticed Ettinger's white mustache and baby-pink skin in the rearview mirror. Ettinger was driving a black Austin today; the FBI provided him with a different car every time. The Austin stuck to them like a magnet, with a buffer of about ten feet; no one could get in between them. Crossing Knickerbocker Avenue, Josef sped up. Ettinger sped up too, also ignoring the red light. "Hey, careful," said Max behind him. "We don't want any trouble, remember?"

He steered the truck carefully past clusters of pedestrians who stood in the median, driving at normal speed again. When the road ahead of them was clear of people, he floored it.

"Are you trying to get us thrown in jail?" shouted Max.

That's exactly what I'm trying to do, thought Josef. He wanted to finally put an end to it. He stepped on the brake, there was a squeal, then crunching and shattering. His knee hurt, plus something on his arm.

"Shit, Josef!" Max shouted.

So Max was still alive. And he was still alive. He took a breath and waited.

"That was nothing," Max called up to him. "Drive away, right now. We're not at fault, he ran into us."

"That's precisely why we have to wait." He had said it calmly and deliberately.

Max swore.

No, he wasn't going to drive away. He waited. Ettinger's face popped up in the driver's window. His eyes twitched searchingly left and right. He seemed to be working hard trying to figure out the meaning of this situation. "Hey, mister, why'd you just slam on the brakes like that?"

"There was a dog," said Josef, his voice firm.

"Here's my card. We'll settle things ourselves. No need to get the police involved."

Josef got out. Saw with satisfaction that Ettinger shrank back. On the sidewalk people had stopped and were looking at them with curiosity. The front end of the black Austin was crumpled. The delivery truck's bumper was hanging off. The license plate had come off completely. A man was sitting in the Austin. Josef thought he saw a small shiny radio in his hand.

"You ran into that delivery truck," someone called out.

"Get the police!" cried Josef.

"You're doing it all wrong, Joe," whispered Ettinger.

They waited in silence. Ettinger kept staring at him. It was a probing look. At one point he said, "Think about this. It's not too late," but Josef turned away.

When a cop showed up fifteen minutes later, Ettinger said, "All right, then," hurried toward the cop, and planted himself in front of him.

Josef tugged at the back door of the truck. He wanted to show everyone what they were hauling around town—not just drinks but a radio. The door was locked. Liquid dripped onto the pavement.

Ettinger stood talking with the cop. He was sure to have shown him his FBI badge. The cop gave the people standing around the sign to move along, the situation broke up into its separate components.

Josef climbed back into the cab, and when Ettinger drove past him he heard him say in German, *"Das war ein Fehler"*—*That was a mistake.*

Then there was heavy breathing. Josef turned around. Max sat in a glittering pile of broken glass and puddles of lemonade, his hands bloody. "That guy's got something to hide—how much you wanna bet? I've got a nose for these things. He bribed the cop."

"Are you hurt?"

"I'll live. No comparison with Sonnenstaub." He gave an indecent laugh.

Josef had already started the engine. Now he turned it off again.

"What's wrong?" cried Max. "Drive already!"

"You'd like to take credit for Sonnenstaub, huh? For people getting maimed or killed?"

"It's war, Josef. You don't know what war is—you were never in one. So shut your mouth and take me to a hospital."

He drove off. Thoughts flew through his head. *Your life will grow smaller from now on, ever smaller. You won't amount to anything more here in America.* Something inside him let go and relaxed.

Peace.

33

BUENOS AIRES, NOVEMBER 1949

HE'S BEEN WEARING THE SAME SUIT FOR FOUR WEEKS. HE has no money to buy himself a new one, and no friends to lend him one. He shares a rathole with two Argentinians who are kind enough to let him sleep on the floor. His suitcase might have come long ago, but without his freight note he can't get it. He goes to the post office every day. Still no letter from Carl. Meanwhile, he has already written five, with the increasingly urgent request to send the freight note at all costs, or at least to find out the number from the shipping company.

It's hot; there's no wind. His face is covered in a film of sweat. At the laundry he has his suit ironed for the third time this week, which hardly helps—the sweat and the dust eat their way into it. While he waits in underwear and socks behind a crooked curtain, the girl runs the iron over the suit, her face blank.

Gracias—that's one thing he can say. *Hasta luego* is another. He has a Spanish–English dictionary; he opted for it over the Spanish–German one. His stomach is making problems for him too. He often sits in a filthy food stall and spoons up soup with bits of meat in it. The milk usually curdles when he pours it in his coffee.

Buenos Aires also has massive buildings and geometry, like New York, but the buildings aren't as tall and there's more space in between them. On the grand boulevards he hears European languages. Near the post office is a large square with an obelisk, a neatly scrubbed park with a statue of a man on horseback, with pools of water and hysterical fountains. Hotels with white, curved awnings like seashells over every window. Every city has these little spots that act like they know nothing of the other little spots.

His spot: he has to ride half an hour on the bus to a neighborhood of low buildings, unfinished or already stripped. There's always something missing on each of them—a windowpane, a doorbell, a wall. Chickens in the unpaved streets. At night the electricity goes out. *Villa miseria*, his new friends call it. There's no need to translate.

It doesn't matter, he doesn't plan to stay here long. It's just a city like any other. He will keep moving, back to America.

He nears the harbor. The siesta is over, the Porteños are slowly rising from sleep. "Down there," someone tells him when he asks for the *aduana principal*, the customs office for parcel post. The ships bear names like *Rotterdam, London, Bilbao, Genoa*. He walks among shipping containers and sleeping people. The Rio de la Plata is mud-brown as usual.

He knocks on a half-open iron door and hears a noise from within. The man behind the desk, his slick hair combed back, speaks a little English.

"I'm sorry. We need the freight note." He knows voices like this, unyielding, final. At regular intervals an oscillating fan blows air past the sitting man and ruffles his hair.

"Can't I just go and take a look myself?"

"There are hundreds of packages! And I can't possibly let you in there. Surely you understand that."

No, he doesn't understand.

His clothing is in this package: two suits from Carl, a few shoes (which Edith traded a clock for), a comb, razors, towels, an alarm clock, a lamp, a travel typewriter, tools, mettwurst.

He roams the streets. He hears a lot of German, sees German businesses: Großman's Bakery; W. Tolle Furs; Casa Schill Doll Repair; Dr. Dinkeldein, Dermatology; Adlerhorst Cervecería. Up to now he hasn't spoken with any Germans here, although he can spot them. How? He just can. And so he walks past them and tries to seem Argentinian.

He should make himself useful, Dörsam had said.

In a German bookstore on Avenida Flores he floats among the tables like a ghost, worried the bespectacled young man will throw him out—him, the tramp. He shuffles over to a wall covered in notices. A Bach choir is seeking a tenor, a chess club has announced the dates for its next tournament, a German meetup at Restaurant ABC (he would meet Schmuederrich there, said Dörsam). No job postings. They seem to be above such things here, or they have a different system. His fingers trail over spines. "*A Hamburg novel full of sun and longing for the wind and the sea.*" And another: *Daily Hygiene.*

The door chime rings and two women step inside, break the uncomfortable silence between the bookseller and him, even if it's only to say "*Guten Tag*" and to whisper something to each other every now and then.

He picks up a book by a French author, *Nuremberg or the Promised Land,* and reads on the back cover: "*The Germans weren't monsters, as Nuremberg would have you believe.*"

A fly lands on his hand. He shakes it off and puts the book back.

The young man is standing in front of him. "Here, just came in."

Josef takes the magazine from him with a nod, as if he knew what it was. *DER WEG—Monthly Magazine for Cultural Preservation and Development.* He pages through it. *"Only those who surrender are lost,"* quoting a certain Colonel Rudel, who, he reads, was a highly decorated Stuka pilot and is now head of the Argentinian branch of the Siemens corporation. One article works out how it couldn't have been six million. *"We have to throw off the straitjacket,"* he reads. *"We know that our newspapers are lying."* He flips to the end. The magazine is published in Argentina and in Germany. *"Chess Problem: Which side can mate in two moves? Solution given by Messrs. . . ."* He sets the magazine down on the table and leaves the store, uttering something more like a noise than a word.

Another week passes. His rounds shrink, limited to the places where he can get credit. The girl irons his suit every day. A Madonna on a household altar stares at the ceiling, eyes rolled up toward the ceiling (as if she'd had her fill of Josef). The two Argentinians will be moving soon. They pantomime working in the fields, make the international sign for money. *You can come along, repay your debt.* He doesn't want to. Then again, if they move, he won't even have a floor to sleep on anymore.

A man is rich in proportion to the number of things which he can afford to let alone.

Once his favorite line from Thoreau, but that was then. That time is over. The older he gets, the less interested he is in other people's insights.

The last night he lets the Argentinians take him to a wedding and gets drunk. Corn on the cob and meat on a charcoal grill—a delicious smell wafts through his shantytown neighborhood. He feels like he's only had to sit out one dance and is ready to jump back in, just a few goddamn years behind bars and now onward and upward—but he doesn't know how. He doesn't know anymore what he should do with his life. He's lost the beat, and here at the shantytown wedding he has to confront this insight, here where all he understands is *Salud*, rum, whiskey, gin.

An image pops into his head, and he closes his eyes in shame. Him in the *New York Times*. Shoulders slumping forward, his hands in handcuffs. The remarkably brazen grin. He never understood this grin.

Ettinger had told him that same day. After the car accident he hadn't heard from him again, but then, half a year later, Ettinger called him. "Tonight."

He neatly folded Lauren's sweater, smelled it, unfolded it, then smelled it again.

At 8:30 that night they knocked on his door. Put him in handcuffs, put him into a car downstairs. He sat in the back seat, pinned in between them. End of June. A hot day. At Grand Central he saw two policemen on a side street shooting water pistols at each other and laughing loudly; he could hear the laughter over the sound of the traffic. It wasn't just him who was arrested that night but all of them, thirty-three agents.

The next morning dust floats through the shafts of light as both Argentinians put their hats on and say goodbye. They make it clear somehow that, next time, he should pay.

Restaurant ABC is pinned between two tall buildings at 545 Lavalle. Tiny, with a red-tiled roof, it looks like it's made of gingerbread. Over the waist-high curtains in the windows he sees crumpled cloth napkins and little cups of *cortado*. It's late afternoon. He nods to the waiter as he walks inside, cranes his neck to make clear that he's looking for someone, sees as far as the giant painting on the back wall, a mountain landscape with a castle. He doesn't see anyone he knows seated between the wood-paneled walls. But a young man squeezes his way between tables and heads right for him, as if he knew more about him than Josef did himself. "You're looking for someone?"

Josef hesitates. On the other hand, he has nothing to lose, and so he mentions Schmuederrich's name. Schmuederrich won't be here until tomorrow night. Is he new here? Josef nods.

"No place to stay?"

He can barely bring himself to nod a second time.

"I know a boarding house—there might be a room available. I'll call them. One second." The young man notices Josef's hesitation and smiles. "Don't worry. It's a German couple from the Saarland, the Griebels."

The Pension Aleman is just a few blocks away. They walk up a long flight of stairs. Josef feels lines of sweat running down his neck. The door opens—that must be Frau Griebel, and behind her, on the shelf against the wall, the Führer. A bust. So that's what was meant by "Don't worry."

"Did you have a taxing journey, Herr Klein? Did everything go all right?"

"Yes, it's only here that it's been difficult."

"No, now you're safe. It's good that you've made it. You won't lack for a thing here!"

"Pardon me, but how much are you asking for the room? I'm a bit hard up, don't have a job either."

"You'll find a good job in no time, I'm sure. You can pay at the end of the month."

Upstairs a strong smell of oil. The corner room that she gives him was just repainted, she says. It's clean and bright, with a table and two chairs.

On the wall hangs a framed metal engraving with a quote: TO YOU, MY HOMELAND, SMOKE ON THE HEATH, I SHALL REMAIN TRUE TILL MY FINAL BREATH.

In the hall bathroom he dabs shaving cream onto his chin and shaves carefully. Then he lies down in the freshly made bed. He thinks of Edith as the strange noises fill his ears, the rattling of a streetcar, the trilling of a canary, and somewhere a radio. He doesn't even know the name of the young man who led him here. So this is what he is now: a Nazi on the lam.

The next day Schmuederrich is standing at the door to his room, two bottles of cold *cerveza* in his hands, beads of condensation dripping off them. He wears a pale suit and a straw hat, he's lost a little weight. "There you are, little man!" Schmuederrich laughs, showing the gap in his teeth.

For the span of a second, nothing happens—no handshake and of course no embrace. Then Schmuederrich simply barrels his way inside, opens the beer bottles, and starts talking. He works at La Plata Aid; they send care packages to Germany: cooking oil, lard, bacon, beef, meat extract, cheese. He handles the advertising and new client acquisition— very much his métier, but still, a step down for him. There's nothing to be done about it. Yes, a rather large step down. He's got his eye on something better, but he can't say anything about it just yet. The German community in Buenos Aires is very well respected and sticks together, no matter what. There is a universal desire to wrest Germany back from the Allies, to liberate Germany. Josef frowns.

"Now don't go pissing yourself. This time we won't run into any trouble with the government. Perón loves the Germans! German expertise is going to help Argentina become the major power in South America. We're trying to make the tail wag the dog. Nothing's lost yet. It's simply a matter of pulling the Germans up out of their depression and getting them excited again!"

Schmuederrich sips his beer contentedly, prattles on, and every now and then calls out for "Irma, doll!" He means the goodly Frau Griebel. With great gusto she brings beer and sandwiches, opens the windows, and hauls a large fan into the room, which churns up the humid mixture of heat, paint, beer smell, and cigarette smoke. Josef feels dazed. Through a fog he hears words like "rocket scientists," "air squadron generals," "physicists," "doctors," "military advisers," "representatives of German industry," "former diplomats"—in short: big fish, but they couldn't stay in Germany. Despite their proud past they would be persecuted there.

Only when Schmuederrich says something about a job does Josef start paying attention—sure, at the Casa Schirmer print shop. They're in urgent need of extra help for Christmas card production, what with Christmas being just around the corner. Josef sits up and has Schmuederrich give him precise directions for how to get there, Schmuederrich adding that he could start tomorrow. Schmuederrich raises his bottle: "To freedom!"

Josef drinks in large gulps. He hopes Schmuederrich will leave soon. Then he hears him say, "You should make yourself useful to us at some point. We're overthrowing the German government."

Josef looks away. "Not interested."

"We helped you out."

"Without you and your friends I wouldn't have needed any help."

"You know what I think? That little girlfriend of yours. She was FBI."

"That's ridiculous."

"Oh no it's not."

"No, Hans. She wasn't FBI."

He leaves the room, walks outside through the piercing light of the afternoon sun. Lauren is in the past. An eternity ago. But the pain is fresh. It's there with him every second.

34

BUENOS AIRES, CHRISTMAS 1949

H E WATCHES THE MEN CLOSELY. FACES TURNING GROTESQUE when they laugh, neighing like horses. These are the men Schmueder-rich looks up to. That he eagerly stares at. They, on the other hand, don't seem to notice Schmuederrich, even though two of them are his custom-ers at La Plata Aid.

Schmuederrich swirls the martini in his glass expectantly and points out the fantastic view they have out here on the terrace. They can see all the way to the Rio de la Plata, which glitters golden in the setting sun. True, it is nice at the Schlüters: stately palm trees adorn their garden, a wreath of deck chairs wraps around the circular pool, a Christmas tree drowns in tinsel.

Herr Schlüter, the successful German industrialist, appears before his guests in folk costume, complete with staghorn buttons. He nods at them—he is also a La Plata customer—but joins the more impor-tant gentlemen. Frau Schlüter, a slender vision in green silk, her posture ramrod straight, smiles graciously as she walks past them and vanishes back into the villa; the doorbell is ringing every minute now. The ter-race fills up. A pair of young ladies wearing hats draped in netting park themselves next to them and start chatting away without even a glance in their direction. They're complaining about the beautiful but impractical New Look from Dior, which they themselves have shown up wearing: high heels, long flowing skirts, cinched waists. A Yuletide boys' choir is playing on the record player.

"There, you see what all I can offer you outside the penitentiary?"

Beads of sweat on Schmuederrich's forehead and cheeks. By the time the sun has sunk behind the trees, about two hundred guests fill the terrace and garden. Schmuederrich runs into acquaintances every now and then, mostly care-package subscribers, but he just gives a brief nod; he wants to keep himself free for the big shots. Josef asks if they all got here after the war. "Of course, what do you think?" Schmueder-rich replies curtly. Josef just wanted to hear it said. Cigars are passed around. Dior chitchat to the left, war chitchat to the right. "What a mistake, blowing Germany to shreds, the only bulwark against the Red hordes!" "America's got another thing coming to them!" A special fury is reserved for the cowardly generals, the cowardly suicides.

Something is wrong with Josef's new shoes; the leather in the front has split off from the sole. Must be the heat. Cheap shoes, you end up paying for it later.

"Some crackers and cheese cubes, gentlemen?"

Schmuederrich sets down his empty martini glass, asks for cigars, and stares over at the men. He seems as lost as Josef, who notices that some of the men even seem to make a point of looking past them.

"What are they calling you here now, José?" Schmuederrich asks absently.

"I don't care what people call me."

"Don't you go along with it. They keep trying to call me Juan here. No way. The *putas* say it all the time."

"*Putas?*"

"Whores. Got some pretty kitties out here."

One of the Schlüter children skips among the assembled guests in a nightshirt, hiding behind the ladies' evening gowns. The nanny walks around in a crouch, arms outspread, searching, then gathers up the child, who bubbles over with laughter.

"How's your job at Casa Schirmer?"

"They're not keeping me on. End of the month, that's it."

"It's because you run your mouth too much about America. How you're saving your money and want to go back. It's gotten back to me."

"I might have my problems with the American government. But not with America."

Schmuederrich rolls his eyes.

Frau Schlüter claps her hands and asks everyone to please join her in the salon for the Christmas festivities. He has to lift his foot well off the ground so the sole doesn't drag on the floor. Schmuederrich doesn't notice anything. In the salon, lined with fabric wallpaper, an old man is waiting at the piano, his face obscured by bushy white eyebrows. "*Oh, du goldenes Meer!*" he calls out. *Oh, you golden sea!* Some listeners close their eyes, gripped with emotion. "Oh, you stars!" he cries. "How you look down upon us and think of us, though we're no longer here!"

After the singing, a man in horn-rimmed glasses gives a lecture. The thrust, as far as Josef can tell, is that abstract art is a failure because it does not have the capacity to move the soul. Nodding all around. The ashtrays are overflowing; the maid slips quietly through the salon and empties them. The learned man complains that the omnipresent scourge of advertising and the tangos of Hollywood have a ruinous effect on the calm contemplation of art. The young Dior ladies exchange glances. Quiet snorting. They remind him of Lauren—she could laugh like that too. Afterward a hefty woman sings a Schubert song, "Du bist die Ruh," then the buffet is opened. Schmuederrich simply walks off. Apparently Josef has served his time.

His stomach is out of sorts. He limps outside, reaches for his cigarettes. The terrace is empty, but the group of gentlemen has stayed right where it was, as if in scornful indifference to whatever might be happening around them. They look at him, sizing him up. One of them, still young, has a prosthetic leg, a defiant smile in his well-chiseled face; Josef noticed him earlier. He doesn't even know if he's allowed to nod at them. Just as he's about to leave, he hears the question: "Where did you serve?" He turns around, incredulous at the fact that they would speak to him. He identifies the source of the hoarse voice: a man with very white, well-manicured hands, who wears a uniform covered in medals, the only one of them so dressed.

"Nowhere. I lived in New York. Happily, I might add."

"We thought you'd injured your leg in the war. You're limping."

He suddenly feels inside him a strange mix of lightness and mirth. "My shoe's busted. The sole is coming off. I have to lift my foot so it doesn't drag across the ground, see, like this."

He lifts his foot, stands on one leg. The sole is dangling pitifully by this point. The gentlemen laugh; the one with the prosthetic leg laughs loudest.

"Did you buy the shoes here?"

He nods.

"Looks like you got ripped off."

"They were cheap. I picked the wrong thing to skimp on."

"There are certain things one should never skimp on. A good pair of shoes is important. Without shoes you'll never get ahead in life."

"I'll make a note of that."

He wishes the gentlemen a good evening and starts making his way toward the other end of the terrace, where he runs straight into Schmuederrich.

"What were they asking you about?" he whispers excitedly.

"Where I served."

Schmuederrich looks over at the gentlemen, seems to take a moment to collect himself, and then calls out, "He was imprisoned! In New York!"

"Oh, so you mean your adjutant isn't an FBI agent? That's a relief."

Laughter. "What about you?" one of them calls out, making it clear that there's no need for him to come any closer.

"We worked for Germany. We kept the faith." Schmuederrich seems full of expectation.

"You didn't exactly do much over there, did you? What's your name, anyway?"

When Schmuederrich doesn't answer, one of the gentlemen says in a conciliatory tone, "Oh, that's just old Hans Schmuederrich. He's the one who sells us the care packages."

Laughter.

Schmuederrich wishes them a pleasant evening and walks off into the garden. They're still talking. Scornful laughter. "You have to be charitable. After all, they never really knew the Third Reich." "They weren't even allowed to carry a weapon over there." "Supposedly there were traitors among them."

Angels made of silver paper are hanging from the trees; a striped cat sets them to dancing. The river is lost in the darkness.

Josef takes his shoes off, walks barefoot over the lawn. He sees Schmuederrich by the pool; he sits slumped on a deck chair, bending over and reaching for a cigarette that's rolling away from him.

I should have turned you in, thinks Josef. *You, myself, everyone.*

35

ELLIS ISLAND, MAY 1946

EVERY MORNING WHEN HE WOKE UP HE SAW THE STATUE OF Liberty in the right half of the window frame. She was trapped, just like him. Every morning like that moment in the past. When he sailed toward Manhattan on the steamer. The moment lingered for the rest of the day, then night erased everything completely. At night, when he turned onto his side in his bed in the dormitory, it felt like he was falling. As if the rumble of the fishing boats, the lapping of the waves, were pushing him over a cliff, pushing him away, into another world almost.

In the morning it all started over again. To the right the Statue of Liberty, in the distance the city, rising up out of the water, its slender, smooth towers pressed together like people holding their breath in a crowded elevator, keeping their outward calm and dignity at any price.

When he was transferred, surprisingly, to Ellis Island in the fall of 1945, what it meant more than anything else was that he would see Lauren again. At Sandstone, high up in the north, she hadn't been able to visit him. He had understood that; he had even thought it was for the best.

This way she wouldn't have to see him in a striped prison uniform—crossed out, from head to foot, the bars still on his body.

Every year they had written each other less, but from the start it was without any romance. The letters were screened. He wondered, however, if that was the only reason she left out anything of interest, any warmth.

His letters always went to the same address in Brooklyn, which led him to assume that Lauren lived alone. No husband, no kids. Something about that pleased him, and he examined the feeling—was it schadenfreude? Or the hope that things might still turn out between them? Forgiveness, a fresh start, and maybe America would even take him back in. Everything would be good again.

He now found himself close to Lauren, and Lauren wanted to come visit him. Could she bring him anything, a bean pie for example? The second he read this, he knew that she was actually going to come. A few weeks had passed since, but today she would be here. It would be their first time seeing each other in five years.

He was still sitting by himself. It was ten past three. The room had filled up. He kept his eye on the door and the guard, and sometimes he looked at the two-tone Florsheim slippers worn by the German man next to him. He was having a discussion with his wife, an American, about her taking over the business, a shoe store in Bushwick. He knew that the two of them had children, and they were very lucky that their American mother hadn't been taken onto the island with them.

There were so many young people here. They played badminton in the afternoons in the giant registry room, where once someone had looked into his mouth, eyes, and ears. And no one told them how long they would have to stay on the island. Or what would happen after they left. Lawyers pocketed their money, then regretfully informed them that things hadn't gone their way in court.

Sometimes his favorite line from Thoreau would echo in his head, something about how a man's wealth had nothing to do with his outer circumstances, but he'd long found it questionable.

A woman had appeared, seeming somewhat antsy as she looked around, craning her neck shortsightedly. And then she was standing there in front of him, looking down at him with a little smile; without meaning to he had remained seated, and now he decided to stay seated. Her breasts fuller, her face rounder. Her hair styled in a helmet of stiff curls—it made her look stuffy. She was thirty-one now.

"You have to go through a tunnel and then through all these different doors before you finally get here."

"I wasn't checking the time," he said and tried to understand what she was saying. She was still telling him about her trip here.

Because she was so close and yet so different, he couldn't look her in the eye. He looked at the shoes next to him, the Florsheim slippers, and nodded, yes, a tunnel when you get off the ferry, and then the room where they search you. "But it wasn't so bad," she said quickly.

"Are you dying your hair now?"

"This is my natural hair color. Did you never notice that I dyed it?"

He shook his head.

Hotel manager, she said, when he asked, but she had to pitch in herself every now and then, making beds when the girls didn't come in on time. It was a small hotel on Long Island. What had become of her dream of being a journalist? He didn't dare ask the question.

She clasped her hands together and set them on the table. These familiar hands that he had held so many times. The red polish so pristine that he figured it was for him; there was no doubt she had just painted her nails today. Now here she sat, where she didn't belong—where no one belonged; they were only warehoused. Suddenly he saw everything in a kind of double vision, saw the artificiality of it all becoming even greater: their island container, which they were stuck in, and this small portion of freedom that was contained within Lauren and that she had brought with her here, her connection to the outside world. He could sense how she too suffered from it: they were two people who sat here in unequal circumstances.

"How's Princess?"

"She's an old girl now. Her hearing's bad."

They smiled at each other. For a fraction of a second he saw something in her eyes from back then.

"That meant a lot to me, you taking care of her. It was like a part of me had remained free."

She looked at him with interest as he spoke, and under her gaze he realized what she was noticing: he spoke too slowly. As if the stopped time on Ellis Island had crept into his speech.

"How's your family in Germany? Have you heard from them?"

"Not yet."

"You have to write them."

He played the doltish immigrant with the thick accent. "I haff done zat. I vait for answer."

She smiled indulgently.

"And your family," he now asked, making an effort to be polite. "Your parents in the Catskills, how are they?"

She made a dismissive hand gesture that could have meant anything from *Not worth talking about* to *They're all fine.*

So this was about him. All right, then.

In the window he saw the waves rising and breaking with a peaceful irregularity that was all their own.

He didn't know if his family was still alive.

He could have written from Sandstone to try to find out, but he had been ashamed to write from a prison. Only when he got to Ellis Island had he dared to write a letter. Two weeks ago. From an internment camp. That didn't sound quite as bad.

He leaned forward. He would start with the generals. Throughout his years in prison he had clipped out all the articles he'd seen about their executions.

"Canaris was executed in 1945 in a concentration camp. Canaris. You know who that was? The head of military intelligence. He had been fired not long before then on account of there being too many slipups."

She interrupted him. "What are you trying to get at, Joe?"

"Do you remember the Nazi agents in the movie? Those saps? Don't you think they had better people?"

"What exactly are you trying to say?"

He leaned forward and whispered, "They intentionally took on people who were incompetent, or people like me who weren't involved voluntarily and ended up betraying the whole effort. They didn't want to see America reduced to rubble and ash. They always made it look like they were carrying out Hitler's plans, but they were secretly working against him. It was a kind of resistance."

She seemed reluctant to hear this. Only little by little did she grasp his meaning, and when she did she put on an empty smile. As if she wanted to give him a chance to drop the subject.

"There was opposition! For a long time they weren't talking about it here at all!"

"I understand. You want to be one of the good guys." She smiled icily. Her lipstick had rubbed off on her front teeth.

"No. I want to know what happened!" he said angrily.

She pushed back from the table a bit, looked over at the window, the glass clouded with salt.

He gave her an imploring look. He had imagined this moment being different, easier.

Finally she raised an eyebrow. "Joe, in Germany today they're claiming every little thing was resistance and opposition. Suddenly everybody was a resistance fighter. And now you're saying you were too?"

He now pulled the newspaper article with the tear down the middle fold from his pants pocket and handed it to her, just like she'd always done with him.

"Look, Lauren. Here it is in black and white. In summer 1942 eight saboteurs were sent to America by U-boat, without any training, without anything. Canaris was head of military intelligence. All he said was 'Well, I guess we'll lose eight good Nazis.' It was a sham operation, put on for show."

She looked at him dismissively, with hostility, even. He didn't have anything else to offer. That was his biggest argument, the eight good Nazis.

"When is the article from? And who's the source?"

"The head of sabotage, Lahousen, gave an interview to the international press in Nuremberg in December 1945." He was afraid of what Lauren's reaction would be and looked at the feet in the Florsheim slippers, feet that jittered nervously—everybody was nervous here.

"He's saying it *after* the war. At that point they can say *anything* to try and present themselves in a good light."

"But what could they have said about it at the time? It's not the kind of thing you brag about!"

"Joe, there's no point in clinging to something for which there's no proof."

Did she really not understand him? He laughed bitterly. He wanted to stand up and leave, as if he were a free man—and in fact he *would* be a free man for those few seconds in which he left a woman behind, but of course he could only shuffle back to his group cell.

"Lauren, I've lost everything. And I don't know what to think about myself anymore."

"I can imagine that. But your theory is pure speculation."

He looked at her thoughtfully. Of course it was all in his head. There it was, clear and radiant; it blazed a glittering path through the gloom of the day. He felt humiliated.

"Joe, even if it is true, that would mean they sacrificed those people. Six months later and you'd be dead now too. You'd have been sentenced by a court martial. The people who could accept others' sacrifice like that are no heroes."

"I don't care about heroism. I care about the truth." He said it so weakly that he barely believed it himself.

"Yeah? This is the truth." She took the article, crumpled it, and let it drop back on the table.

He stared at Lauren in disbelief, tried to imagine her treating the girls at the hotel this way when they forgot to change a towel.

She wet her lips, then she scooted her chair forward a bit and said in a conciliatory tone, "You'll never know what the others' motives were. But you do know what you did. And if you find you have something to reproach yourself for, learn to live with it."

He couldn't remember them saying goodbye to each other, but suddenly he felt her hand in his once more. Yes, she had given him her hand after all, saying, "So long, Joe. Take care of yourself." The paper bag with the bean pie in it sat on the table in front of him. And that's where he left it.

When he got back to his cell he saw Carl's handwriting. He saw that Carl was alive. On his bed was the letter. The way it was lying there it was like his brother was suddenly in the room with him.

And then he read the letter and learned that they were all alive—all the Kleins had survived. Edith, the two children, and all their relatives in Düsseldorf and Aachen.

"You always have a home here with us," Carl wrote. He knew it wasn't true. But it felt good to read the words.

He immediately set all the wheels in motion and found an agency to send a care package to Neuss. Chocolate. Coffee. Aspirin. Sausage. Pepper. Jerky. Adhesive tape.

36

SAN JOSÉ, COSTA RICA, JUNE 1953

H E FEELS THE HEAT WHEN HE STEPS OUT OF HIS ROOM, ITS force and intensity. The green hurts his eyes. He looks longingly at the river. The water is cool. He dipped his foot in once.

He knocks on Maria's door. She has her wet hair wrapped in a towel and seems happy that he's encountering her in a more intimate setting.

Maria warned him about the river. She didn't mention a reason. Crocodiles? The current? Now he stands facing her and asks.

"It's so deep, Don José!"

He stares at her in amazement.

"The men say thirty feet in the deepest parts."

"But I can swim."

"But it's so deep."

So Maria can't swim, he takes it. She doesn't know what swimming is.

"It doesn't matter how deep the river is," he tells her. "You can drown as soon as you don't feel the ground beneath you anymore."

She rubs her hair with the towel and looks at him like he's pulling her leg.

"Maria, drowning isn't like falling from a building, where you're more likely to survive a fall from two meters up than from eight meters."

"Fine, go give it a try, then."

Again and again. Even when Maria has closed the door, he's still explaining it to her. Again and again. Like the squirrel that keeps looking desperately for a way out of the wire cage. During the day the cage hangs from the terrace awning. When you move closer, it starts shaking violently this way and that.

"It would rather die than be trapped," he said to Maria yesterday. She doesn't like hearing it, her mouth a stubborn dash.

He lies back down on the bed, which is small, without bedposts or a headboard, and watches the patient spinning of the ceiling fan. The blades slice through the air and make a thin, high sound. On the floor, the maps. All of Costa Rica is lying around him. To map a country. The mountains, the roads, the rivers, the towns. Colors of light blue, lime green, eggshell white.

Buenos Aires: Two years of being stuck in a city that was either muddy from the rain or dusty from the sun. In which you couldn't make any money if you hadn't already brought a lot of money with you. He had torn down houses and painted the garden fences of rich exiles. Men with a past. A married couple from Austria let him live in the gardener's shed of their vacation home outside the city. He kept their garden in good shape. Mowing the grass, trimming the hedges, pulling weeds. Sometimes on the weekends he saw the couple from a distance. He breathed, he slept, he ate beans and rice. *Now I'm like Thoreau in his cabin*, he thought then. And soon it had been two years. Only when an invitation came from Schmuederrich did he show himself among the Germans. When he had saved enough money, he set out. His plan was to travel to the US via Mexico. It was in Costa Rica that, for the first time, someone took a closer look at his homemade passport. He sat in prison for three days. Yes, he was German. They sent someone from the German Embassy. He believed him but needed proof, which Josef didn't have. Finally he asked for a telephone and called Dörsam. He knew someone here. Two hours later he was free and had an address in his pocket, which led him to Maria. And then he got the job at the Geographic Institute.

Music in the ceiling fan. He hasn't done much, just poked through the maps, spreading them over the floor, letting them get out of order, happy that he knows how to produce such things. He still hasn't learned to deal with the dizziness in the little plane, an old three-engine sesquiplane. They work in a team; he enjoys great esteem. *Americano* they call him, José the *Americano*.

Sometimes he flips through the issues of *Stern*. He's received them all by now, except for the last one; it should be coming today. He flips through the pages and he searches, even though he already knows there's nothing in there about him. He's happy about that. But then why is Dörsam coming?

He pauses when he sees a picture of the German American Bund's rally at Madison Square Garden. *"But they do it in good faith and with a self-evident sense of connection with the motherland."*

How touching.

And all throughout there are women hanging up laundry, demonstrating their ease of movement in advertisements for sanitary towels, and still more women showing off their waists in ads for tights, hands on their hips, legs crossed, back foot up, elegantly modest.

A car drives into the courtyard. The driver is a young man, cigarette dangling from one side of his mouth, hat pushed back on his head. He gets out and strikes a pose: one arm on the roof of the car, eyes gazing up at Josef. Josef nods to him from the veranda. This will all belong to him someday. Maria's oldest son. Maria comes running out of the house and throws her arms around the young rascal. The smell of perfume wafts up from below. She turns around and waves goodbye. He waves back. "See you Monday, Don José!" she calls out. Her spending the weekend with her children in town is perfectly all right with him. Maybe he'll find the courage in the next two days to free the squirrel.

From the veranda he can see out to the road in front of the house. The neighbor's three dogs are there, out for their evening walk. Ever since her husband died, Maria has kept her dog on a leash. He's dangerous, she says. Everything here is dangerous, apparently.

He can hear the dog breathing sometimes, depending on which way the wind is blowing. It's just a watchdog. He's supposed to bark when someone gets too close, that's all. On her nightstand, she tells him, there's a pistol.

At first the dog would bark at him whenever he came loping across the courtyard toward the house; by now, though, the dog recognizes his shambling gait.

Next he hears the mailman's creaky bicycle. He's already holding the brown envelope with Carl's handwriting in his hand. It's the last *Stern* issue. Now it makes him nervous after all—why else would Dörsam announce his visit?

His heart is pounding when he opens the magazine. He sees the picture of the accused in the courtroom, framed by DR. SCHOLL'S SHOE INSERTS and REFORMA RHEUMA-EASE COMFORTERS. Him on the far right, head cocked and looking off to the side. Who was he looking at? Lauren? He remembers looking away, how each of them kept trying to avoid the other's gaze. He felt hollowed out on the inside. He couldn't run away and couldn't speak. He remembers the scraping of feet, the murmur in the courtroom; he remembers Judge Mortimer Byers. He remembers the absence, the whispering—where's Sebold? The only one missing at the trial was this man who, thanks to Ettinger, he hadn't met once. Maybe he would have gotten an even longer sentence if he had. Sebold's office was a trap. The FBI was waiting behind a mirror and everyone he lured to the office was captured on film forever. He remembers the films being shown in the courtroom, one agent after the other blundering into Sebold's office. There had never been anything like it. The papers the next day couldn't get enough of this spectacular method for unmasking criminal activity.

The one person who didn't show up in the film was him. Ettinger had vanished, just like Sebold. And he, Josef, was sitting with twenty-three Nazis and couldn't open his mouth.

Carefully he opens Carl's letter.

> Since I haven't gotten any mail from you for some time, I assume that you're in the process of writing your report to me.

No, he's only started it. Carl had asked him to finally explain everything once and for all.

The other letters are carbon copies. Carl is sending letters all over the place—to the journalists, to the editors at *Stern*, to the surviving agents.

> Dear Herr Thorwald,
>
> My brother, who is traveling the world without papers . . . may I ask for your help . . . we must combine our efforts to . . .

Josef swallows. He needs a break and puts on Duke Ellington.

Later he stares at a photo of Nikolaus Ritter for a long time and thinks about the Old Heidelberg again. The greasy hair, the smug, broad smile. Now Ritter is sitting with reporters in his apartment in Hamburg, reminiscing. For him, the exporter, things couldn't be better. He pompously explains that the Jew Lily Stein received assistance in leaving the country, and in exchange she was to perform a few services for military intelligence.

Right at the bottom his eye is caught by a letter from a reader. A former agent guesses that military intelligence had already calculated in advance that the operation would be uncovered. So he's not the only one this idea has occurred to.

He sighs and closes the magazine. It's over.

SAN JOSÉ, COSTA RICA, JUNE 1953

RICARDO IS COUNTING AGAIN. FOUR BOTTLES OF SODA WATER. Two cartons of milk. Five bananas. While he counts he taps every object with his finger. Starts over from the beginning and then adds another banana so the price is easier to calculate. His glasses are greasy and there's a crack down the middle of one lens. Everything he does he does slowly, and depending on Josef's mood this can either drive him into a white-hot rage or impart a feeling of deep peacefulness.

Edith's quick movements. The way she closed the door behind her with her foot, bread pinned beneath her chin, the laundry in her arms.

With Ricardo he thinks hard beforehand about what exactly he's going to have him pull off the shelves. Sometimes he shortens the list halfway through because things are moving too slowly for him. Ricardo likes to grab each item off the shelf separately. It doesn't help to list off three items at once that are right next to each other—rice, lentils, beans. He only comes back with one.

Every single thing is given its dignity. Here's the semolina. Here's the tobacco. Here's the milk.

Oh, how he's come to love this.

On the way back a car passes him, trailing a brown cloud of dust. He holds his breath. He rides past the old pochote tree that has grown so crooked that no one wants to cut it down.

The car that passed him is waiting in the driveway. A taxi. Dörsam has gotten out and holds up a bag of crackers. "You live up there, right?"

Josef goes up the stairs ahead of him. At the top he points toward the veranda. "Have a seat, Herr Dörsam."

"Well, well," mumbles Dörsam. "In Buenos Aires you always made yourself scarce, true. But I heard only good things about you. That you were a hard worker. A good handyman. The Germans have you to thank for all their garden fences. How's the work at the Geographic Institute? Good?"

What is Dörsam getting at? That it's thanks to Dörsam that he has a good job? Yes, that he knows.

"I can't complain."

"You never could complain. You always had it good."

The midday heat has settled in on the veranda. Josef goes into the kitchen, grabs two glasses, hesitates, then tosses a few ice cubes in them before filling them with water. He has a thought: he could grab Dörsam and throw him over the railing, or go get Maria's revolver from the nightstand and gun him down, then throw his body in the river, which of course is nice and deep.

When he comes back, Dörsam has taken off his jacket, even slipped off his suspenders.

"This fall there are parliamentary elections in Germany," says Dörsam with his mouth full and offers him a cracker. He wants to keep him up to speed, he says as Josef furrows his brow. The leading candidate for the Deutsche Reichspartei is Rudel. "The gentleman from Buenos Aires. You met him a few times. The one with the prosthetic leg."

Josef doesn't know if he should nod or laugh.

The dog barks in the courtyard.

Josef takes advantage of the interruption. "Have you heard about the report in *Stern*? Isn't that why you're here?"

Dörsam looks at him, taken aback. Josef stands up, grabs the magazines, and throws them on the table. Dörsam nods and pages through them a little. "Our efforts are getting the recognition they deserve. Oh, look at that. Söderbaum has a new movie out."

"That's all you have to say?" Josef's voice is louder than usual, almost shrill. Dörsam sets the magazine back down. Cranes his neck and looks over the balustrade. Jungle. Green. Banana bushes, leaves hanging limply like exhausted flag bearers. Still no answer. Did Dörsam not hear him?

"You used us," says Josef.

"Used you?" Dörsam moves an ice cube around in his mouth. There's a soft crunch when he bites down.

Josef wipes his forehead with his hand and decides to bring the matter to a head: "What are you doing in Costa Rica, Herr Dörsam?"

Dörsam leans back. "I'll be visiting a few more Germans while I'm here. I want to know who I can count on. When we win in the fall and start putting Germany's house back in order, will you be with us?"

"No, Herr Dörsam."

Dörsam nods. Doesn't seem at all disappointed. Praises the magnificent view. "You've really got it nice here! A little slice of paradise on earth. Maybe I'll come back to Costa Rica someday myself."

Soon after that Dörsam stands up, takes his time putting his jacket back on—"Get yourself an air conditioner!"—and goes stomping down the stairs, Josef following after him. Then he hears him howling.

"Look at this! Typical, these primitive country people. Don't know that you can't keep a squirrel in a cage."

"Herr Dörsam?"

Dörsam keeps walking and just gives a quick glance back over his shoulder. "Yes?"

"I went to the FBI back then and told them about us."

Dörsam's hand is on the car door. He freezes for a moment. Then turns around with a jerk.

"Oh, almost forgot. Schmuederrich sends his regards."

"Please send him mine as well."

The black taxi disappears behind the brown dust cloud. He sees only this rising tower of dust, a ghost that slowly collapses in on itself, and hears the *takatakataka* of the motor growing thinner and thinner, then the sounds of the jungle take over again, chirping and croaking and cawing.

He has a piece of cracker stuck in his teeth.

That evening he listens to the German international radio service broadcasting out of Cologne, which comes in as clear as a local station. He looks at the letter he started yesterday. He's started several such letters.

> I'll keep writing the letter tonight. Or start it over again. I'll write it in such a way, Carl, that you understand.

Then he crosses out the last sentence.

> I don't know if I can explain it all to you. I just think I was too stupid, simple as that. And now it's all too late.

This too he crosses out.

A storm rolls in, the electricity drops out, the ceiling fan makes one last tired revolution. The sky grows dark, the trees start to sway. He stands on the veranda, feels the cool wind and the silence. A baffled silence. Everything is reshaping itself.

In the morning he is awakened by a sound, a regular *rip, rip* that tears him away from his dreams. Maria is back. She is sitting on the stairs in front of the house and tearing leaves off a bulky stalk of herbs; a whole pile lies in front of her. *Rip, rip, rip.* The sound triggers a feeling of uneasiness within him, as if he'd done something wrong.

He pulls himself out of bed, puts on the first clothes that come to hand, and goes down to join her. She welcomes him with a big smile. "Don José, your hair is too long. May I cut it for you?"

"Gladly." He hesitates, but then he says in a firm voice, "But first let's free the squirrel."

Her smile stiffens, but to his surprise, she then assents and gestures invitingly over toward the cage. He carries it over to the lawn as she watches. Maria crouches down and looks at the squirrel. It's hanging from the side of the cage, fully outstretched, its leathery claws clinging to the bars. A silent, patient exchange of glances, as if the animal knew what was going on.

"It'll always be close by, Maria. It'll live here in the garden."

"It'll get as far away as it can."

"Yes, maybe," he has to admit.

Once she's opened the little door, it leaps off into the jungle, fast as lightning, cutting arcs in the fluttering air. Quick, agile, like a good idea in your head, as light and quick as the air itself. Where was it he'd seen the electronics store in town? He looks up at the house. Sure, he could attach an antenna up there.

"Don José?" Maria fishes a key out from her clothes. "For the boathouse. You can take the boat out and go fishing. Like the men. But be careful."

Maybe he'll stay here.

ACKNOWLEDGMENTS

For historical guidance, I thank Dr. Florian Altenhöner, Professor Dr. Wolfgang Krieger, Dr. Christoph Selzer, and Dr. Monika Siedentopf. I also thank Barry Moreno and Kevin Daley at the Ellis Island National Museum of Immigration and the amateur radio operators at the Chaos Computer Club, Berlin. Thanks also to Ernst Vranka (OE3EVA), who alerted me to a few technical inaccuracies. Not everything stands up to literary adaptation—may amateur operators forgive me!

For conversations and thoughtful reading, I thank my editor, Corinna Kroker, and also Isabel Fargo Cole, Hannah Dübgen, Rolf-Bernhard Essig, Lucy Fricke, Karin Graf, Christian Jeukens, Sünje Lewejohann, Inger-Maria Mahlke, Lydia Mechtenberg, Klaus Sellge, and Liliana Marinho de Sousa.

Finally, I owe a very special thank you to my mother, who remembered everything for my benefit.

BIBLIOGRAPHY

For readers who wish to delve deeper into the subject, the following is a selection of books, films, and documentaries I recommend.

Nonfiction

Bernstein, Arnie. *Swastika Nation: Fritz Kuhn and the Rise and Fall of the German-American Bund.* New York: St. Martin's Press, 2013.

Breuer, William. *Hitler's Undercover War: The Nazi Espionage Invasion of the USA.* New York: St. Martin's Press, 1989.

Brown, Anthony Cave. *Die unsichtbare Front: Entschieden Geheimdienste den Zweiten Weltkrieg?* Munich: Desch, 1976.

Carlson, John Roy. *Under Cover: My Four Years in the Nazi Underworld of America.* New York: E. P. Dutton, 1943.

Duffy, Peter. *Double Agent: The First Hero of World War II and How the FBI Outwitted and Destroyed a Nazi Spy Ring.* New York: Scribner, 2014.

Hynd, Alan. *Passport to Treason: The Inside Story of Spies in America.* New York: National Travel Club, 1943.

Mader, Julius. *Hitler's Spionagegenerale sagen aus.* Berlin: Verlag der Nation, 1979.

Nesper, Eugen. *Der Radio-Amateur "Broadcasting": ein Lehr-und Hilfsbuch fur die Radio-Amateure aller Länder.* Berlin: Springer, 1923.

Ritter, Nikolaus. *Cover Name: Dr. Rantzau.* Edited and translated by Katharine R. Wallace. Lexington: Univ. Press of Kentucky, 2019.

Siedentopf, Monika. *Unternehmen Seelöwe: Widerstand im deutschen Geheimdienst.* Munich: Deutscher Taschenbuch Verlag, 2014.

Thorwald, Jürgen. "Die unsichtbare Front." *Der Stern*, March 1953.

Wighton, Charles, and Günter Peis. *Hitler's Spies and Saboteurs.* London: Award Publications, 1973.

Novels

Di Donato, Pietro. *Christ in Concrete*. New York: New American Library, 2004.

Glaeser, Ernst. *Class 1902*. Columbia: Univ. of South Carolina Press, 2008.

Gold, Michael. *Jews Without Money*. New York: PublicAffairs, 2009.

Miller, Arthur. *Focus*. New York: Avon Books, 1965.

Roth, Philip. *The Plot Against America*. New York: Houghton Mifflin, 2004.

Films and Documentaries

Hathaway, Henry, dir. *The House on 92nd Street*. Los Angeles: 20th Century Fox, 1945. 88 min.

Kirst, Michaela, dir. *Zum Nazi Verdammt: Deutsche in amerikanischen Lagern*. Munich: Tangram International, 2008. 52 min.

Nitvak, Anatole, dir. *Confessions of a Nazi Spy*. Los Angeles: Warner Bros., 1939. 104 min.

A NOTE FROM THE TRANSLATOR

Every translation requires research, but this translation was unique in that so much of the research was centered around my home, New York City. Given the novel's historical setting, I felt the need to be as accurate as I could, which meant not only quoting primary sources verbatim wherever possible when referring to real-life events—the German-American Bund's rally at Madison Square Garden on February 20, 1939; the explosion at the Hercules powder plant on September 12, 1940—but also making sure I had a clear sense of the geography of New York at the time. Was the layout of Carl Schurz Park, where Josef meets Lauren for a date, different in 1939, before the FDR Drive was built along the East River? What about Brooklyn Heights before the Brooklyn-Queens Expressway was forced through? And how did Lower Manhattan's street grid look prior to the construction of the World Trade Center?

Resources like *Hagstrom's New York Atlas*, *The WPA Guide to New York City*, and the *AIA Guide to New York City* were invaluable, as were the New York Public Library's online databases. It was particularly enjoyable to look through the NYPL's collection of early 20th century menus, thanks to which I was able to confirm that chop suey was indeed available in New York in the 1930s—in 1938 you could order it at the Shanghai Food Shop on W. 45th St.—and that at least one diner, the Restaurant Longchamps at Madison and 59th, offered "alligator pear"—served on the half-shell, with crab meat and your choice of Russian or French dressing, it would cost you $1.25 in 1936.

It was not just a concern for historical accuracy, however, that made me so intent on capturing Ulla Lenze's vivid, tangible evocation of New York. The city holds a special place in the heart of the book's protagonist, Josef Klein. Indeed, though Josef's thoughts and motivations are so often unclear—most notably his response to the Nazi activity he finds himself enmeshed in—the affection he feels for his adopted home is unambiguous. It may be exceeded only by his devotion to the radio.

The Radio Operator's original German title is *Der Empfänger*, "the receiver." The title has a double meaning, referring specifically to an electronic component—a radio receiver—and by extension to Josef himself, "one who receives." Josef is a figure uniquely attuned to the activity around him, a sensitive antenna picking up disturbances in the fraught atmosphere of a city on the verge of war. The passive nature of this receptivity has dire consequences, as Josef is unable to assert himself against the negative influence of the Duquesne spy ring.

But there is nevertheless a positive side to Josef's receptive nature. He maintains a poignant openness to the world around him. The sense of connectivity, of oneness with the world that he experiences at his radio terminal can be seen as well in his deep identification with New York City. Living in New York, Josef doesn't need to assert himself; the city itself has personality enough for him. Josef's model for himself—and others' for him—might be Thoreau in his cabin on Walden pond, but another, more suitable comparison might be Ishmael from *Moby Dick*, perched on the masthead aboard the *Pequod* and so entranced, so at one with his surroundings that he is unable to perform his watch duties. Josef is not a heroic character, but his openness to the world makes him a sympathetic one—and in the end, his receptivity gives him a chance at redemption.

—Marshall Yarbrough

Here ends Ulla Lenze's
The Radio Operator.

The first edition of this book was printed and
bound at LSC Communications in
Harrisonburg, Virginia, April 2021.

A NOTE ON THE TYPE

This novel was set in Adobe Jenson, a typeface designed in 1996
by Robert Slimbach. It is based on two distinctive designs from
15th century Venetian type pioneers: a Roman type by Nicolas
Jenson (c. 1420–1480) and an Italic type by Ludovico Vicentino
degli Arrighi (1475–1527). Adobe Jenson is an organic design,
well-regarded for its elegance. Its high readability makes it
suited for a broad spectrum of applications, but it shines
brightest on the printed page.

HarperVia

An imprint dedicated to publishing international voices,
offering readers a chance to encounter other lives and other
points of view via the language of the imagination.